D0175424

DT._____

MADE IN KOREA

SARAH SUK

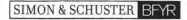
SIMON & SCHUSTER BFYR

NEW YORK LONDON TORONTO SYDNEY NEW DELHI

SIMON & SCHUSTER BFYR

An imprint of Simon & Schuster Children's Publishing Division
1230 Avenue of the Americas, New York, New York 10020
This book is a work of fiction. Any references to historical events, real people,
or real places are used fictitiously. Other names, characters, places, and events are
products of the author's imagination, and any resemblance to actual events
or places or persons, living or dead, is entirely coincidental.
Text © 2021 by Sarah Suk
Jacket illustration © 2021 by Anne Pomel
Jacket design by Sarah Creech © 2021 by Simon & Schuster, Inc.
All rights reserved, including the right of reproduction in whole or in part in any form.
SIMON & SCHUSTER BOOKS FOR YOUNG READERS
and related marks are trademarks of Simon & Schuster, Inc.
For information about special discounts for bulk purchases, please contact Simon & Schuster
Special Sales at 1-866-506-1949 or business@simonandschuster.com.
The Simon & Schuster Speakers Bureau can bring authors to your live event.
For more information or to book an event, contact the Simon & Schuster Speakers Bureau
at 1-866-248-3049 or visit our website at www.simonspeakers.com.
Interior design by Tom Daly
The text for this book was set in EB Garamond.
Manufactured in the United States of America
First Edition
2 4 6 8 10 9 7 5 3 1
Library of Congress Cataloging-in-Publication Data
Names: Suk, Sarah, author.
Title: Made in Korea / Sarah Suk.
Description: First edition. | New York : Simon & Schuster Books for Young Readers, [2021] |
Audience: Ages 12 up. | Audience: Grades 7-9. |
Summary: "Two entrepreneurial Korean-American teens butt heads-and fall in love-while
running competing Korean beauty businesses at their high school"—Provided by publisher.
Identifiers: LCCN 2020038934 (print) | LCCN 2020038935 (ebook)
ISBN 9781534474376 (hardcover) | ISBN 9781534474390 (ebook)
Subjects: LCSH: Korean Americans—Juvenile fiction. | CYAC: Korean Americans—Fiction.
| Entrepreneurship—Fiction. | Business enterprises—Fiction. | Love—Fiction. |
Beauty culture—Fiction.
Classification: LCC PZ7.1.S846 Mad 2021 (print) | LCC PZ7.1.S846 (ebook) |
DDC [Fic]—dc23
LC record available at https://lccn.loc.gov/2020038934
LC ebook record available at https://lccn.loc.gov/2020038935

For 아빠, 엄마, 언니, and 오빠,
who loved me since day one

CHAPTER ONE

VALERIE

Monday / September 9

There's a Hi-Chew flavor for every occasion. Grape to focus. Mango to celebrate. Strawberry to calm the hell down when things aren't going the way I planned. Like this afternoon. The first sales day of a new school year was always, without a doubt, one of the most unpredictable. I mean, I definitely hadn't expected two of my classmates to have a major throwdown right in front of my locker. Talk about high stress.

At least I'd come prepared. My fanny pack was filled to the zipper with emergency strawberry Hi-Chews. I tore one open and popped the chewy sweet into my mouth as I surveyed the situation before me. The lineup to my locker twisted all the way down the hall, comprised of the familiar faces of regulars who had been shopping with me for years, plus freshmen who were eager to get a glimpse of V&C K-BEAUTY, Crescent Brook High School's most popular student-run business. The line hadn't moved for a good thirty seconds thanks to Natalie Castillo and Amelia Perry's big blowup, and it was making me seriously antsy. Thirty seconds was thirty seconds too long.

The object of their desire: a brand-new citrus-honey hydrating moisture gel.

Quantity: one.

"I got here first!" Amelia said, elbowing Natalie out of the way with her tiger-striped tote bag. "I've been eyeing this gel since Valerie posted it on Instagram this morning."

"Excuse you, but I was in front," Natalie snapped back. Her curly hair was practically springing out of her scrunchie in shopping-induced rage. "You cut the line."

"Just let it go! You can get this same gel on Amazon."

"You know my dad puts a limit on my online shopping. I'm already capped out! *You* buy it on Amazon."

"Uh, no, not for the price that V&C charges. Besides, I don't have my own credit card, and my parents will kill me if I take theirs without asking. Again."

It was true about the prices. You couldn't find a deal like ours anywhere else, thanks to my uncle. He worked in Seoul as a manager at a Korean beauty company and sent my aunt a box of products every month. Too bad for him, Sunhee Eemo couldn't care less about face masks. What she really wanted was for her husband to send more money so she could work fewer hours at the soondubu restaurant.

"Money! Send more money!" she'd yell during their phone calls. "What am I going to do with all these face creams?"

"I know you love them," he'd always tease. "Only the best products for my wife!"

The man was extravagant or just plain clueless. Either way, the packages continued, and my cousin Charlie and I had the brilliant idea to sell them to our classmates at a discount. Charlie's dad was cool with it as long as we gave Sunhee Eemo first pick, not that she ever took us up on the offer. He got us a permission slip allowing us to resell his products as a student business project, and bam: V&C K-BEAUTY was born.

We'd built up this business since our sophomore year, and I wasn't about to let Amelia and Natalie bring it all down now. People at the back of the line were starting to lose patience and trickle away. Enough was enough.

"Okay, executive decision," I said. "The only fair way to decide this. Rock-paper-scissors."

"Are you serious?" Amelia said. "You're going to hinge this life-altering decision on a juvenile game of rock-paper-scissors?"

Amelia was a theater student. I had very little patience for theater students and their dramatics. "Rock-paper-scissors," I said, my voice firm. "Unless you'd rather surrender the gel to Natalie in peace?"

A look of determination flashed across Amelia's eyes. She held out her fist in front of Natalie. "Let's do this."

Natalie followed suit and they chanted, "Rock-paper-scissors." The entire line sucked in a collective gasp as Natalie's hand came down in a peace sign and Amelia's formed a flat open palm.

"Yes!" Natalie cheered, while Amelia groaned, slapping her paper hand against her face.

"A plague on all your houses!" she cried.

I reached into my locker for the citrus-honey moisture gel. I could feel everybody watching me, their gaze following my reach into my infamous school locker–turned–K-beauty storefront. It was the stuff of Crescent Brook High legends. The inside was lit up with battery-powered fairy lights. A glittery laundry-clip hanger dangled from the top, but instead of mismatched socks and underwear, packets of glossy Korean face masks hung from the clips. Clear drawers lined the faux marble shelves that Charlie and I had painted and installed ourselves, filled with every kind of Korean beauty product imaginable. You name it, I had it. Toners, cleansers, serums, lip tints, and BB cream galore. Everything was arranged by type, size, color, and scent. The bottom corner was reserved for my schoolbooks, but nobody cared about that.

What people cared about was the product. And I always delivered on what the people wanted.

I bagged the gel for Natalie and tucked her payment into my fanny pack in a separate pocket from my Hi-Chews. Amelia bought five lip tints to make up for her loss, and the line started moving again. Crisis averted. My heart rate eased back down.

"Finally. That took *forever*." Kristy Lo stepped up in line, sequined wallet already in hand. Aside from her Starburst-colored hairstyles, which changed weekly, Kristy was known for having the biggest mouth in our senior class. She sniffed out gossip like a bear tracking honey, which suited me just fine. Kristy was my best customer, and there was no better advertising than word of mouth.

She smiled brightly. This week her hair was the color of pink cotton candy. "Did you have a good summer, Val? Sucks that we don't have any classes together this year. I don't have any with Charlie, either." She pouted. "Tell him I say hi, will you?"

I narrowed my eyes. Unspoken rule of shopping with V&C: Don't try to flirt with my cousin through me. Kristy giggled nervously.

"Okay, got it—you're not my messenger," she said. "By the way, did you hear Tina Pierce and Matt Whitman broke up over the summer? Ten bucks says they'll spend all of senior year trying to make each other jealous and then hook up again during prom. Oh, and have you met the new guy yet? Wes Jung?" She leaned forward and whispered, "He's seriously hot. Maybe even hotter than Charlie."

"What can I get for you?" I asked, tapping my fingers against my locker door.

"Oh, I'll take five packages of the green-tea eye masks and one tub of the coconut body cream," Kristy said, opening her wallet. She pursed her lips thoughtfully, in deep contemplation. "I guess Charlie is more cute than hot, though. There is a difference, you know?"

I plucked the bills out of Kristy's hand. "Always a pleasure, Kristy. Next in line, please."

As the line rolled smoothly along, the anxiety in my chest continued to lift. The beginning of this school year had me feeling seriously on edge. Would students come back? Or would they find a better deal elsewhere while we were on vacation? To my relief, it looked like summer break hadn't done anything to hurt our sales.

"Sorry, all sold out." I zipped up my fanny pack and looked at the time. Twenty minutes, even with Amelia and Natalie's squabble. We cleaned out fast. "See you next week, everybody. Remember, we restock and sell every Monday."

The students still in line grumbled as they dispersed through the hall. I stepped back and took a satisfied look at my now-empty locker. My favorite sight. I pulled out my phone and snapped a photo for my Instagram story. *Senior year starting strong!* I typed. I added a GIF of a SOLD OUT sign with dancing donuts for the *O*s.

Just as I was about to lock up, I felt someone tug at the fanny pack around my waist. I whirled around, ready to beat the thief to a pulp. Charlie Song, my cousin and business partner, grinned back at me, dangling the fanny pack in my face, his hair sweaty and matted on his forehead from basketball practice.

"How'd we do today, Val?" he asked.

"*I* did great," I said, swiping the pack out of his hands. "You, on the other hand, will get a black eye if you sneak up on me like that again."

Charlie laughed, bouncing around me as I locked up. "Really, though. Did our reputation hold up over the summer like I said it would?"

At this, I couldn't help but grin. "Yeah. Yeah it did."

Charlie fist-pumped the air as we made our way outside. "See! I told you we'd be okay. We always are."

He wasn't wrong. Ever since we'd started our sales, we'd been growing at a steady rate. At first, it was just a few girls who were interested in our discounted prices, but soon word of mouth (thank you, Kristy Lo) gave us more business than we were prepared for. Over time, we built up a solid client base and an even more solid reputation. Now Charlie asked his dad for a specific list of the hottest products every month.

If I had just looked at how things had gone after last year's summer break, I supposed I wouldn't have had much reason to be worried. We'd survived between school years once before; we would survive again. But that was then and this was now, and I could never quite shake the feeling that something would swoop in and topple everything we'd built. A new online store with competing prices, maybe. Or waning interest in our products. But today reassured me that we were still strong, and I was more determined than ever to make sure that V&C had a great final year. After all, not only did I want to round us off with a solid ending, but this was also the year I would be highlighting in my college applications.

We walked out to the parking lot and climbed into Sunhee Eemo's car. Bless her for letting Charlie drive it when she was at the soondubu restaurant. Hauling a box of beauty products to school every week would be a serious pain without it, and I say that from experience. Before Charlie got his license, we would lug all our products around in a wagon that's since lots its wheels to a speed bump incident. RIP. Charlie revved the engine as I pulled the day's earnings from my fanny pack and counted out the cash.

"So," Charlie said, backing out of the parking lot. His tongue stuck out between his teeth in concentration. "Senior year is officially underway and I think I know who I'm going to ask to prom. Curious?"

"Not even a little bit." I held up a wad of cash. "Here, this is yours." We split all our profits seventy-thirty. We used to do an even fifty-fifty before Charlie became co-captain of the basketball team and didn't have as much time for the business anymore. Still, he helped out where he could, and he earned his 30 percent. I stuck the money in the glove compartment before folding up my own share and tucking it back into my fanny pack.

"Okay, first off, rude, and second, I think you'll be surprised to hear my answer."

I sighed. "All right, I'm sorry. Go ahead." Senior prom was ages away, but Charlie had been talking about it since we started high school. He was a hopeless romantic. I was also looking forward to prom, mostly because I wouldn't have to listen to him talk about it anymore.

"Apology accepted. Now guess."

"You think I keep track of all the girls you've gone on dates with? I'm not guessing."

"All right, fine." He straightened up in his seat. "I'm going to ask Pauline."

My eyebrows shot up. "Pauline as in Pauline Lim? The girl you had a major crush on in sophomore year?"

"Told you you'd be surprised," he said smugly.

"The same girl you were friends with until she ghosted you out of nowhere and totally broke your heart?"

His smile faded a touch. "Yeah, her."

"Why? I thought you were over her."

"I was. I am! I think." He shook his head. "I don't know. I just

8

feel like I never got closure between us. I never even got to ask her out on a proper date like I wanted to back then. And this is our last year of high school. I don't want to have any regrets and always wonder what could have been."

Like I said, hopeless romantic. I sighed. "I'm pretty sure you'll regret it more if you reopen this jjak sarang."

He groaned. "Why do you have to call it that?"

"Because that's what it is. Jjak sarang. One-sided, unrequited love."

"That's what it *was*," he corrected me. "It's been two years. You never know what can change. Besides, I've grown up a lot since then. I'm more mature and, let's face it, way better looking. Sophomore year was not my year."

"Speaking of which, Kristy Lo was saying there's a new guy who's 'even hotter than Charlie.'" I raised my fingers into air quotes at that last part.

"Oh yeah? What else did she say?"

"That's it. And that she thinks you're actually more cute than hot. There's a difference, she said."

Charlie frowned. "Untrue. I'm definitely both. Tell me I'm both."

"We're done talking about this."

I rolled down the window. It was an old car, so I had to use the manual hand roller to get the window down. I loved the feeling of the crisp September air blowing strands of hair out of my fishtail braid. I slid my tortoiseshell sunglasses from the top of my head onto my face, snuggling deeper into my thrifted corduroy jacket.

Fall is definitely my favorite season. "By the way, did you talk to Ms. Jackson about setting up our mentorship meetings for the year?" I asked.

"Yep. The last Wednesday of the month over lunch. Is that cool with you?"

"Yeah. Thanks for doing that."

He grinned and flashed me a thumbs-up. Crescent Brook High was big on creativity and innovation in all departments: they encouraged new science experiments, out-of-the box art programs, and, of course, student-run businesses. To run a business, you needed permission from the principal and a teacher to mentor you, and Ms. Jackson had been our mentor since we first started V&C. She was whip-smart and one of the first people to encourage my goals as an entrepreneur. She ran her own start-up with a team of all Black women before she switched gears and became a social studies teacher. "I missed being around teens," she said when I asked her why she'd changed careers. "Now if only I could get these start-up CEOs to stop calling and trying to poach me!" Basically, she's goals. I plugged in our monthly meetings into my phone calendar as Charlie turned up the radio.

We drove through the suburbs, passing playgrounds, corner stores, and tree-lined streets, admiring the outline of mountains through the open windows. I'd spent my entire life in the Pacific Northwest, but I didn't think I could ever get tired of this view. Mountains called out home to me and even though their snow-capped tops scraped against the sky, the sight of them always left me feeling more grounded.

Ten minutes later, we pulled up in front of my town house. "Are you going to hang out with me and Halmeoni today?" I asked, unbuckling my seat belt.

"I would, but I gotta pick up my mom from the restaurant," Charlie said.

"She asks about you."

"Does she? I'll have to come by soon, then. Can't deprive our grandmother of Charlie time."

He laughed and I rolled my eyes even as my lips quirked up in a smile. Charlie could be annoying sometimes, but he was genuine and he always kept his word. I respected that about him.

"Hey, Val?" he called as I got out of the car.

I turned. "Yeah?"

"You really think it's a bad idea to ask Pauline out?"

I sighed. Genuine, reliable, and utterly hopeless. "I just don't want you to get crushed again."

"Okay, but what if this is my last shot? I know it's been a while, but obviously I'd be lying if I said I don't think about her still. Don't I owe it to myself to at least try?"

I slammed the door shut and leaned down to look at my cousin through the open window. I didn't want to see him get hurt, but Charlie wore his heart on his sleeve, which basically increased his chances of getting hurt by ten as far as I was concerned. I had to give him some tough love. "Listen, Charlie, you do what you gotta do, but don't say I didn't warn you. And don't let it get in the way of our business. Last time she stopped talking to you, you were in such a funk, you were no help for months. If you want to put yourself through that again, I can't stop you, but don't leave me hanging." I patted the side of the car. "Thanks for the ride."

I turned and jogged into the house. Charlie honked the horn behind me, and I raised a hand to wave without looking back.

As soon as I stepped through the front door, I heard yelling in Korean. I knew what that meant. Umma and Halmeoni were fighting. Again.

I toed off my sneakers and tried to tiptoe through the living room unnoticed.

"You can't just keep me locked up in the house!" Halmeoni cried. She was dressed in her walking outfit, complete with a puffy purple vest, track pants, and a reflective visor over her short, curly permed hair. Her hands were on her hips, her round chin jutting out in defiance. Puffy purple had never looked so fierce. "I'm only seventy-six. I'm *healthy*. Healthy! The doctor said so herself!"

"Well, you can't just disappear without telling someone where you're going," Umma said, throwing her hands in the air. Her clothes were splattered with what looked like fresh paint stains, as if she had been right in the middle of her most recent home-renovation project when the fight had begun. When she isn't setting up staging rooms for Appa's real estate open houses, Umma is always remodeling something around our own house. She also gets into way more fights with Halmeoni. "What if something happens to you and no one knows where you are?"

"You're my daughter, not the other way around," Halmeoni said, narrowing her eyes. Her gaze fell on me and she waved me over. "Valerie, come here and tell your mom to let me go on walks without her supervision."

I froze, halfway up the stairs to my room. I turned back around, lifting my sunglasses up and clearing my throat. Something told me rock-paper-scissors wasn't the way to go with this fight. "Halmeoni should be allowed to go wherever she wants."

"Valerie," Umma said, pinching her nose like she was already exhausted by this conversation. "Please. What did I tell you about listening when adults are speaking?"

"I'm almost an adult," I said.

"No. You're seventeen. What kind of mother would I be if I let you talk back to me, huh? Now stay out of matters you don't understand."

I winced, shrinking at Umma's words. I wanted to run up to my room and disappear, but for Halmeoni's sake, I would stand my ground. "Well, I think Halmeoni knows what she's talking about. Not to mention the doctor, who said she was doing fine at her last checkup." I walked down the rest of the stairs, linking arms with my grandma. "If she wants to go out, you can't keep her locked up here like a prisoner."

Halmeoni straightened up, nodding her head. "Like a prisoner," she repeated.

Umma looked back and forth between the two of us, pressing her lips together. "You two always gang up on me. Umma, the doctor might say you're fine, but there's nothing wrong with being extra careful at your age. You're not as healthy as you once were, no matter what you want to believe. Why must you be so stubborn?

And you, Valerie." She shook her head. "You need to learn how to listen like your sister. Samantha never disrespects me like this."

With that, she turned on her heel and disappeared into the kitchen, where she started vigorously painting the cabinets again. I scowled, feeling the tips of my ears heat up in anger. Why did Umma always have to compare me to Samantha? This wasn't even about her. Leave it to Umma to take any opportunity she could to highlight my older sister and make me feel like I was too young to know anything. Fuming, I dug into my fanny pack and tore open a strawberry Hi-Chew. I chewed furiously.

Halmeoni's wrinkled hand covered mine. "Don't listen to your mom," she said gently. "You are doing me a favor. You're my girl."

She patted my hand and I smiled back, relaxing a little. Umma might not understand me, but Halmeoni always did. She made me feel like I was fine just as I was.

"How about I go for a walk with you and then we can have a spa day inside?" I suggested. "I'll dye your hair again."

"My girl," Halmeoni said, patting me on the arm. "You know just how to cheer me up."

And so we did. As I dyed Halmeoni's hair that evening, with a Korean drama that we'd seen a hundred times already playing on my laptop, I couldn't help but notice how stooped her shoulders were. She used to be so much taller than me, even just a couple of years ago.

"Halmeoni, you're shrinking," I said, trying to keep my voice jokey and light.

"Yah, you silly girl," she said, swatting me in the arm. "I'm not shrinking. You're just growing. You're at a growing age right now. You'll keep on getting taller for a long, long time, much taller than your halmeoni."

I smiled. "Yeah, you're right."

She stared at the laptop screen, where the couple in the Korean drama was dancing in front of the Eiffel Tower. "What do you think it's like there?" she asked. "Paris? Wouldn't it be wonderful to go?" Her nose wrinkled in displeasure. "I don't know why your mom has a fit anytime I talk about going anywhere. She thinks I can't think for myself anymore."

I said nothing, dyeing her curls in silence. When Halmeoni had first emigrated from South Korea with her two teenage daughters, she'd had big dreams of exploration. But between raising a family and getting older, she never had a chance to travel the world like she wanted to, even though she was always talking about the endless list of places she longed to see. I thought of the cash in my fanny pack and the rest of the money I'd been saving since my sophomore year. Halmeoni didn't know it, but I'd been saving all that money so I could take her on a trip of a lifetime. We would go to Paris and visit art museums and eat cheese from charcuterie boards with gochujang, because Halmeoni never went anywhere without a travel-sized tube of her favorite spicy paste.

She deserved to see everything she wanted to, and I would take her there. Umma would disapprove, of course, but like I said, we weren't her prisoners. How could she hold us back if I was the one funding everything and Halmeoni was healthy enough to go? I was going to make this happen no matter what, and when I did, Umma would finally see that I wasn't just a child who knew nothing. I was way more capable than she thought I was.

I'd prove it.

Monday / September 16

The following Monday, I was still mulling over Umma and Halmeoni's never-ending argument while I waited for my customers. I leaned against my locker, chewing on a green-apple Hi-Chew, the best flavor for thinking. I didn't understand why Umma couldn't see how trapped she was making Halmeoni feel. Besides, everyone knew that fresh air was good for your health. Why wouldn't Umma want that for Halmeoni?

I looked at the time. Ten seconds until the final bell. I put my thoughts on hold and got into business mode. Three, two, one.

The lineup arrived but felt shorter than usual as I sold face masks and cleansers. Maybe people were held up in class? Or maybe there had been a field trip today. By the time school emptied out, I stared at the products in my locker. There were still a few things left. Usually, I would have sold out by now.

"Valerie!" a voice called down the hall. Kristy came jogging toward me. "Sorry I'm late. Do you have anything left?"

"Um, yeah," I said, half closing my locker so Kristy couldn't see inside. "Barely anything, though." I didn't want people to think V&C was losing its touch, especially not Kristy. Once Kristy knew something, it wasn't long before the entire school knew too.

"Oh good," she said. "I'll take one of the peach lily masks."

"Just one?" Strange. Kristy was usually a serial shopper.

"Yeah. You know Wes Jung, the new kid? Turns out his mom works for a huge entertainment company in Korea." Her eyes widened as she spoke. "He was selling Crown Tiger lip balm in band class, and I spent half my week's allowance on it."

My jaw tightened. "What? What are you talking about?"

"You don't know Crown Tiger? They're only the biggest K-pop boy band around."

"No, not that. What do you mean he was selling lip balm?"

"Oh yeah! Crown Tiger's new lip-balm line. They're all sold out everywhere else, but Wes had a bunch from his mom, and he was selling them. He literally made a hundred bucks like *this*." She snapped her fingers. "Natalie and Amelia were fighting over all the flavors. I swear, those girls are out to kill each other."

Natalie and Amelia? They were *my* regular customers, and they'd been noticeably missing from the line today. "Do you know if they'll be coming by the locker today?" I asked, trying to keep my voice even.

"I don't think so. I'm pretty sure they spent all their money with Wes," Kristy said. "If he keeps this up, he won't just be the hottest guy in our grade. He'll be the richest." She peered over my shoulder. "So, where's Charlie today?"

I clenched my teeth. Wes Jung. I didn't have any classes with him, but maybe it was time I met this new kid. Someone had to teach him that there was only room for one K-beauty business around here.

CHAPTER TWO

WES

Monday / September 16

Breakfast was always the same. A bowl of white rice with a package of dried seaweed. Sometimes, if I was feeling fancy, I would add extra things. When we lived in Seoul, it was mostly Spam with kimchi. Then we moved to Tokyo and I experimented with different kinds of fish. Salmon, tuna, mackerel. I would have made my way through the whole sea if we'd stayed. But of course we left, and Los Angeles brought around a strong hot-sauce phase. Now, in the Pacific Northwest, I was all about the avocado. Maybe with a touch of soy sauce.

It was nice to have a routine. Something good that stayed consistent when everything else felt like it was in constant motion.

I sat at the jade marble island in the kitchen, slicing up an avocado as Mom whirled around like a tornado in a power suit, already late for the hundred and one things that were on her to-do list for the day.

"Good morning," she said, kissing me on the side of the face as she breezed past me on her way to the freezer. She grabbed a bag of frozen berries and poured them into the Vitamix for her morning smoothie.

"Morning, Mom," I said, adjusting my glasses. They always went askew when she kissed me on the cheek. "Long time no see."

She shot me an apologetic look. "Sorry, Wes. I've been so busy with work since we moved here." She didn't stop moving the whole time she spoke, throwing coconut milk and Greek yogurt into the Vitamix with sharp staccato movements. Her voice rose as she flipped on the blender. "There's been a lot going on with Crown Tiger's new merch release."

"No worries," I said, speaking loudly over the whir of the Vitamix. Her sorry expression made me feel instantly guilty. The city might be new to me, but my mom's hectic work schedule was as familiar as ever. I should be used to it. No point in making her feel bad about it.

"Tell me how you're liking the new school," Mom prompted, nearly shouting to be heard. "Has it been exciting making new friends?"

I stuck the blade of the knife into the avocado pit with a swift thwack. *Exciting.* That wasn't exactly the word I would use. Exciting was nailing the climax of a saxophone solo. It was hearing a live jazz band and feeling the music come alive inside me. It wasn't starting a new school for the fourth time in ten years. I had just been starting to fit in at my last school in LA when I was whisked away yet again. Now I was at Crescent Brook High with no friends to my name. Hmm. Exciting? Not quite.

"Mmm," I said in lieu of a real answer. Traveling was just part of Mom's job in the Korean entertainment industry. When you were in charge of marketing and promoting K-pop stars to an international audience, it often required you to, well, go international. It was what it was, and I didn't want to upset her by telling the truth.

The blender stopped, and she poured her smoothie into a glass tumbler, eyeing me the whole time. "Remember, if you're not liking this school, we can always send you to private school."

"No, it's fine," I said quickly. When we'd first moved here, right before the start of my senior year, my parents had wanted to send me to a small private school with a specialized math program, but I'd opted for the local public school instead, saying that it was a better option for me to meet more people. That was a lie. Really, I chose it because it had a more popular music program. My parents didn't know it, but I was planning on going to college for music, and I wanted the best musical experience I could get in the last year of high school leading up to it.

Speaking of which, I was going to be late for band class if I didn't hurry up. I wolfed down the rest of my breakfast and reached for my saxophone case.

"Wait, before you go!" Mom lowered her smoothie and lifted a small shopping bag from the kitchen table. "I got these for you. There's enough for you to share with your new friends!"

I peered into the bag and pulled out a tube of lip balm illustrated with a cartoon white tiger wearing a sweater vest. There were four other designs: an orange tiger wearing sunglasses, a blue tiger wearing a hanbok, a black tiger on a surfboard, and a silver tiger eating a corn dog. "Uh, what is this?"

"It's Crown Tiger's new merch line," she said excitedly. "Five members, five flavors of lip balm!"

Crown Tiger was the latest K-pop boy band Mom was promoting. I tried not to get any more sucked into her work life than I already was, but I knew that Crown Tiger was pretty big these days. They were dominating music charts all over the world. Hence their own lip-balm line. My forehead scrunched, holding up the one with the silver tiger. "And this one is corn dog–scented?"

"No, it's mint. That's Namkyu's scent. He's just known for loving corn dogs."

Right. Of course.

She stuffed my backpack with the shopping bag full of lip balm. This was another thing I could always rely on: Mom packing my bag with advertising materials to hand out at school under the guise of helping me make new friends. Classic Mom move.

"You'll be so popular," she gushed. "All the kids your age love Crown Tiger."

I didn't have the heart to tell her that there was no way I was going to hand out lip balm at my new school to my nonexistent friends. So instead I gave her a quick kiss on the cheek and grabbed my saxophone case, jogging out the door before she could slip anything else into my pockets.

"You're new, right?"

I looked up from the music stand, pausing from putting a new reed in my saxophone. A freckled girl with pretty red hair smiled back at me.

"I'm Lisa Carol. First name, last name, not a two-word first name." She laughed. Her laugh sounded like a chorus of bells. "Sorry, people always get confused."

"Um." I fumbled with the reed. Blame it on all the moving, but I could get weirdly awkward around new people. Not that I didn't have social skills. I just didn't know where they were half the time. "Hi. I'm Wes. Wes Jung."

"Cool," Lisa said. "Well, welcome to Crescent Brook High, Wes Jung. Let me know if you have any questions about anything, especially anything band-related. I've had Mr. Reyes since freshman year." She tilted her head to the side, her red waterfall hair spilling over her shoulder. "I play the clarinet. Maybe you noticed?"

Was she flirting with me? Maybe she was. I was terrible at flirting. I tried to think of something interesting to say. I could not.

"Clarinet is neat," I said blankly. I blinked at her through my glasses and she blinked back.

"Okay, then." She smiled brightly. "You know where to find me."

With a wave, she disappeared to the clarinet section. Her friends immediately began to giggle, nudging her teasingly and raising their eyebrows suggestively in my direction. I turned away, but my cheeks were growing warmer by the second. I knew what those looks meant. I'd always heard people whispering behind me in the halls: "He's so handsome. He looks like a model! And his glasses are so stylish."

It's not that I was completely oblivious. When I looked in the mirror, I could see, objectively, why people would call me handsome. I'm tall and broad-shouldered, and I'd gotten enough compliments about my face to know that there was something appealing there. The problem was that I didn't know what to do with any of it. I felt like people expected me to be some cool guy who could charm Lisa with a single word and make her swoon into her clarinet seat. Honestly, I wished I were that guy too. But most of the time, I just felt painfully awkward in my own skin.

I wasn't immune to the whispers that followed me. It was definitely flattering, but it was also equal parts panic-inducing. I could never figure out a way to be myself. Sometimes I wasn't even sure who *myself* was.

"Warm-up scales, everybody, warm-up scales!" Mr. Reyes said, entering the room with a Venti Starbucks cup in his hand. The yellow polka dots on his socks, visible beneath the high cuff of his pants, were in the shape of little suns. "This room is far too quiet."

I brought my saxophone to my lips. Correction: I did know who I was. At least, when I played music I did. I blew into the mouthpiece and felt a familiar warm buzz rush through me. When I play the saxophone, I'm creative. Free. Wild. There's nothing I love more. Throughout all the moves, music had been my constant companion. It was the one thing that kept me grounded when it felt like everything else was up in the air, the thing that felt like home when home was always a question mark.

Just one year, I told myself. *Just one more year of high school, and then I'll be off to music school, where I can enjoy this every minute of every day. I can start building my career as a musician and feel like my best self all the time, doing what I love.* Music is my refuge, the place where I feel simultaneously most safe and most alive. I can't imagine doing anything else. Not only that, but I'd finally be able to stay in one city at one school with one community. No more uprooting.

I began my warm-up scales, feeling my shoulders relax as soon as I started playing. Or at least they started to relax. A few minutes in and some of my notes weren't playing as smooth as they used to. It took double the air to get the sound out, if I could get it out at all. Uh-oh. This had been happening here and there over the past couple of days—having to use more air or press harder on the keys to get the sound out—but the problem was definitely getting worse. I'd have to get it checked out.

In the meantime, I played what I could. Even with the saxophone issue, I was blissfully in my happy zone for the hour of class, bobbing my head to the *How to Train Your Dragon* score we were practicing. Apparently, Mr. Reyes loved movie soundtracks, which meant that 90 percent of our song list came from the big screen. I didn't mind. In fact, I loved it. I secretly hoped that one day I might play in a professional orchestra for a movie soundtrack.

At the end of class, Lisa the clarinet player reappeared at my music stand. I froze, my fingers slipping on the clasps of my saxophone case. Why was she here again? I felt the back of my neck get sweaty the way it does when I get nervous.

"Hey, I was wondering if you wanted to have lunch together

later?" She hugged her clarinet case to her chest and smiled. She had even, sparkly teeth. I was entranced by them. She would be great for dentistry ads. Her brow furrowed at my non-response. "Um, Wes?"

"Huh? Oh. Sorry. Yeah, lunch." I fumbled with my case, accidentally swinging it into my music stand and tipping the stand onto Lisa. "Oh God, sorry!" I lunged for the stand, only to kick my backpack over. Tubes of lip balm spilled out, tumbling across the floor like a synchronized gymnastics routine.

"No worries," Lisa laughed. She picked up a lip balm. "Is this yours?"

"Um, no, they're my mom's."

Lisa stared. "You use your mom's lip balm?"

"What? No!" I was *really* sweaty now. "It's a new line of lip balm from this K-pop group. My mom advertises for them." I scuttled across the floor like a crab, snatching up the lip balm tubes as I talked.

"Wait, hold up," Lisa said, looking closer at the lip balm in her hand. A bunch of her friends were watching us, probably wondering what on earth was going on. Obviously, this conversation was no longer about lunch. Her eyes widened. "Oh my God. This is Crown Tiger, isn't it?"

At the mention of Crown Tiger, all her friends gasped and came running toward us.

"Wait, what? What about Crown Tiger?" A pink-haired flute player rushed over, nearly tripping over her own feet.

"Is that their new lip-balm line?" one of the percussion players gasped. "Those literally *just* launched in Korea and sold out in ten minutes."

"I can't believe you have a whole bag of them!" Lisa said.

"Are they for sale?" the pink-haired girl asked eagerly. She was already pulling out her sequined wallet. "I'll give you ten bucks for one."

Before I knew what was happening, everyone else was pulling out their wallets too. I was too stunned to say anything. *Actually, they're free,* I should have said. *Just take it.* But instead I held out the bag, totally lost for words as they snatched lip balm from my arms and stuffed my hands with ten-dollar bills, running around the band room, screaming, "I got Crown Tiger's lip balm!" Two girls were viciously fighting over the Namkyu corn-dog mint flavor.

"You're so cool, Wes," Lisa said, shaking her head in disbelief. "I can't believe your mom works with Crown Tiger!"

I gulped. *I'm not cool. I'm the opposite of cool.* I looked down at my hand. Cool or not, I'd gotten one hundred dollars richer in the span of five minutes. *How did* that *happen?*

"How was school, son?"

How was school indeed. I was still trying to wrap my mind around what had happened in band class. I'd been so flustered that I'd immediately fled after the lip-balm sale, dodging Lisa's lunch invitation. I sat through the rest of my classes wondering why I'd let my classmates pay for something that was meant to be free. Should I find all of them and refund their money? But that would involve explaining the situation to them. I didn't like this at all.

Dad spun around in his computer chair. He's a software developer who works from home, but he always dresses as if he's about to go to an important business lunch. He was wearing a crisp blue dress shirt tucked into a pair of freshly ironed slacks, his hair combed neatly back, his glasses sitting perfectly on the bridge of his nose. People say I'm the spitting image of my dad. I can see it. I definitely get my height and bad eyesight from him, but that's about where the similarities end.

"School was fine," I said.

"Math and science going well?"

"As well as ever."

Dad nodded in approval, adjusting his glasses. "We'll have to get started on your college applications soon. I've added a couple schools to our list for you to consider."

I said nothing. To my dad, music was a hobby, not a career. He wanted me to study science and become a doctor, his personal dream that got sidetracked when he married my mom and had a kid. It was like he believed that his dreams were just another gene that got passed down to me.

"Son?" Dad prodded. "Did you hear me?"

"Hmm? Right. Yeah."

Dad frowned. "You're getting spacey. Don't zone out now that you're a senior. This is the most important year." He tapped his temple. "A man has to stay clear-headed to strive for excellence, right?"

"Right. Excellence." For a second, I thought about saying what I really wanted to say. That maybe excellence for me was music and maybe the best thing I could possibly do would be to follow the dream I'd had since I first picked up a saxophone when I was seven years old. Heart hammering, I opened my mouth to speak. "Listen, Dad, I—"

But before I could say anything more, his phone dinged with a Kakao message. He looked at the screen and pursed his lips before glancing back at me.

"Who's that?" I asked.

"Oh, just your uncle," he said. He was trying to sound casual, but I could already see the stress lines forming between his eyebrows. "It's okay, I'll reply later. You and I were in the middle of a conversation."

"You sure?"

"Yeah, nothing urgent. He's just being stubborn again, like always." He laughed, strained. "You know how Uncle Hojin is."

And there it was. Uncle Hojin is Dad's younger brother and was my very first saxophone teacher back in Korea. He and Dad had both played music when they were kids, but for Dad it was just a childhood hobby. For Uncle Hojin, it was a lifeline. "Smartest kid in our whole family," Dad always said when he talked about his brother. "So much potential. He could've been anything, but instead he chose to be a musician."

He'd say the word "musician" like it was the most disappointing word in the world. And I guess to Dad it was. It was no secret that Uncle Hojin struggled to make ends meet. Dad was constantly trying to send him money and help him out, but Uncle Hojin always refused, which stressed Dad out to no end.

Probably all the more because their parents had passed away when they were pretty young, so Dad felt like it was his responsibility to take care of his younger brother. I never even got to meet my grandparents on Dad's side. I wonder if they were musical too.

"Anyway, what were you going to say?" Dad said.

"I . . . was just going to say that I've been having some problems with my saxophone. Air leaks, I think. The pads might be wearing out, so I probably have to get it repaired."

Kakao! Dad's phone dinged again, and he glanced at the screen, his eyes skimming the message before looking back up at me. "Doesn't your school do free rentals? Let's just rent one for you for the rest of the year instead of wasting money fixing that old sax. You'll only be playing it for a little while longer anyway, since you won't have time for it in college."

Under his confident gaze, I felt myself lock up inside. Any courage I had mustered earlier to try to speak my mind was gone. His phone dinged again.

"You should reply," I said. "I need to go study now anyway."

Dad nodded, already reaching for his phone. "Okay, yeah. Study hard so you don't end up like your uncle, got it?" He laughed like he was joking, even though we both knew he wasn't. "Let me know if you have any homework questions. I'm always here for you."

Always here for me except in the ways I needed him to be.

That night, I scrolled through the internet, looking at all the music schools I had bookmarked. For the longest time, I hadn't even considered music school as a real option. I knew I loved music and that I wanted to play it for the rest of my life, but it wasn't until recently, when the future had started becoming more tangible, that I'd realized there was no way I could pursue anything else. Even if it meant totally disappointing my parents. I just couldn't shake the feeling that if I chose a field I had zero interest in when I knew so clearly what my passions were, I'd regret it for the rest of my life—and, worse, be trapped forever doing something I hated.

This was tricky, though. Mom and Dad had been saving for my college tuition since I was a kid. I was seriously grateful for that, but I knew there was no way they'd use that tuition money for a music school. I'd have to pave my own way. I imagined telling them as much and felt my hands go clammy. Ah. Well. I could cross the telling-parents bridge when I got there. No need to think about it now.

I'd have to see if it was financially possible first. Maybe if I got a part-time job? Though Dad wasn't a big fan of the idea of me working while I was in high school. He always told me to focus on my studies for now, and, really, what did I need money for anyway? Still. Maybe I could work secretly. Or convince him that I actually really needed a part-time job for work experience. Colleges love work experience. And I could apply for financial aid.

Let's see . . . The most urgent thing I had to pay for were application fees, which were due in December for the schools I was looking at. Then the enrollment and housing deposits in May. Oh, and

I had to get my saxophone fixed ASAP. Maybe it was sentimental, but I couldn't just ditch my saxophone for a rental. Not after everything we'd been through together.

I pulled up my phone calculator, adding up how much I needed for one school. The application, enrollment and housing deposits, and repair fees would come up to around . . . two thousand dollars. Wow. I flipped my phone facedown and dropped my head on the desk.

This was going to be harder than I thought.

"Nothing worthwhile ever comes easy," Uncle Hojin used to say during our saxophone lessons. He'd point to his forehead with a twinkle in his eye. "Just look at my wrinkles! All these wrinkles are a sign of something I worked hard for. A fair trade-off, I think."

I still had his email scrawled on the back of some sheet music he'd given me. "Contact me anytime," he'd said. "Really, anytime. I love getting email, but no one ever emails me, not even your dad." Even with messenger apps like KakaoTalk and video-chatting apps, Uncle Hojin and I mostly stayed in touch through email. It was kind of our thing: writing long updates to each other, attaching music links that we thought the other would like, not replying for months, and then picking up right where we left off with a video of an amazing busker we saw on the street. But with all the moving I'd been doing, our emails had slowly tapered out. We hadn't spoken in years, except for the occasional hello during his phone calls with Dad.

I found myself pulling out the folded piece of sheet music

now, creased from years of bouncing from country to country. I chewed my lip and opened up a new email draft on my computer.

Subject: Annyeonghaseyo
Dear Uncle Hojin,

Hello! It's been a long time since we talked (really talked, not just hello) and even longer since we've seen each other in person. I think the last time was in middle school, and now I'm nearly a high school graduate. Well, almost. Graduation is in the spring, and I've been thinking a lot about what I want to do after. . . .

I know this is out of the blue, but you're the only person I know who went into music after school, and I think I want to do the same. Actually, I know I do. It's the only thing I love enough to even imagine pursuing. But my dad thinks I'll be making a huge mistake if I do. I guess I just wanted to ask—have you ever regretted your decision?

It's kind of funny that we've never talked about this before even though we talked so much about music. But I feel like you would understand. Writing to you makes me feel less alone, like I'm not the only person in the world who's felt this way. Maybe you even had these exact same thoughts when you were my age.

I stared at the screen. What would Dad say if he found out I'd tried to contact his brother, saying these kinds of things? He would probably flip out. But he never had to know.

Hope you are well, I added at the end. Then, before I could think too much about it, I hit send: a call for help into cyberspace.

Tuesday / September 17

The next morning, I dragged my feet to school. I'd decided I would return everybody's money, which meant I had to hunt them all down and explain the mistake I'd made. I was not looking forward to that.

When I turned the corner to my locker, though, I found two people already standing in front of it. One was a girl in an oversized corduroy jacket, a pair of sunglasses perched on top of her head. I didn't recognize her, but there was something about the way she stood, shoulders back, posture straight, emanating confidence, that made me feel like I should. The other was a boy in my math class: Charlie Song. He was wearing a basketball jersey and had a backpack slung over one shoulder. They were talking in low voices. When Charlie saw me, he abruptly stopped speaking and nudged the girl in the side. Her eyes locked on mine as I approached, sharp and appraising, making my palms sweat.

I hesitated. They were standing directly in front of my locker. "Sorry. Excuse me . . ."

I shuffled to the left. They moved to their right, blocking me. I moved to the right and they shadowed me, blocking me again.

"What's up?" I asked in alarm.

"Wes Jung, right? Second row, calculus?" Charlie said, giving me a quick once-over. "You probably know me already. I'm Charlie Song. This is my cousin, Valerie Kwon."

My eyes shifted to Valerie. I smiled cautiously. She stared back, raising an eyebrow. The smile slipped off my face.

"We know about your lip-balm sales," she said, cutting straight to the chase.

I sucked in my breath. Shit. How did they find out that the lip balm was actually supposed to be free? Were they the school's FBI going undercover as teens or something?

"I can explain," I said.

"Actually, I'll do the explaining," she said. She pointed back and forth between Charlie and herself. "See us? We're V&C K-BEAUTY. We sell Korean beauty products at this school. I heard you've been selling lip balm, and I'm going to have to ask you to stop. You're new here, so I'll assume you didn't mean anything by it, but you're kind of stealing our customers."

I blinked. Well, that was unexpected.

"I . . . um, what do you mean?" *Real smooth, Wes.* Why did my tongue always stop working in situations like this?

"It's a small school," she said, shrugging her shoulders like *What can you do?* "There's no room for two of us. And we're not interested in sharing our profits. You get what I mean?"

She cocked her head to the side and looked up at me, her gaze unwavering. This close, I could smell the faint scent of some kind of strawberry candy on her lips. Unlike the sharp intensity in her eyes, her lips looked soft and gentle. She had a pretty mouth. I wondered what it would look like to see her smile.

"Hello?" She waved her hand in front of my face, making my eyes dart back to hers. "Did you hear what I said?"

"Um. Yes." I swallowed hard. When I didn't say anything more, her pretty mouth turned down in a scowl. Pretty and also scary as hell. I was even sweatier than I had been yesterday. What was she talking about anyway? Stealing her customers? No room for two of us? My brain was working double time, trying to piece together what she was saying.

"So?" she said.

"So . . ."

She sighed. "Do you get what I mean?"

"Oh. Right." I nodded rapidly. "Yes. Got it." I definitely didn't, but it seemed safer to agree.

We stared at each other. I held my breath as she surveyed me, calculating, like she was trying to gauge how honest I was being. She must have been satisfied by what she saw, because she finally gave me one curt nod back, breaking eye contact. "Okay. Good." Then she turned on her heel and walked down the hall.

"Smart move," Charlie said. "You don't want to get on her bad side." He clapped a sympathetic hand on my shoulder before disappearing after Valerie.

I leaned against my locker and put a hand over my chest, letting out a breath. My heart was hammering. It felt like I had just had a near-death experience.

One part of my brain was relieved to have escaped Valerie's glare alive. The other part was turning over something she had said: "We're not interested in sharing our profits."

I thought of the hundred dollars that had come so easily into my hands yesterday. The students at Crescent Brook High were hungry buyers, there was no doubt about that. Not to mention there were a lot of K-pop fans. And, clearly, they had some extra spending money if V&C K-BEAUTY could be successful. How much did V&C make, exactly? Enough that they had a stable market.

Enough to help me fix my saxophone and pay my application fees?

"Excuse me," a voice said. I turned my head. A girl who had the locker next to me stood beside me, books in her arms. I tried to recall her name. Pauline Lim. We were in the same biology class. We'd played Two Truths and a Lie as an icebreaker, and her two truths were that she was half-Korean, half-Irish, and that she was an aspiring marine biologist. Her lie was that she was allergic to kiwis. "I'm really allergic to arugula," she'd said.

In the same moment, I also realized I was leaning against her locker. "Sorry," I said, sliding out of the way.

"Don't worry about it," she said. As she dialed the combination, I couldn't shake the thought of Valerie. Her words tumbled around inside my head.

"Hey," I said to Pauline. She looked up. "What do you know about V&C K-BEAUTY?"

CHAPTER THREE

VALERIE

Saturday / September 28

The smell of sizzling pajeon wafted in the air as I walked into the kitchen, wearing my Pompompurin pajamas. I yawned and rubbed the sleep out of my eyes. The kitchen was way too busy for a Saturday morning. Charlie stood over the frying pan in a red-checkered apron, whistling along to his Chill Rap Spotify playlist, while Samantha, who came home every weekend from college, was mixing pajeon batter in a big glass bowl. *Don't people know that Saturday mornings are for sleeping in?*

"Hi," Charlie said, expertly flipping the scallion pancake in his frying pan.

"Hi." I looked him up and down. "You look like a picnic table."

"Wow. Good morning to you, too."

"Not exactly morning anymore," Samantha teased. A few wisps of hair fell out of her ponytail and into her face like they always did, probably because she used the same stretched-out spiral hair ties that she bought in bulk at the beginning of the year and wore until they snapped. "It's nearly noon."

"It's eleven forty-seven a.m.," I said. "And 'a.m.' still means morning, in case you've forgotten."

Growing up, Samantha and I fought all the time over stuff like who got the last Yakult drink or who got to choose which movie to watch. Physical fights, where we'd bite each other's arms and sit on each other until the other person couldn't breathe. You know, sister stuff. We don't fight like that anymore, but God knows she loves to drag me any chance she gets. It's like she gets actual joy from annoying me. And, okay, maybe I get a little bit of joy from annoying her too. Maybe. Just a little.

"Why don't you ever use the new hair ties I got you?" I said, tugging on her loose ponytail. "Yours are so old."

"Hey, they're comfy. They're perfectly stretched out to my hair thickness, thank you very much." She swatted my hand away and gave me a once-over. "Besides, you're one to talk. When are you going to get rid of those pajamas? Aren't you a little old for cartoons?"

"What's wrong with Pompompurin?" I said defensively. He's a dog that looks like pudding. What's there not to like?

"Oh, nothing." She shrugged, clearly pleased at having bested me. She passed the remaining batter to Charlie. "Here, Charlie, this is ready."

I racked my brain for a comeback, but before I could think of one, Umma walked into the kitchen carrying a container of kimchi from the kimchi fridge in our garage. "Oh, Valerie, you're awake?"

she said, setting the container down on the countertop. "Finally. You know your sister's been here since eight a.m.? You should learn to wake up earlier like her. I was just reading an article about how morning people are more productive and successful in life."

I made a face at her offhand comparison and folded my arms across my chest. As far as I knew, Umma didn't read anything except for the home-improvement magazines she subscribed to. "I didn't know *Living Room Today* had tips for life success."

"As a matter of fact, they do. It's a column called Happy Spaces, Happy People. I'll leave it on your desk for you to read." She raised her eyebrows at me as she began cutting up the kimchi. "Maybe after you read it, you'll finally let me redecorate your room. That space is so messy. I don't even know how you can think in there."

"It's not messy," I said. It wasn't. I knew exactly where everything was. It just wasn't the same pristine, polished, minimalist look Umma was so into these days. "Besides, not *all* successful people are morning people." That was statistically impossible. Still, Umma was so certain of herself, I made a mental note to google it later. I hated how she made me doubt myself.

Umma sighed. "I wish you would just trust me for once. Samantha, scoop the rice, will you?"

"Ne, Umma." Samantha hurried over to the rice cooker. She popped it open and a cloud of steam billowed out, filling the kitchen with the warm smell of freshly cooked rice. She then gathered a stack of ceramic white bowls and filled each one until they all looked like real-life replicas of the rice-bowl emoji. As much as she was an annoying sister to me, she was a dutiful daughter to Umma.

I sighed inwardly. Perfect bowls of rice for my perfect grown-up sister who never slept in and hated pudding dogs.

"You know, even Charlie came over early to help," Umma said, continuing the conversation as she arranged the kimchi onto side plates.

I grabbed a glass of water, biting my tongue. I would not snap back. I would not yell. No matter how much I wanted to tell her to let me breathe, I'd just woken up. Saturday mornings were not for yelling.

"Actually, Minhee Eemo, I'm just early because I caught a ride with my mom on her way to work," Charlie said. "And I had to wake up early to FaceTime with my dad. Otherwise I would have slept in too."

"See, Valerie," Umma said, glossing over the entire second half of what Charlie said. "Look how much Charlie was able to do because he woke up early. More productive, just like that article said."

Charlie frowned. "Oh. That's not what I—"

"Charlie, the pajeon is burning!" Samantha cried.

"My pajeon!" Charlie dove for the frying pan, flipping the crispy scallion pancake just in time. He breathed a sigh of relief.

"Good catch, Samantha," Umma said.

Fuming, I chugged the water down, trying to swallow my feelings with it. What was wrong with sleeping in on the weekend anyway? It wasn't like anyone had told me there was going to be a pajeon-making party that I was expected to be at. Why did Umma always have to make me feel so guilty about everything?

The worst part was that I actually *did* feel a little guilty. Maybe I should have just known. Samantha always "just knew." She was only four years older than me, but it felt like we were light-years apart, at least in terms of how Umma saw us. It had always been this way, ever since we were kids.

When I was ten years old, I had a trade going on with a girl in my school. Her name was Elaine and she loved sweets, but her mom never let her have any. Every day she would stare at the Choco Pie that Halmeoni had packed for me in my lunch bag.

"Wanna trade?" she would say, holding up her pumpkin-seed granola bar.

"No way," I said.

"How about these?" she asked, offering her carrot sticks.

I shook my head. "Nuh-uh."

"How about I do your math homework for you?"

My ears perked up. Math was one of my worst subjects back then, and Elaine was the smartest kid in our grade. So I agreed. From then on, we had a deal. Every time we had math homework, she would get my Choco Pie and do my worksheets for me.

It was awesome. I was so pleased with the deal that I bragged about it to Samantha. Only, she didn't think I was so smart. Instead she turned around and immediately told Umma.

"I can't believe this. I didn't raise my daughter to be a cheater!" Umma yelled. She was so angry her face literally turned as red as a tomato. "Do you see your sister doing things like this? No. She earns her grades! She works hard! How will you survive in this world if you can't even do these things for yourself?" She sighed

41

and shook her head, muttering to herself but loud enough for me to hear, "Where did I go wrong with you?"

I cried the whole time she yelled at me, and then she made me sit on my knees in the hallway, holding my arms above my head, for a whole ten minutes. After I was finally allowed to leave, I ran into Halmeoni's room and sobbed into her lap.

"My girl," she said, stroking my hair. "Don't take your mom's words too much to heart. She says them in the heat of the moment, but she doesn't mean them the way it sounds. She just wants you to grow up to be a good person who can take care of herself."

"She hates me," I said between my sobs. "She only likes Samantha."

"It is not true. Who could hate you? My Valerie is smart and kind. Everybody makes mistakes. You will learn from them."

Later that same day, Umma did end up feeling guilty for her harsh punishment. She never outright apologized, but she showed up in my room with a plate of sliced-up peaches, which was the closest to "sorry" she ever got. Still, I knew deep in my heart that she saw me and Samantha differently. Samantha was the golden child, the one who got everything right, and I was like one of her home-renovation projects. Could be better and never enough.

I snapped back to the present moment as Halmeoni walked into the kitchen, stretching her arms over her head. "Good morning everybody!" she said. She was wearing yellow house slippers and her Pompompurin nightgown. "Mmm, smells good in here."

Samantha's eyes flicked between our matching pj's, the slightest frown crossing her face like she was realizing that maybe

Pompompurin wasn't so ridiculous if there were two of us wearing it. *Ha. Take that.* Leave it to Halmeoni to take care of my comeback for me. Samantha recovered quickly, bowing at a perfect ninety-degree angle from the waist. "Annyeonghaseyo, Halmeoni. Did you sleep well?"

"What's up, Halmeoni?" Charlie said, waving his spatula.

Samantha pinched his elbow and he yelped. "Manners to your elders," she chided him.

Halmeoni chuckled. "All right, all right. Look at this pajeon. So perfectly done! We will eat breakfast like kings today."

"Actually, it's lunchtime now," Umma said.

"Nonsense. It's the first meal after a good night's sleep, so that makes it breakfast." Halmeoni winked at me. "Isn't that right, Valerie?"

I grinned, feeling a weight lift off my chest. Halmeoni knew what was up. She loved sleeping in even more than I did. "Exactly."

Halmeoni rolled up her sleeves. "Now, it wouldn't be pajeon without the dipping sauce. Valerie, bring me the soy sauce, vinegar, and honey. We'll make it together. It will be our contribution to breakfast."

Umma sighed and shook her head, turning away to finish setting the table. Samantha sniffed the air as a burning smell filled the kitchen. "Charlie! The pajeon!" she cried again.

"I'm on it!" He flipped the pancake. It was blackened to a crisp. "Um . . ." He smiled sheepishly. "Who likes their pajeon well done?"

• • •

After breakfast, Charlie and I sat cross-legged in Appa's home office, a big cardboard package from Seoul open between us. Appa is the number one real estate agent in our Korean community, or so his business card says. That means he spends most of his weekends hosting open houses and meeting clients, so Charlie and I were free to use his office as we pleased. When I was younger, I used to hate that Appa was never home. I got along better with him than I did with Umma, but he was hardly around. Now I was grateful for the extra space to have my own business meetings, away from Umma's prying eyes.

"Have you told your mom how well V&C K-BEAUTY is doing these days?" Charlie asked. He reached into the package and pulled out a box of snail-jelly face masks. He wrinkled his nose and gagged, setting the masks far away from him. "Gross."

I sighed. He brought up this conversation at least once a month. "I told you already—"

"I know, I know, you try not to talk to your mom about the business," he said, leaning back on his hands. "But we're seniors now, Val. That means it's officially our *third* year of running this business. And it's doing really, really well. That's pretty impressive, isn't it? I think Minhee Eemo would be proud of you, even if she wasn't so enthusiastic when we first started."

"Not so enthusiastic is an understatement," I said. "Remember when she called it a cute hobby as long as it doesn't get in the way of my grades? And then she launched into a full fifteen-minute monologue about how Samantha was taking a business elective in college and maybe if I studied hard enough I could follow in her footsteps. Yeah, no thanks. I don't want to revisit that conversation." I shook my head, rifling through the package and pulling out a bottle of snail-mucin essence. Ooh. This stuff was perfect for getting smooth skin. This would fly out of my locker in no time.

"I still think she would be proud if she knew how hard you work on this," he said.

"That's because you and your mom are best friends and she's proud of everything you do. Not everyone can be a mama's boy."

"Yeah, I guess . . . Wait, what did you call me?"

I grinned teasingly. He rolled his eyes and reached into the box again, pulling out tube after tube of snail foam cleansers. "Um, I'm sensing a theme in this month's package," he said. "A very nasty theme."

"Hey, watch your mouth. Snail mucin is all the rage in K-beauty."

"Mucin?"

"Slime."

He dropped the cleansers. "What is wrong with Korean people?"

"What are you talking about? They're beauty geniuses. Besides, *we're* Korean, remember?"

"Yeah, that's why I can say these things," he said matter-of-factly. "I say it with love."

I laughed and flipped open the Moleskine notebook on my lap. I had a new notebook for each new business year to write down everything related to V&C: inventory count, sales records, ideas for Instagram posts, and, of course, meeting agendas. I tapped my fingers against today's agenda, chewing the cap of my pen.

"We've got a lot of ground to cover today. We only have one

Monday left in September, which means we need to do a final social-media push for our September stock. We also have to finish taking inventory of all this new snail stuff and think about how we want to spread it out over October. You'll call your dad later to thank him for the package, right? And then—what? Why are you looking at me like that?"

"Oh, nothing," Charlie said. "I just don't understand why you won't talk to your mom about something you're so obviously good at, especially when you want to impress her so badly." He held up his hands with a shrug. "Not to sound like a broken record or anything."

My mouth dropped open. "I do *not* want to impress her."

"Yeah, you do. That's why you want to go to Paris, right? I mean, partly, yeah, it's for you and Halmeoni to go on a trip together, but it's also for you to prove a point to your mom, isn't it?"

I fell silent. I didn't want to admit it, but it was true. Paris was for Halmeoni, but it was also for me. It was something that Samantha had never done before, had never even come close to doing—funding a whole trip, exploring the world, taking Halmeoni on an adventure. Umma wouldn't be able to compare this to anything Samantha had done, and it was real, tangible proof that I could work hard for the things I wanted to achieve, morning person or not.

She would disapprove at first. In fact, she might disapprove so much that she wouldn't even realize how impressive it was. But she'd come around. I knew she would. Because the thing was, as much as Umma worried about Halmeoni, I knew that what

Halmeoni really needed wasn't to be locked up inside the house. It was to do what she'd always wanted to while she still could. Umma might not see that right away, but one day she would.

In the meantime, I wanted to prove her wrong—about me and about Halmeoni—and, okay, maybe a petty part of me wanted to say, *Hey, if you'd supported me, I might have taken you to Paris too.* It was small of me, but everything about Umma made me feel small. I couldn't help it. A sudden lump of emotion rose in my throat, and I swallowed it down. I wished things were different between us, but they weren't. I would never be enough to her until I could prove that I was worthy of it, and Paris would be my proof.

"Charlie, listen," I said. "It's not that I won't talk to her about it. It's that every time we do talk about, I feel like shit after. The last time it came up in conversation, she asked me how my 'little makeup club' was going and then, immediately after, started talking about how Samantha is president of some club at her school. That's how it always is with Umma. She just doesn't get me. And I don't know if I have it in me to try to make her understand. I'd rather show her with something big. Like Paris."

"Yeah, I see what you're saying," Charlie said solemnly.

"Besides, business is the one thing that comes naturally to me. I love that every decision I make means something for someone. I don't want Umma to ruin that for me and make me second-guess everything about myself the way she always makes me do. Especially not now, when we have so much work to get through."

He hesitated as if he wanted to say something more. But he

pressed his lips together and nodded. "Okay. You're right. Let's get to work."

We spent the next several hours digging through the package, taking photos for Instagram, and making an action plan for October. Making action plans always sent a thrill of excitement racing through my veins. It was as if writing things down in ink gave me momentum, reminding me that every great venture began with a small idea just like this one. I really meant it when I told Charlie that I loved this business. Whether it was matching someone with the perfect product or figuring out a really sweet deal, I liked the feeling that I had a presence, that everything I did mattered and made an impact.

Even after Charlie's mom came to pick him up, I kept on working. I might not have been an early bird, but once I got into the zone, I could burn the midnight oil, completely losing track of time. Umma's voice played in a loop around my head as the sun began to set outside.

Where did I go wrong with you? Wrong with you? Wrong with you? I clenched my jaw and tried to shove down Umma's voice. I thought instead of Halmeoni: *You're my girl.*

I flipped to the front of my Moleskine notebook, where I had made a chart of all the Paris expenses I was saving for. Flights, hotels, museum fees. The total goal was five thousand dollars. So far, since sophomore year, I had saved up $2,074. Estimating my growth and income from previous years, this year I would be able to get that number up to around $3,500, which was still short of my goal. I had to figure out a way to work extra hard and nearly double my income if I wanted to take Halmeoni to Paris this summer. It was the perfect time for our trip: before I went to college and while she was still healthy enough.

Don't worry, Halmeoni, I promised in my head. *I'll take us to your dream city no matter what it takes. I'll find a way.*

Her voice alongside Umma's warred inside my mind, my constant companions as I worked late into the night.

Monday / October 7

October at Crescent Brook High was about to become the month of the snail.

I got to school an hour early to set up for the day. Charlie and I had decided to release one featured snail product a week, starting with the snail-jelly face masks. I clipped them to the laundry-clip hanger in my locker, giving it a spin for good measure. They looked good. Real good. Amelia and Natalie were going to throw a fistfight over these.

After making sure that all my shelves were plentifully restocked with toners and creams, I took a step back to survey my handiwork. Perfect. Everything was ready for business. Just as I locked up, I heard rapid footsteps coming down the hall. I turned to see Charlie racing toward me, out of breath and sweaty in his number two basketball jersey.

"Valerie," he said, grabbing my arm. "You're not going to believe this."

"What? What's wrong?" My eyes widened in alarm. "Is

everything okay? Did something happen to Sunhee Eemo?"

"No, she's okay; everyone's okay." He took a breath, biting his lip. "It's just . . . there's something you gotta see. Follow me."

I followed Charlie down to the first floor, my heart thudding in my ears. We turned the corner into the band room, and I heard it before I saw it.

The sound of buyers. A whole crowd of them.

And they were buzzing.

"Oh my God, oh my God, which face mask are you going to get? I'm going to get the one that Shiyoon Oppa designed."

"Girl, you know Alex Oppa is my bias. But honestly, I'm probably going to buy one of each. You know these masks are sold exclusively in Korea, right? We can't even get these online, so we should just stock up as much as we can now."

"Yeah, yeah, you're so right. That's the way to go. I hope they're not sold out by the time we get to the front!"

I stood on my tiptoes to look past the chattering line. And then I spotted them.

Wes Jung and Pauline Lim were standing at the front of the room with a row of music stands behind them and a cash box in Pauline's arms. Each music stand was lined with face-mask packages. There were dozens of them, and five different colors to choose from: silver, blue, black, orange, and white. Each package was printed with a different cartoon tiger, corresponding to the color of the mask inside. I recognized those tigers immediately. Crown Tiger beauty merch.

What. The. Hell.

"What is this?" I demanded, my voice coming out sharp and clipped.

Charlie narrowed his eyes, looking back and forth between Wes and Pauline. "That's what I'd like to know."

Whatever it was, I was going to put a stop to it right now. I pushed through the crowd, ignoring the complaints of the students in line and Charlie calling out behind me. Amelia was at the front, batting her eyes at Wes as she filled her tiger-striped tote bag with face masks. A tote bag that said CROWN TIGER in big metallic letters across the front.

"Oh, hey, Valerie!" Amelia said, spotting me. "Are you a Royal Stripe too?"

"A what?" It was taking all of my control to keep my voice level.

She pursed her lips. "Well, if you don't know, you obviously aren't one. It's the name of Crown Tiger's fandom."

"That's great." I turned to Wes, who was desperately trying to avoid eye contact with me, even though I was literally standing right in front of him. *How dare he pretend I'm not here?* "Hey. Wes Jung. Can I have a word?"

"Oh, hey, Valerie," he said in an *Oh, I didn't see you there!* kind of way. I wanted to take Amelia's tote bag and throw it at him. "Sure. Um, Pauline? Will you be okay on your own for a sec?"

Pauline glanced at me before giving him a nod. The angry, coiling feeling in my stomach grew tighter. Of all people, why was Pauline Lim helping him? She didn't even care about beauty products. She'd never shopped with us once since we started our business.

Wes followed me to the side of the room. The first time we'd met, I thought I'd set him straight. I hadn't heard anything otherwise last week, so I thought things were back to normal, as they should be. So why was he back? And the better question was, why was he back selling *face masks*?

I stared hard at him, trying to figure him out. He was tall with cool glasses that made me wonder if he really needed them or if they were just for fashion. With his strong jawline and full lips, he could probably be a model if he wanted to. He even had that deep, soulful look in his eyes that people loved in models. Ugh. Kristy Lo was right. He was annoyingly handsome. I shook my head quickly, clearing my thoughts to focus. He kept rubbing the back of his neck with his hand, like he was nervous around me. As he should be. He had no idea.

"This, um, this isn't what it looks like," he said, looking at me with something like hope. "Can I explain? Please?"

For a second, I considered taking a deep breath and saying *yes, fine, go ahead*—like an adult would do, like Samantha would probably do. If I tempered my anger and looked at Wes, *really* looked at him beyond his potentially fake glasses, I could see that he had an air of open honesty to him that made me want to give him the benefit of the doubt. But then I heard Kristy Lo's voice carry across the band room, exclaiming, "Give me two of everything. I won't need another face mask for weeks!"

My walls immediately snapped back into place. The tight feeling in my stomach grew into flames. I knew what that fire was. Anger. Pure, unfiltered anger.

"You mean you're not selling face masks at school and stealing my business?" I said, my voice faux cheerful.

"I'm not stealing—"

"You're new, so maybe you don't know how things work around here, but are you aware that you can't just sell products at school without the principal's permission?"

He mumbled something unintelligible. I leaned forward with my hand cupped around my ear. It was a petty action, and I hated it when Samantha did that kind of thing to me, but I did it anyway. "What? I can't hear you."

His cheeks turned pink as I got closer to him. He glanced down at my mouth and then looked away, mumbling, "I said I did get the principal's permission."

My smile faltered. "Oh? Well, do you also have a teacher mentor? Because you can't run your own business at school without a mentor from the faculty."

"Mr. Reyes," he said. "Mr. Reyes is my mentor. He said I can use the band room to sell."

"What?" I blinked fast. It felt like someone had knocked the wind out of me. "You . . . you got permission to start your own K-beauty business?"

"K-pop merch," Wes said quickly. "It's different from V&C. Today's merch just happens to be face masks."

"And your last sale just happened to be lip balm?" I asked, my voice rising.

He paused for a long moment. "People can still buy from both of us?" he said finally, but it came out as a question, uncertain and naive.

"We're high school students. You think we grow money trees in our backyard?" I cried. I glanced at the crowd, where I spotted Natalie, Amelia, and Lisa Carol, who had been shopping with me since I first opened, gushing over their new face masks. I turned back to Wes, gritting my teeth. "And it looks like our buyers do overlap, whether you think so or not."

I can't believe this. It took me years to build up my business, and this new guy thinks he can just waltz in here and steal all my customers? Who the hell does he think he is? Does he even know anything about running a business? He looked genuinely upset at how distressed I was, but before he could say anything, Pauline slammed her cash box closed and cried, "That's it, everybody! We're all sold out! Thanks for coming."

I stiffened. I felt a lump rise in my throat. Shit, was I going to start crying? *Now?* I had to get out of there. Shouldering past Wes, I ran as fast as I could out of the band room. I heard him call my name, but I didn't turn back.

Someone grabbed my arm and I whirled around, tugging my arm away.

"Hey, hey," Charlie said. "It's just me."

"Oh. Sorry." I inhaled deeply through my nose, pressing the heels of my palms into my eyes to stop the tears from coming. I would not cry at school. I would not.

"I didn't want to cut in, but I overheard your conversation with Wes," Charlie said, putting an arm around me. "And you know what? He's a dick. But he might be right. Just because he's starting a business doesn't mean that it's the end of ours. People could still buy from both of us, and I bet lots of people won't even buy from him at all. Not everyone's a Crown Tiger fan. Besides, we've been around for years. This guy sells like two things and suddenly he's competition? Nah."

I said nothing. Could Charlie be right? Maybe I had overreacted. I was too emotional. Samantha wouldn't have lost her cool like that. She would have been precise and collected, easily accepting that potential competition is just another part of running a business like the mature grown-up she is. I could almost hear Umma's disapproving voice in my head.

"Let's just wait to see how our sales go today," Charlie said. "I'm sure everything will be fine."

I nodded. Okay. I could do that. "You're right." I smiled feebly. "Thanks. Honestly, I was surprised to see Pauline working with Wes. I didn't know she was into K-beauty or business stuff."

"Same." He frowned, and I knew what he was thinking. He still hadn't had a chance to ask Pauline out. Would he get to take his last shot, or was there something going on with her and Wes? "I have calculus with Wes later. I'll try to see what I can find out about his new business." He gave my shoulders a tight squeeze before releasing me, replacing his frown with an encouraging smile. "See you later. And remember, keep your chin up!"

The day dragged by. I sat through all my classes, completely listless. Whenever my teachers weren't looking, I pulled up Instagram under my desk. My feed was infested with photos of my classmates taking selfies with their new Crown Tiger face masks with hashtags like *#RoyalStripes* and *#TakeMyMoney*. The photo that I'd posted on V&C's account had fewer likes than we'd had on anything since sophomore year. Everyone was too busy obsessing over the newest thing. I was falling behind.

No. I couldn't let this happen. I had to take Halmeoni to Paris. My mind flashed to the expense sheet in my notebook. I needed every single dollar I could make this year.

I took a deep breath, tapping my fingers against my desk. I had to stay calm. It was just social media. It wasn't cold hard facts. The sales would speak for themselves.

My last period on Monday was free, a strategic move I'd carefully curated my school schedule around. I stood by my locker the whole time, counting down the minutes.

Three, two, one.

The bell rang, and customers began to line up, but I could feel the difference in energy. The line was shorter. Kristy only bought one snail mask. Amelia and Natalie didn't even show, and neither did Lisa.

By the time the hallways cleared, over a third of my stock was left. Six out of ten snail masks still hung from the laundry clips. They spun around on the hanger in slow motion, creaking back and forth.

I couldn't move. I just stared at my locker. This couldn't be happening.

"Well, shit," Charlie said, coming up behind me. "What now?"

I snapped back to myself. No way was I going down without a fight. I pulled out a grape Hi-Chew from my fanny pack, tearing the wrapper open. "He got his warning and he still wants to play the game. So, fine." I popped the Hi-Chew into my mouth and turned down the hallway. "We'll play the game."

CHAPTER FOUR

WES

Monday / October 7

I didn't mean for it go down this way. Really, I didn't.

I called out Valerie's name as she ran out of the band room, but she didn't look back. A terrible sinking sensation filled my stomach. I hate when people are mad at me, no matter who it is, and Valerie was definitely furious.

The students in the band room were buzzing with excited energy, comparing their face masks and snapping photos for their Instagram. Squeals of "I can't believe we got these half off—and no shipping!" bounced off the walls. I tried to feel happy. My first non-accidental sale had been a success. But I couldn't get the look on Valerie's face, right before she ran away, out of my mind. The way the fire in her eyes had dimmed to shock, and how obviously she'd been trying to keep it together. I couldn't shake the feeling that I had offended her personally, beyond a business level.

Pauline appeared at my side, hugging the cash box to her chest.

Her wavy brown bob was pulled back in a headband patterned with starfish, and she wore a blue sailboat-printed dress. I could practically hear ocean waves every time she came near.

"Congratulations, Wes," she said with a smile. "We completely sold out."

"Congratulations to you, business partner," I said, smiling back. But my heart wasn't in it. I cleared my throat, trying not to let my distress show. "Are you sure you don't want a free face mask? I kept an extra in my locker in case you changed your mind."

She shook her head and pointed to her face. There were dry red patches around her eyelids, on her forehead, and in the space between her nose and lips. "Face masks make my eczema flare up. As do most products." She laughed lightly. "Just boring old dermatologist-recommended face creams for me. Thanks, though." She cocked her head to the side, appraising me with her curious eyes. "You're upset about Valerie," she said.

"Huh?" I blinked, a sudden blush warming my cheeks. "No. That's not true."

"You're a terrible liar," Pauline said simply. "It's written all over your face."

"Well," I said. It was disarming to be called out so swiftly.

"It's all right. She looked pretty angry. You weren't surprised, though, were you? You must have seen it coming."

I bit my lip. Surprised? No, I couldn't say that I was. But I had also been hoping—foolishly, in hindsight—that things wouldn't be so bad when I decided to give the sales thing a go. I thought back to Valerie's confrontation at my locker and how I'd turned to Pauline right after, asking her the question that had launched everything into motion: "What do you know about V&C K-BEAUTY?"

"V&C?" Pauline had said. She tapped thoughtfully on her chin. "They sell K-beauty products every Monday after school out of Valerie Kwon's locker. She runs the business with her cousin, Charlie Song. They do quite well for themselves. They're the only student-run business in our school that's lasted longer than a year."

"Are you friends with them?" I asked. The question came out without me even thinking about it. I was curious about these two students. Students who were my age and had somehow found a way to make a profit at school.

"Um, not exactly," she said, an awkwardness in her voice that made me think there was more to the story. "I worked with Charlie on a science project once, but we don't really run in the same circles anymore."

"Cool," I said, not pushing it. I felt suddenly embarrassed. Pauline and I weren't even friends. She probably thought I was a total weirdo, interrogating her like this. "Thanks."

I shifted on my feet, one last question burning in my mind. Should I ask it? Or should I walk away before Pauline got completely freaked out by my awkwardness and asked for a locker transfer? She stared at me patiently, like she knew I had something more to say.

"When I don't ask a question that's on my mind, I stay up all night thinking about it," she said. "You may as well ask now."

My mouth dropped open. "How did you know?"

"I'm a scientist in training. I can spot a question from a mile away. Also, you are very easy to read. Go on."

"This is just a hypothetical question," I said. "But if someone wanted to start a student business, how would they go about it?" I tried to keep my voice casual, even as my heart started pounding in my ears. Was there really a way for me to make money right here at school? From my research, it was going to cost between four and five hundred dollars to get my saxophone repadded. And the application fee for my top-choice school, Toblie School of Music, was a hundred and ten dollars. I would need that money by the December application deadline, and sooner for my saxophone repairs.

"You'll have to propose your idea to the principal and get it approved," Pauline said. "And you'd need a teacher to agree to mentor you. Someone to keep you accountable. You'd also need permission to resell from wherever you're getting your products if you're not making them yourself. And of course you'd need something to sell." She raised her eyebrows. "Do you have something to sell?"

Did I have something to sell? An excellent question. And also a ludicrous one. I thought of Valerie's warning and gulped. *There's no room for two of us.* It was probably best that I put this out of my mind.

I went home that day and emailed my resume to a list of potential part-time jobs, including the local music store and the Starbucks closest to my house. I could find another way to make money for music school.

And then the quartet happened.

Four people who somehow came together in perfect harmony in the following weeks to resurface the idea in my mind.

The first: Mom.

"Wes, I never asked you, how did your friends like the Crown Tiger lip balm?"

It was the first day of October, two weeks after the accidental lip-balm sale. I sat at the kitchen island with my breakfast avocado, checking my phone for any callbacks from jobs as Mom sipped her smoothie. Nothing yet. I turned off my phone.

"My friends?" Gulp. "They, uh, loved the lip balm."

"Really?" Mom perked up, probably eager to get a read on how the kids at school were responding to her marketing tactics. "They're big fans?"

"Yeah. Big fans. They call themselves the Royal Stripes."

"Yes! Crown Tiger's fandom name!" Mom clapped her hands together, pleased as punch. "Well, if your friends like them, I have some more freebies. I'll be getting a bunch of samples from Crown Tiger's new face-mask line soon. Why don't you take them to your friends?"

I nearly choked on my avocado. "More products?"

"We're really focusing on their partnerships with beauty brands." Mom beamed. "Tell your friends to Instagram them, okay? That'll be great publicity."

Pauline's question came floating back to my mind. *Do you have something to sell?* It looked like the answer was yes.

"I'll, uh, need a permission slip to distribute stuff at school," I said, choosing my words carefully. Distribute stuff, sell stuff . . .

same thing, right? "It has to be written in a specific kind of way. Really strict school." My mouth felt dry like all the words I weren't saying were cotton balls weighing against my tongue. But Mom didn't bat an eye.

"Sure," she said, already distracted by a message on her phone. "I'll write you one right now."

The second: Mr. Reyes.

I headed to school after my talk with Mom, making an immediate beeline for the band room to see Mr. Reyes before class began. Okay, so I had something to sell. That didn't mean I had to sell it. But what if I did? The idea had latched onto my brain and I needed to know if it was a real possibility or not. I could casually talk to Mr. Reyes about mentorship. It didn't mean I was going to pursue anything, I told myself. I just wanted to know if I could. And if I couldn't, fine. Great, even. I would peacefully put it out of my mind for good.

"I'd be happy to mentor you for your K-pop business!" Mr. Reyes said, beaming over his venti americano. "I've mentored quite a few student businesses in my time. I had one student who liked to sell her own bubbles. Made them from scratch with soap."

Whoa. That was much faster than I was expecting. "Thanks, Mr. Reyes," I said. "I mean, this is all hypothetical, of course. I was just wondering for *if* I wanted to do it."

"Certainly. You can use my room Monday mornings to sell if you'd like."

Mondays? Those were V&C selling days. "Um, are any other days a possibility?"

"No can do. Other days I'm not in that early, or there's choir practice going on. But Monday morning is all yours."

Band-class students started to trickle in, and Mr. Reyes smiled, raising his Starbucks cup to me. "We'll talk more later. For now, let's get those warm-up scales going!"

The third: Kristy Lo.

"Psst. Wes."

I looked up from my sheet music to see Kristy Lo, the pink-haired girl, waving at me from the flute section. Only now her hair was more orange than pink, like an ombré sunrise. Mr. Reyes was working with the percussion students at the back of the room. The rest of us were supposed to be studying our music, but I was pretty sure the second saxophone player, Aubrey Mills, had fallen asleep in the chair next to me.

"Will you be selling any more Crown Tiger merch?" Kristy asked in a loud whisper.

Everyone around us perked up at her question, their eyes immediately turning to me.

"Maybe." I smiled nervously, suddenly paranoid that Kristy had mind-reading abilities and knew exactly what I had been contemplating. "I don't know yet."

"Because I told a bunch of people about the lip-balm sale, and they're so choked they missed it. They told me to text them ASAP once I hear about your next sale."

"Ah, Wes, telling everyone that you'll be using the band room on Monday mornings for your business, are we?" Mr. Reyes said, reappearing from the back of the room. My eyes widened in alarm and I was about to protest when he wagged his finger, making a tutting sound with his tongue. "Right now is rehearsal time, not business-promotion time. Though I do admire your hustle."

Kristy's phone was already in her hands, her fingers flying across the screen, while the rest of the eavesdropping students burst into excited whispers. She grinned, flashing me a big thumbs-up as I sat completely stunned in my seat. "I just let everybody know. This is going to be so great!"

"All right, all right," Mr. Reyes said, waving his conductor's baton in the air. "Let's get back on track everybody. From the top!"

Um. What just happened?

The fourth: Pauline, again.

"I heard about your new business. K-pop, huh?"

I looked up from my locker to see Pauline standing next to me, wearing a denim jacket over a jumpsuit patterned in turtles. Kristy's text had just gone out a few hours before. News had traveled fast. "Ah, yeah. Well, kind of. It's a long story. . . ."

She tucked her thumbs under the straps of her backpack, rocking back on her heels. She looked nervous. "I could help you."

I paused. "Help me? Like a business partner?"

She nodded. "Exactly like that. Administrative stuff, tracking sales, helping you with school rules you might not know. That sort of thing."

"I mean, that would be amazing. But why would you help me?"

"I need more extracurriculars for my college applications," she said. She dropped her gaze from mine, scuffing the floor with her shoe. "And, also, my dad. When I told him there was a new kid at school selling K-pop merch, he got so excited. He's always wanting me to get more into Korean culture. He keeps hounding me about it, and he won't let me volunteer at the aquarium unless I also do something Korean-related. Sorry." She lifted her eyes up, an apologetic frown on her face. "I hope it doesn't feel like I'm using you."

"I don't feel that way at all. If anything, I feel like you're doing me a huge favor." I had been so hesitant about tackling this whole business thing, but maybe with someone to navigate it with me, it wouldn't be so overwhelming. There was still one thing holding me back, though. "I have to ask. Do you think this is a good idea? It feels weird. I don't know, like I'm copying V&C or something."

"Hmm." She considered this seriously, taking her time to answer. "K-pop is different enough that you could make it work," she said finally. "There might be some overlap in your buyers, since a lot of your products are from a K-pop beauty line. But it's a free-for-all at Crescent Brook. No one can stop you if you follow the rules."

I nodded slowly. That made sense. "All right," I said. "Let's give this a try."

We shook hands.

It was so strange how everything had come together. I stared at Pauline now, standing before me in the band room, cash box in her hands, with our first day of sales behind us.

"Here's all the money we made today," she said, passing the cash box over to me. "I took my cut already."

"Are you sure we can't split it more? You've helped so much."

She shook her head. "You source all the products and do the

majority of the work. I'm just here to help with some side things. It's the experience for me that's worth it. Besides, thirty percent is already more than enough." A smile lifted the corners of her lips. "My dad said if I keep this up, I can volunteer at the aquarium."

I smiled back, genuinely this time. "That's great, Pauline."

"Let me know when you want to have our next sales day," she said. The first bell rang, and she waved, heading out of the band room. I held up a hand to wave back, but she was already gone, leaving just me, the students trickling in for class, and my cash box full of money.

My eyes were starting to glaze over as I stared at the whiteboard where Mr. McAvoy was writing the day's warm-up math problems. I took my glasses off and polished them with the edge of my T-shirt, as if cleaning them would help me focus more. I had no idea how I was going to sit through calculus when my mind was still whirring from this morning's sale, and the look on Valerie's face. I had no idea what to make of her still. She was difficult to read, but clearly sensitive when it came to her business. I didn't want any enemies, but I was starting to worry that maybe I had just made one.

"Is this seat taken?"

I looked up to see Charlie standing at the seat next to me, backpack draped loosely over one shoulder. He grinned and scraped the chair back before I could answer, taking a seat.

"Great. Thanks, man," he said.

"Uh, sure." I awkwardly shifted my binder over to make room

for Charlie as he spread out his notebook, textbook, and water bottle on his desk. My shoulders tensed, on guard. Something told me he wasn't sitting next to me because he wanted to be friends.

Mr. McAvoy's marker squeaked across the whiteboard as he finished writing his final problem. "All right, everybody, who wants to volunteer for our morning math warm-ups?" he asked enthusiastically. The entire class groaned.

Charlie leaned over to look at me, propping his chin in one hand as he examined the side of my face. I tried to look straight ahead, focusing on Matt Whitman's back as he got up to volunteer for a question. My eyes darted over to Charlie. He was still staring. He wasn't as scary as his cousin, but still, his stare was unnerving.

"Can I help you?" I whispered so Mr. McAvoy wouldn't hear.

"I was just taking a second look at you," he whispered back. He narrowed his eyes. "I thought you looked like a pretty honest guy when we first met. But seeing as you totally ignored Valerie's and my warning, I'm having doubts. What's up with your business, Wes? You really want to be our competition?"

My eyebrows shot up in surprise. I hadn't expected something so direct. I opened my mouth and then closed it again. How did you answer a question like that? I turned back to the front of the classroom instead, where Mr. McAvoy was fixing Matt's mistakes with excited flourishes of his red whiteboard marker, my leg nervously jittering beneath my desk.

"Okay, you don't want to talk about it—that's cool." Charlie stared straight ahead at the whiteboard as well, his face impassive.

A moment later, he cleared his throat and whispered, "Just answer this one question for me."

His tone was different now, less offensive, more uncertain. I paused for a moment and then gave a slight nod.

"Are you and Pauline dating?"

"Huh?" I gave him a sharp look and then quickly looked ahead again. "No!"

"No?" A visible look of relief crossed his face. "Okay, cool. I mean, it'd be fine if you were, obviously. She can date whoever she wants. But that's cool, that's cool." He paused, and when he spoke again, his voice was back to being all business. "Are you going to keep selling together?"

"I don't know. Maybe. Yes."

"So you're really keeping this business going even after what Valerie said?"

"Maybe."

"What about at the Halloween Market?"

"The what?"

"Oh. Never mind. Forget I said anything. One last question, then."

I was getting flustered. We were going to get in trouble if he kept talking to me like this. "What?"

"It takes one hour for Cameron to mow the lawn. It takes Tim thirty minutes to mow the same lawn. How long will it take Cameron and Tim to mow the lawn if they work together?"

I stared at him. "Huh?"

"You don't know? Well, you better think fast. Mr. McAvoy!"

Charlie raised his hand, waving it in the air. "Wes would like to volunteer for the next question!"

"Excellent, Wes," Mr. McAvoy said, beaming. He held out the whiteboard marker. "Why don't you come up here and show us how it's done."

Oh God. I got up from my desk, looking back at Charlie as I did. He gave me an angelic smile, leaning back in his seat and leisurely folding his hands behind his head.

That night, I lay in bed, staring up at the ceiling and listening to music. I had a lot to think about, and there was nothing like instrumental jazz to help clear my head. Something about the smooth and silky rhythm helped line up my thoughts, like they needed a melody to flow to in order for me to make sense of them.

Was this whole business thing a good idea? I had obviously crossed a line with V&C. Was it worth it?

Yes. The answer came immediately. Selling things at school was a huge opportunity. From today's sale alone, I was one step closer to getting my saxophone fixed and my application fees covered. One giant $112 step to be exact. At this rate, I would definitely be able to save up enough by December. But . . . Valerie's face flashed through my mind. I sighed. Maybe there was another way I could make the money, without stepping on anyone's toes.

I scrolled through my phone to see if anyone had gotten back to me about my job applications. Nothing yet. But I did have one new email.

My fingers froze over the screen.

It was from Uncle Hojin.

I glanced at the door as if Dad would suddenly burst into my room and catch me red-handed. No sign of him. Obviously. That would be weird. I quickly tapped on the email.

Dear Wes,

Wow! So good to hear from you! It's been so long since we've done these emails. I don't know why we stopped. They really make my day.

I'm so happy to hear that you are thinking of pursuing music. I've always thought you had something special in you when you played. You asked me if I've ever regretted my decision to do the same. Hmm. What can I say, Wes? When you choose the path of an artist, nothing is promised, but everything is possible. I have never regretted opening myself up to those possibilities, even when they were unclear. Your dad was always worried for me because of that uncertainty, but for me, it was simply a calling I couldn't ignore. Difficult? Yes. Regret? Never.

I hope you are happy and healthy, Wes! What else is new? What are you listening to these days?

Uncle Hojin

PS. Of course I'll keep your email between us. Your secret is safe with me!

Something like hope took root in my heart at Uncle Hojin's words. It was exactly what I needed to hear, but at the same time I wondered if I should delete his email and pretend I'd never seen it. It felt like I was betraying Dad somehow to commiserate with Uncle Hojin over this.

And yet. I stared at my desk, where I had put my cash box. Next to the cash box was a stack of college brochures that Dad had left in my room, colleges with the most amazing and reputable science programs. Just the sight of those brochures made me want to take my saxophone and run as fast as I could. Dad would want me to apply to those schools soon. How was I supposed to tell him that not only was I not going to do that, but I was going to apply to a music school instead?

And yet and yet.

Valerie's face flashed through my mind. I thought of how I could barely get the words out to explain myself when she was glaring at me with those angry eyes today. Her confrontation had made me seriously consider giving up on this business thing, and it was only day one. If I couldn't even stand up to Valerie Kwon, who I barely knew, how would I ever be able to stand up to my parents?

Nothing is promised, but everything is possible. The words made my heart beat faster. *Everything is possible.* I wanted that. I wanted everything, even if there was a chance I'd end up with nothing.

I closed my eyes and let the music seep into my skin. The sounds of the piano-saxophone instrumental soothed me, but, more than that, they gave me courage to do what I had to do for myself. Open up to the possibilities.

I opened my eyes and texted Pauline.

Me: Hey. What can you tell me about the Halloween Market?

Thursday / October 31

Pauline had said that Halloween night at Crescent Brook High was a big deal, but I hadn't realized just how big it would be.

I walked into the courtyard, where students were putting the finishing touches on the outdoor carnival. There were rows and rows of game stalls, including a dunk tank, balloon darts, and a whack-a-mole game with spooky ghosts instead of moles. The aroma of caramel apples and candy corn filled my nose as I walked by the sweets stands, followed by the savory scent of grilled cheese and shawarma wraps as food trucks began to roll into place.

The entire carnival was lit up with strings of lights and candlelit jack-o'-lanterns. The doors of the school building, on the other hand, were strung with spiderwebs and caution tape. The first floor had been converted into a haunted house for the evening. I made a mental note to check it out later. But first I had to go to the marketplace.

I passed by people dressed up as everything from Kermit the Frog to the Jonas Brothers. Lisa Carol, who was wearing a Supergirl costume, waved at me from the other side of the courtyard, where she was lining up pumpkins. I waved back, tugging uncomfortably at the collar of my cape. I hadn't worn a Halloween costume in years, but Pauline had insisted it was mandatory. A quick trip to the mall and a dollop of hair gel later, I was maybe the world's worst vampire. My fake fangs kept jiggling around in my mouth, and I was pretty sure I'd never seen a vampire with glasses before. I smoothed out the white collared shirt I'd borrowed from Dad and tucked into a pair of ripped black jeans, hoping I blended in well enough.

The marketplace was at the end of the carnival, a series of tables covered in orange tablecloths and bowls of candy. Sweet treats to entice people to shop while they trick-or-treated. A few students who had signed up for the marketplace were already there, setting up their tables, while Ms. Jackson, my social studies teacher, supervised and directed everyone to their places. She was dressed up as Buzz Lightyear from *Toy Story*.

"Wes, you're at table number seven," Ms. Jackson said. "Remember, whoever makes the most sales by the end of the night wins the Halloween Market ribbon! Good luck!"

"Thanks, Ms. Jackson," I said, making my way to my table. I took off my backpack and started setting up the products I had. More Crown Tiger lip balm and face masks. It would be my first sale since that day in the band room. I had to think of a way to get products faster, and more of them at once, too.

I was so lost in my thoughts that I didn't notice someone appearing at the table next to me until they cleared their throat. I looked up and froze.

Valerie stared back at me, Minnie Mouse ears on her head. She wore what looked like a vintage red velvet dress with fishnet stockings and cherry lipstick. Without even thinking, my eyes flicked down to her legs and then back up to her eyes, my face burning. *Oh*

God, seriously, Wes? She already hates you. Do not check out her legs and freak her out even more.

"Hi," she said.

"Hi," I managed to say back.

"Looks like we're neighbors."

"All right, everyone, people are trickling in," Ms. Jackson said, clapping to get our attention. "Finish setting up and get ready! The marketplace is always a hot spot on Halloween night."

Valerie and I stared at each other. I swallowed hard. The air was charged between us, silent static like the moment when the conductor raises his baton, right before the music begins. The moment that says, *Hold your breath. The show's about to start.*

Ms. Jackson lifted her arms, the wings of her astronaut suit rising with her.

"Let the sales begin!"

CHAPTER FIVE

VALERIE

Thursday / October 31

I'd already known Wes would be at the Halloween Market before
I got there. Not just because fate is cruel, which it definitely is, but
because I'd seen the list of marketplace vendors on Ms. Jackson's
desk during our mentorship meeting yesterday. I didn't mean to
see it. It was literally just sitting right there next to her WORLD'S
BEST TEACHER coffee mug. How was I supposed to resist?

"Valerie? Did you hear me?"

"Huh?" I looked up from the Halloween list to see Ms. Jackson
staring at me, her eyebrows pinched together in concern.

"I asked if business is going okay for you two." She glanced back
and forth between me and Charlie before turning back to me and
pointing her pencil at my face, eraser end first. "You look stressed."

"Me? I'm fine," I said at the same time Charlie said, "She's
totally stressed." I pinched him in the elbow, making him yelp.

"Really, I'm fine," I said. I meant it too, if "fine" meant trying to think of a way to squash the sudden competition that was Wes Jung and his K-pop beauty products. He hadn't had another sale since the face masks, but I knew the competition wasn't over yet. I had to stay ready.

"Just remember not to get too caught up in your sales," Ms. Jackson said. "It's important to focus on your studies, too. Those colleges will be interested in V&C, but it won't mean squat if you start flunking all your classes. You hear me?"

"Loud and clear, Ms. J," Charlie said, but my mind was already on the Halloween Market. If Wes was going to be there, I'd have to bring my A game. He was the one who had started the war, but I was going to finish it.

He stood in front of me now, smiling hesitantly and revealing his vampire fangs. With his slicked-back hair and glasses, he looked like *Grease* meets nerdy Count Dracula. It would have actually been kind of cute if he wasn't the enemy.

I kept my face neutral and gave him a stony look until the smile slipped off his face. He cleared his throat, running his hand through the back of his hair.

"Um, I like your costume," he said, trying for a different approach. "It looks vintage."

I blinked, surprised that he'd noticed. Halloween was my favorite holiday because it gave me the perfect excuse to go thrifting for a costume. Umma hated it when I went thrifting. She couldn't understand why I'd want to wear someone else's old clothes when I could wear something brand-new. But even she couldn't argue the fact that it was the perfect place to find a Halloween costume.

Before I could respond to Wes, a Teenage Mutant Ninja Turtle jumped out from behind me, whirling a pair of nunchucks over his head. "Boo!" he yelled.

Wes and I both jumped. Charlie grinned, his eyes crinkling behind his orange eye mask. He was wearing a plastic turtle shell on his back and a full-body green jumpsuit with a yellow turtle belly across his torso.

"Hey, Donatello, you scared the crap out of me," I said, pressing a hand against my heart.

"Uh, I'm Michelangelo," Charlie said. "I was Donatello last year."

True, for the record. Charlie had been reusing the same Teenage Mutant Ninja Turtle costume since freshman year, just swapping out the eye-mask color and weapon of choice to be a different character each year. Lucky for him, he'd hit his growth spurt early and the costume still fit, albeit a little short around his ankles.

"How's it going, Wes Jung?" Charlie said coolly.

Apparently, Charlie's version of getting back at Wes had been to volunteer him for a math problem during class. When he'd told me about it, he was so proud of himself. "I did it in vengeance for V&C."

"That was your version of vengeance?" I'd said. "You've never seen *John Wick*, have you?"

"Trust me, Val. You gotta wear down the competition from all sides. He was definitely fazed."

Well, he definitely had some creative ways of taking out the competition. As for me, I had some strategies of my own up my sleeve.

I watched Wes out of the corner of my eye as he began to set up his table of products. He had nothing I hadn't seen before. More Crown Tiger lip balms and face masks. Was that all he had? He was going to have to try harder than that if he wanted to stand a chance against V&C. "Did you bring our stuff?" I asked Charlie.

"Yep," he said. He slid off his turtle shell. The shell was hollow on the inside, doubling as a huge backpack. He zipped it open and pulled out our beauty products.

The Halloween Market was one of my favorite places to sell, because it wasn't just about beauty. It was about enhancing people's costumes. I had products that I held on to for the whole year so I could release them around Halloween. I'd split them into two piles: one to sell on the Monday before Halloween, so people could prepare for their costumes (we're talking hair dyes, lipsticks, and eyeliners in all different colors) and one to sell on Halloween day, with products that people could use to add a little extra glamour to their costumes on the spot.

Out of Charlie's turtle shell came a parade of nail stickers, red lipsticks, liquid glitter eye shadows, and special-edition two-tone lip tints. Adrenaline rushed through me as I looked at the items I had so carefully curated just for this day. This was my element, and I was ready to make some sales.

As students began to trickle into the market, I took a scan at the other vendors setting up their tables. Among them were Matt Whitman, dressed up as a bee with his homemade honey; Ethan Phan (at least I thought it was Ethan Phan—it was hard to tell with the white sheet thrown over his head for his ghost costume) with his newest pottery creations; and Joanne Patel and Rebecca Sanders, the school's craftiest couple, selling their Halloween-themed bracelets and dressed up as Sailor Moon and Sailor Moon's cat, Luna. The two girls waved at me, calling, "Cool costume, Valerie!"

I waved back before turning my attention to my table. Joanne and Rebecca were sweet, but it was hard not to see everyone at school as either competition or customers, and right now, they were competition. Charlie and I had won the Halloween Market ribbon the past two years we participated, and I didn't want to lose my streak. It might not have been hard cash, but it was still validation that I was doing well, that I was on the right track. I couldn't let myself get distracted. I popped a grape Hi-Chew into my mouth to get my focus on.

"Valerie, you look so cute!" Kristy said, arriving at my table in a Princess Peach costume. She twirled a parasol over her freshly dyed blond hair, glancing over at Charlie and batting her eyelashes. "Hey, Charlie. How's it going?"

"Well, if it isn't my *Mario Kart* player of choice," Charlie said, making Kristy giggle. He put an arm around her shoulders and gestured to our products. "Can we interest you in anything at our table, Princess Peach?"

"Mm-hmm, I definitely see something that catches my interest," she said, giggling behind her hand.

I suppressed the urge to roll my eyes as Charlie grinned. "Did you see these pink flower nail stickers?" he said. "These were practically *made* for your costume. Not to mention, they really bring out your eyes." It was totally cringe. How the heck did nail stickers even bring out anyone's eyes? But Kristy was eating it up, and I had to admit, Charlie had a way with people that I could never quite imitate. We almost always sold more when he was around.

"Oh, hey, Wes," Kristy said, noticing Wes at the table next to us. She squealed. "Oh my God! You have more Crown Tiger stuff?"

"Happy Halloween, Kristy," Wes said.

Charlie frowned as Kristy slid out from under his arm to check out Wes's table. "Hmm," she said, her excitement dimming as she scanned the products. "I already bought all this stuff during your first sales. You don't have anything new?"

"New?" Wes said, looking genuinely confused. Lord help him. I felt a flash of annoyance. Did he know anything about running a business at this school? It was just as I suspected. He was totally clueless. No way was he going to hold anyone's attention span trying to sell the same product all the time. "No. Not right now."

"Too bad," Kristy said. She turned back to me and Charlie, all smiles. "I'll take the nail stickers."

"If you get two sheets, we'll throw in a bottle of base-coat nail polish for twenty percent off," I said. "It'll help protect your nails when you put the stickers on."

"Ooh, Valerie, you know I love a good deal," Kristy said, her eyes lighting up. "What about the lip tints? I've never seen these before."

"They're two-tone, so they're great for getting that gradient look on your lips," I said. "And they also double as a moisturizing lip balm." I held up two fingers. "If you buy two, you get the third half off."

"Wow, Kristy, nail stickers *and* lip tint?" Charlie said as Kristy surveyed the different colors. "You're not even going to give anyone else a chance to win the costume contest, huh?"

She laughed, swatting Charlie in the arm. Then she turned to me, fishing out her wallet. "Give me everything you told me about, Val. I'm sold."

Charlie high-fived me as Kristy skipped away with her new products, parasol twirling over her head. "Way to start off strong!" he said.

"Like I always say, make deals that feel like steals," I said, ending our high five with a fist bump.

I felt Wes watching the exchange out of the corner of my eye. He was frowning in a way that looked like he was trying to solve a puzzle, like he was realizing for the first time that running a business wasn't just about having a great product. As more and more people shopped at our table, my confidence rose higher. Wes might have Crown Tiger fans, but even fans get tired of the same old product. If all he had was lip balm and face masks, maybe I really didn't have anything to worry about.

"Attention, ghosts and students," a voice came over the loud-speakers. "The Amazing Haunted House Race is about to begin in fifteen minutes, starting with the senior student track. Everyone wanting to participate, please come to the front doors of the school. Remember, the winner of each track gets a fifty-dollar cash prize—if you make it out alive."

The voice cut out with a foreboding crackle.

Wes frowned, glancing around as if hoping someone would

explain what he had just heard. *That's right.* I'd almost forgotten he was new around here. Charlie and I took turns running the Haunted House Race while the other watched the market table—he ran it last year so it was my turn this year—but Wes would have no clue what that even means. For a second, I wondered what that was like. It must be difficult being the new kid, in senior year no less.

Charlie sucked in a breath beside me, grabbing my arm. "It's Pauline," he whispered. He smoothed his hair. "How do I look?"

"As good as a Teenage Mutant Ninja Turtle can look," I said as Pauline approached Wes's table, wearing a lobster costume. I heard him ask her about the Haunted House Race and she began to explain.

"You know that thing she and I used to do back when we were friends where we would share under-the-sea facts with each other?" Charlie said. "After we worked on the aquarium science project together?"

To be honest, I only vaguely remembered this, but I nodded anyway. "Yes."

"Well, I watched this documentary with my mom the other day, and I feel like Pauline would be really into it too. I'm going to tell her about it as a fun fact, like old times. Should I go for it? I'm gonna go for it."

"Go for it." As much as I felt like it would be better for Charlie not to reopen himself to heartache, it seemed like he was determined to live by his motto of "senior year, no regrets." I'd tried to warn him. The least I could do now was to give him a thumbs-up.

"Hey, Pauline!" he called.

Pauline and Wes both turned around.

Charlie froze. "Um. So." He opened his mouth and closed it again before glancing at me, totally panicked. *Hoo-boy.* Charlie had dated a lot of girls, and he sure could charm a crowd, but when it came to Pauline, he completely lost his cool trying to impress her. This I remembered distinctly from sophomore year.

Under the sea, I mouthed to him.

"Right." He nodded, swiveling back to face Pauline. "So. Want to hear a fun fact?"

A flicker of recognition crossed her face. Even if I didn't remember their history of back-and-forth fact swapping, it seemed like she definitely did. She nodded slowly like she wasn't quite sure where this was going. "Okay. Sure."

"I recently just watched a documentary about hacnyeo. Have you heard of them?"

Pauline shook her head, raising her eyebrows. Her cautious expression turned curious.

"Haenyeo are Korean female divers in Jeju Island," Charlie said eagerly. "They're really cool. There's this whole community of women, some even in their seventies and eighties, who go diving for seafood for a living."

"Haenyeo," Pauline repeated, like she was commiting it to memory. She smiled. "That does sound really cool."

Wow. Go, Charlie. Looked like his idea was actually paying off.

She cleared her throat. "Want to hear about something I learned recently?"

By the elated expression on Charlie's face, I guessed this was part of their back-and-forth. She was reciprocating! Truthfully, I was surprised. I'd always taken Pauline to be kind of cold, especially after the way she'd ghosted Charlie. But maybe there was hope for them after all.

"Hey, Charlie, you're cool with watching the table while I run the Haunted House Race, right?" I said. Probably best if I stepped out of the way to give them some alone time. He nodded gratefully, catching the hint.

"Oh, are you running?" Wes asked. He cleared his throat. "Pauline was just telling me about the race and I was, um, thinking about giving it a go myself."

I frowned. Was this guy really going to insist on competing against me in everything? How annoying.

A sudden idea sparked into my head as I remembered what Charlie had said about calculus class. *You gotta wear down the competition from all sides.* Bolstered by the success of our Halloween sales, I locked eyes with Wes and straightened up, a smile spreading across my lips.

"Care to make it a little more interesting?" I asked. "We make it a bet. Whoever beats the other in the Haunted House Race wins."

"Wins?" He frowned, his little vampire teeth poking into his lower lip. I tried not to think about how cute this actually was, because—*focus, Valerie*—this was Wes Jung, business-idea stealer. "Wins what?"

I considered this for a moment. "Loser has to help the winner advertise their business for the rest of the night."

"What kind of advertisement?" he asked, his eyebrows rising in interest.

"No limitations. Winner gets to choose."

"So you'll do anything I say, then?"

My stomach did a weird lurch at his words. This would be a much easier conversation if his vampire teeth weren't so distracting. "No," I said. "*You'll* do anything *I* say. Because I don't plan on losing." I cleared my throat and stuck out my hand. "Do we have a deal?"

"Uh, Val, is this a good idea?" Charlie asked.

I nodded. Yes. I would show Wes once and for all who he was dealing with.

Wes stared at my hand, considering. He looked from me to Pauline, who smiled and held up her lobster claws as if to say, *Your decision, buddy.*

He took a breath and put his hand in mine. My heart beat faster as he shook it once. He looked me in the eye, not letting go right away.

"Okay," he said. "Let's do this."

"Welcome to the Amazing Haunted House Race, seniors," Mr. Reyes said, dressed as one of the aliens from *Toy Story*. All the teachers had coordinated to be Toy Story characters; from Mr. Reyes to Ms. Jackson to Mr. McAvoy, who was helping run the carnival in his Hamm the piggy bank costume. "The rules here are simple. The first floor of the school has been transformed into a haunted house. Whoever can first make it all the way to the band room on the other side of the school wins. But beware: there might be some creatures of the dead that want to stop you from getting there."

He wiggled his fingers and made spooky ghost noises. Half of the twenty seniors in line to race giggled nervously, while the other half rolled their eyes from cheesiness.

I adjusted my Minnie Mouse ears and took my place at the starting line. Wes stood beside me, double-knotting his shoes for the race. I had no idea how fast he was, but regardless, I had the advantage of having run this race before. I knew what to expect.

Mr. Reyes raised his conductor's baton in the air. "On your mark! Get set! Go!"

The doors to the haunted house opened, and we bolted inside.

I zigzagged down the hallway just as a zombie leaped out from behind a column wrapped in fake spiderwebs, jerking his head in creepy movements, his arms outstretched toward us. Two people behind me screamed, changing course, but I ducked under the zombie's arm and kept on running.

A line of creepie Chucky-like dolls blocked the hallway, singing a disturbing lullaby in unison. "Come play with us," said one of the dolls, who I was certain was Amelia Perry. She smiled, the porcelain shine of her doll makeup shining under the pumpkin-shaped string lights. "Come play with us."

Ugh! Gross. I turned the other direction to take another route, racing through a graveyard maze and dodging a group of mummies who were gleefully wrapping some of their captives in toilet paper.

Somewhere along the way, I'd completely lost sight of Wes. Was he behind me? In front of me? All I could hear was the sound of my classmates screaming, shoes skidding against the floor as they ran this way and that, creepy Halloween music pulsing through the halls. And then I saw him.

There! Just ahead. The boy with the vampire cape and the ripped skinny jeans. Somehow he had slipped through everything and was headed down the hall that led straight to the band room. I pushed forward as hard as I could, gaining on him until we were neck and neck. He glanced at me, pumping his arms harder, but I refused to lose. Not now. Not when I was so close.

Just as we were about to turn the corner to the band room, a witch's body dropped from the ceiling, dangling in front of us with her mouth wide open in a wicked snarl. I screamed, falling backward into a bank of lockers strung with cobwebs and pumpkin lights.

Oh my God. That definitely hadn't been there the year before. Heart racing, I tried to pull away from the lockers, but I was stuck. I looked down. *Oh shit. Shit shit shit.* My fishnet stockings were caught in the sticky string of lights and cobwebs. I grasped at the lights, desperately trying to untangle them from my leg, but the more I wrestled, the more my stockings started to rip. Frustration bubbled up in my throat. *This can't be how the race ends.*

Suddenly, Wes was kneeling in front of me, his hands gently untangling the lights from my stockings. His brow was furrowed, his glasses hitching up at the wrinkle in his nose as he concentrated, taking care not to rip my stockings any more than I already had. I stood frozen to the spot as his fingers brushed against my leg, finally freeing me from the string of cobwebbed lights.

He looked up at me, a question in the air. I knew what he was asking without him saying it out loud. I could see it in his eyes, in the way he was still kneeling in front of me instead of bolting for the band room.

Are we still at war?

For a moment, I considered extending my hand and helping him up. After seeing his sales at the market, I knew I had the better business. He wasn't a threat anymore. And there was something about the way he'd stopped to free me, the way his fingers had brushed against my skin and made my breath catch in my throat, the way he was looking at me right now with such hope and seriousness and genuine anticipation, that made me want to say, *All right, the war is over. Good game, Wes Jung.*

But then I heard footsteps coming down the hall and I felt something stronger. The desire to win. To nail in my victory and prove that I was really the best.

"I thought you were competition," I said. "But I guess I was wrong."

I pushed past him and ran to the band room. I heard him leap up, chase after me. But it was too late. I had already won.

"Valerie, you're the best!" Charlie cheered as I held up my Haunted House Race cash prize. "I knew you would win!"

I grinned triumphantly.

"Congratulations, Valerie," Pauline said from the next table over. "Looks like you won fair and square. I suppose Wes owes you some advertising now."

I tried to ignore the twinge of guilt I felt at her words. It was like Pauline knew what had happened in the haunted house. But why should I feel guilty? It *was* fair and square. Nobody had asked Wes to stop and help me. He could have won. "Thanks," I said.

Charlie glanced awkwardly at Pauline and turned away, shoving his hands in his pockets. Pauline quickly looked away as well, busying herself with the table. I looked between the two of them. *Okay, weird.* This had definitely not been the vibe when I left.

"What happened?" I whispered to Charlie.

"Um, I'll tell you later," he said. He glanced up and nodded at someone behind me. "For now, you should cash in your win."

I turned around to see Wes walking toward us, wiping the sweat from his forehead. The guilt in me grew larger. He looked so innocent. I pushed down the feeling, fumbling in my pockets for a mango Hi-Chew. My celebration flavor. Maybe the taste of celebrating would help push the guilt away.

"So I believe you owe me some advertisement, Wes Jung," I said, slipping the mango Hi-Chew into my mouth.

He gave me a steady look and my heart skipped a beat. I couldn't quite read the expression on his face. Disbelief? Anger? Was he going to call me out in front of everyone at the market?

Instead he nodded. "Of course. We shook on it." He held my gaze like he was seeing something new about me, but it wasn't anger in his eyes. It was intrigue. "I'll do whatever you say."

My stomach flipped. Was it the guilt again or something different, something to do with the way Wes was looking at me?

"Time for you to pay up, then," I said too loudly, trying to distract myself from whatever it was I was feeling. I grabbed a red lipstick from my table. "How attached are you to your shirt?"

His eyebrows shot up. "You want my shirt? Um. I mean. Okay. Sure. But what am I going to wear?"

I walked up to Wes, closing the distance between us. He was so tall I only came up to his shoulders, which meant I was eye level with his chest. Perfect. "Don't worry," I said, popping the cap off the lipstick and twisting it up. "You can keep it on." I leaned in to write on his shirt. I felt his breath hitch, but he didn't move away. In big, bold letters across his chest, I spelled out *V&C K-BEAUTY*, stepping back to review my handiwork when I was done.

"Go on, then," I said, capping the lipstick. "The carnival's your catwalk."

For a second he stared at me, stunned. He was blushing furiously, but he quickly cleared his throat, regaining composure. He flashed me a quick smile and turned to Pauline.

"Pauline," he said. "You okay to keep watching the table?"

She nodded, a flicker of amusement in her eyes. "Of course."

He nodded back and, with a swish of his cape, walked into the carnival with my lipstick on his chest.

That night, after Charlie dropped me off, I tiptoed into the house, careful not to wake anyone. The Halloween Market ribbon was pinned to the front of my red velvet dress. I felt good, high off the adrenaline of everything that had happened. I couldn't wait to show Halmeoni. Umma and Appa would be sleeping already, but I knew she would be waiting up for me. She always did on Halloween. I'd go straight up to her room, right after I scoured the leftover candy basket.

"You're home late," a voice said as soon as I walked into the kitchen. My heart nearly leaped into my throat. I flicked on the lights to reveal Samantha standing at the table, digging through the basket of Halloween candy, a black blanket scarf draped over her shoulders and a witch's hat tucked under the crook of her arm.

"You scared me," I said. "What are you doing in the dark?"

"What does it look like I'm doing?" She waved a mini box of Skittles. "I was handing these out to trick-or-treaters all night. Now it's my turn."

I peered into the basket. "Are there any Kit Kats left?"

"Duh. Halloween tradition. I save you the Kit Kats and in return—"

"—you get all the sour candies." I grinned as she tossed me a Kit Kat. "Thanks."

She glanced at the ribbon on my chest. "What's that?"

I looked down at the ribbon, smoothing it out. "V&C K-BEAUTY won the Halloween Market ribbon again."

"Cute," she said, already turning back to the candy basket.

My smile slipped a little. *Cute.* Samantha wasn't as flippant as Umma about my business, but she still saw it as a cute side hobby. Suddenly the ribbon didn't feel so special anymore. In fact, it felt a bit childish.

Samantha sifted through the candy, looking wistful. "I kind of wish I'd gotten to do that at least once during high school. I never went to those Halloween Markets."

"Oh yeah." This was true. In all my childhood memories of Halloween, Samantha was at home handing out candy while Charlie and I went trick-or-treating. I always wondered why she never went to the Halloween Market with her friends instead. "Why didn't you?"

She shrugged. "Someone had to stay home and help Umma and Appa with the candy. You know how many trick-or-treaters we get around here."

Ever-dutiful Samantha. I sighed. "You should have said no at least once. The market is fun. It's part of the high school experience." Come to think of it, weren't Halloween parties part of the *college* experience? Only Samantha would opt out of that to come home and help Umma and Appa hand out candy instead. She really hasn't changed one bit.

She stared at me for a while, not saying anything.

"What?" I said.

"Nothing. It's just . . . it must be nice," she said finally, "to be the youngest child. So carefree."

"Huh? What are you talking about all of a sudden?"

"Never mind." She shrugged, snapping out of whatever weird melancholic state she was in. She grinned instead, hugging her blanket scarf around her shoulders. "Thanks for letting me borrow this, by the way. It was perfect for my costume."

"I thought that looked familiar! When did I say you could borrow it?"

"Never, but it looks better on me anyway, don't you think?" She grinned and popped a sour candy into her mouth before waltzing out of the kitchen. "Good night."

I rolled my eyes and smiled, heading up as well to get ready for bed. I washed the makeup off my face and changed into my Pompompurin pajamas before padding into Halmeoni's room. The lights were still on, but she was already dozing on the floor. Halmeoni likes to sleep on a blanket on the floor like she did back in Korea instead of on a bed. I used to insist on sleeping on the floor with her when I was a kid. Sometimes I still do.

I switched off the lights and curled up on the floor next to Halmeoni, tugging the blanket over both our bodies and snuggling against her. Her eyes flickered open, adjusting to the moonlight.

"My girl, you're home," she said. "How was the Halloween Market?"

I held up the Halloween Market ribbon. "Jjajan! Your granddaughter won this again for the best business at the market."

She gasped, fully awake now. "Aigoo, my girl is so smart!" She patted my cheeks with both her hands. "I'm so proud of you. You must show your parents tomorrow."

My smile slipped a notch, remembering Samantha's earlier comment. "Yeah, maybe. I don't know. It's not that important. It's not even a real prize, really."

"Ridiculous," Halmeoni said. "What's more real than all your hard work? You won this because you deserve it." She smiled, tucking a strand of hair behind my ear. "Now, tell me more about your night. Did you make new friends?"

Halmeoni was always asking if I was making friends, even in my senior year of high school. My cheeks warmed at the thought of Wes freeing my stockings and me writing with lipstick on his shirt. Friends? Maybe more like enemies.

"Um . . . kind of," I said.

"Good, good," she said. "It's important for you to make friends at this age. Charlie's a good boy, but you need more than just your cousin, hmm?"

I smiled in response, choosing to say nothing. Halmeoni didn't know this, but I didn't really have that many friends at school. I had a lot of customers, though. It wasn't quite the same, but I didn't mind. There would be time to make friends later. Right now I had to focus on my sales.

Maybe she had a point that I needed more than Charlie, but I already had her. Wasn't that enough?

"Can I sleep here with you tonight, Halmeoni?" I whispered.

"Of course," she said, already falling back asleep.

I closed my eyes. The last thing I thought of was Wes, the heat of his palm pressed against mine as we shook on the race.

CHAPTER SIX

WES

Friday / November 1

"So, how are you feeling about last night?"

Pauline looked at me as she pulled out a sandwich from her fish-patterned lunch bag, a teasing grin on her face. We were sitting out in the courtyard for lunch, right next to where the Halloween Market had been the night before. My face warmed at the memory of Valerie uncapping her lipstick and writing on my shirt. As soon as I'd gone home last night, I'd unbuttoned my shirt in the bathroom and tried to wash out the lipstick stain, but it was there to stay for good.

I guess I owe Dad a new shirt now.

"To be honest, I'm not sure," I said, unwrapping the chicken burger I got from the cafeteria. "Valerie is . . . something. It was probably not the smartest thing to take a bet against her, huh?"

Valerie Kwon. She wasn't exactly the warmest person I'd ever met. Pretty much the opposite, really. A part of me was stung by the way she'd screwed me over in the haunted house. I'd replayed that moment over and over in my mind, wondering if I should have seen it coming, if I'd made a mistake stopping to help her. If the roles had been reversed, I was almost certain she wouldn't have stopped for me. She would have kept on running, never losing sight of her goal. I'd known it from the moment we met. She was a scary girl.

But another part of me was weirdly impressed. She'd challenged me to that Haunted House Race like she already knew she would win, before betting me anything. From the sales to the race to claiming her prize, she'd basically steamrolled over me. I didn't stand a chance. It was embarrassing, but more than that, it was sobering. I'd always known that I wasn't the most confident guy, but standing next to Valerie made me realize just how unconfident I really was.

"Well, smart or not, you only grow by taking risks, right?" Pauline said as if reading my thoughts. "Though I was meaning to ask you, what happened in the haunted house? The vibe was kind of weird between you two afterward."

Uh . . . I suddenly became very interested in my chicken burger, which was really not very interesting at all. That was a good question. Other than Valerie betraying me, there was that one other thing that happened in the haunted house. That thing I hadn't been able to stop thinking about since. I couldn't even really say what "that thing" was exactly, but it was whatever I was feeling when I was kneeling in front of Valerie, fingers light against her stockinged legs, our eyes fixed on each other, a moment of suspension where suddenly we were the only two people in the world and my heart was a beating crescendo in my ears.

The sound of a bouncing ball jolted me out of my thoughts. I looked up from my burger to see Charlie jogging out to the basketball court with a group of guys, all laughing and passing the ball back and forth.

"Speaking of weird vibes, maybe I should ask you what happened with Charlie while I was in the haunted house," I said, eager to change the subject. "It seemed like you two were getting along pretty well before I left. What happened?"

The corners of her lips turned down in a frown. "Oh. Yeah. I don't know. It started out okay. But then, just out of the blue, he asked me if I had a crush on you. I said, 'What? No. We're friends.' And he got real awkward after that, like he didn't know how to continue the conversation. He kept opening his mouth and closing it without saying anything. Exactly like a goldfish." She shook her head. "I don't know. We used to be friends a long time ago. That fact-sharing thing was something we used to do all the time. Talking with him again at the market felt like we were picking up right where we left off, but . . ." She trailed off and glanced at me, embarrassed. "Sorry. Am I oversharing?"

"No, no, go on," I encouraged her. Truthfully, I was curious about her relationship with Charlie, especially after his weird Q&A with me in calculus class.

"So . . . in sophomore year, Charlie and I were paired together to work on a science project at the aquarium. It was a scavenger hunt, where we had to go around and take notes on different animals. That's how the fact-sharing game started, actually. We'd run around the aquarium and yell things to each other like, 'Did you know that seahorses have no teeth and no stomach?' It was a lot of fun."

She traced an absentminded finger over the fish on her lunch bag. "He was actually the one who encouraged me to get more into marine biology. I've always loved science, and I thought one day I would become a scientist. But while we were eating lunch by the otter tank, he said to me, 'I've never seen someone get as excited about the ocean as you. I feel like it's your calling or something.' And that really stuck with me, you know? It was one of those things that should have been so obvious, but I didn't realize it until he said it."

I nodded. I could understand that feeling of realizing something that had been right in front of your face the whole time. It was how I felt about music school.

"So what happened?" I asked. "What changed?"

"Well, one day I overheard Charlie and Valerie talking in the hallway. Charlie was telling Valerie that he was going to meet me for a study hangout and that she could join us if she wanted to. And Valerie replied, 'Why would I hang out with her? She never even shops with us.'"

I winced. "Oh. Awkward." What a thing to overhear about yourself.

"Yeah. And after that, you know what happened? Charlie texted me and said he couldn't make it to our hangout. He said something came up with the business. I kind of got the feeling that he bailed because of what Valerie had said, and, I don't know, it made me feel weird. I didn't want to assume, but then after that, there was this awkwardness between us that wasn't there before. It was like he didn't know how to be around me anymore. So I started distancing myself, and we just . . . drifted. Hence, present day."

"I think maybe he might like you," I said carefully, thinking again of our conversation in calculus class. It was pretty painfully obvious that Charlie had a thing for Pauline. Even I could tell, and I was new.

"What?" Her brow furrowed like she was considering a tricky science experiment. "But we've barely spoken in years. He doesn't even know me that well anymore. How can you like someone you don't know?"

"He might not know you that well yet, but I think the fact that he wants to get to know you more says something," I said. Valerie flashed through my mind, all Minnie Mouse ears and fishnet stockings. I nearly choked on my burger, coughing on a huge piece of lettuce. Why was she still in my head?

Pauline pounded me on the back. "Are you all right?"

I nodded, tears squeezing out the corners of my eyes. "Yep, all good," I rasped.

She passed me my water bottle and I took it gratefully.

"We should probably talk strategy for our sales," she said as I chugged down the water, trying to get Valerie out of my mind. "We didn't do too well at the Halloween Market. Do you have a plan?"

A plan? Good question. Another thing that had become pain-fully obvious at the market: Valerie knew how to sell. She was a real businesswoman, and I was just a guy with some beauty products and no plan. If I wanted to meet the application deadline and, more urgently, fix my saxophone, I had to step up my game. It was getting harder and harder to play with my old sax in class.

A group of students had gathered to watch the basketball game. Charlie dribbled the basketball between his legs and did a flawless layup, making his fans erupt into cheers. His teammates pumped their fists in the air, jumping up and bumping their chests against his. He grinned, glancing our way to see if Pauline was watching, but she was looking in the other direction and had missed the whole thing. His shoulders slumped slightly, and he turned away, plastering a smile back on for his fans.

Fans. A sudden idea clicked in my head just as the end-of-lunch bell rang.

"Wes?" Pauline said. She waved a hand in front of my face. "Did you hear me? I said, do you have a plan?"

"Yeah," I said. A smile spread slowly across my lips. "I think I just might."

Saturday / November 2

Frank Sinatra's voice crackled on the vinyl record in my bedroom as I sat at my desk, staring at all the products in front of me. At my request, Mom had come through with more Crown Tiger samples to "share" with my "friends." This time it was a lineup of hair dye, each box featuring a different Crown Tiger member, one with red hair, the other with silver, and so on and so forth. Apparently, these had already been released in Korea and were flying off the shelves, giving the entire population neon-colored hair.

Hopefully it would have the same effect at school. Me and my saxophone were counting on it.

I ran through the checklist in my mind. Lesson number one from observing Valerie at the Halloween Market: You couldn't just sell the same product over and over again. You had to offer something new that people wanted to get their hands on. I was pretty sure I had that now. The tricky, more strategic part came next.

Lesson number two from observing Valerie: make deals that feel like steals.

That's what she had said to Charlie, wasn't it? People might initially be interested in one thing, but if you paired it with a second thing at a discounted price, there was a good chance they would buy both, spending more than they'd intended because who could say no to a good deal?

The gears in my mind whirred as Frank sang about playing among the stars.

Stars. Fans of stars. Fans.

My target audience was Crown Tiger fans. Which meant they would probably buy other Crown Tiger–related merch, not just beauty products.

I rose from my desk and padded down the hall to Mom's office. The weekend meant that Mom was out at meetings all day and Dad was out golfing. It was just me and Frank, his voice crooning down the hall as I pushed the office door open and flicked on the lights.

It was utter chaos inside. The dark wood desk was piled high with documents and rolled-up posters. The corner of the room was stacked with boxes spilling with T-shirts, the bookshelf bursting with magazines and more documents. To anyone else, it would have looked like a disaster zone, but I knew she had a system for her mess. She had an office like this in every house we moved to, a place to keep all her excess stuff. Nothing important or new, but overflow merch or promotional material that she didn't know what to do with and often tried to pass off to me. I always said no. I'd never had a reason to say yes, at least not before today.

"One day, I'm going to have a clean office," Mom always said. "We'll do a big spring cleaning. Someday."

Thank God spring cleaning hadn't come yet. It never did. Mom either pushed it off, or we ended up moving and packing the office into boxes to replicate in another city, beginning the cycle again.

It took me a while to find what I was looking for. I unrolled the posters, scanned the bookshelf, and dug through the boxes in the corner of the room. It wasn't until I opened the top drawer of the desk that I found it. Jackpot.

A stack of glossy, signed Crown Tiger postcards gleamed up at me like pirate's treasure. I thumbed through the stack, each featuring a different member. Namkyu. Jun. Alex. Shiyoon. KP. These boys were the key to my success.

Make deals that feel like steals. Get a box of hair dye, or throw in two more dollars and get a postcard with it.

I grinned, sticking the postcards in my pocket. Frank's voice lifted to the climax of his song, and my hopes rose right along with it. I had a good feeling about this plan.

Lesson number three from Valerie: don't take your eyes off your goal.

Music school, here I come.

Monday / November 4

"Did you watch the links I sent you?"

Pauline leaned against the music stand she was setting up, a frown creasing her forehead. It was seven thirty a.m. and Mr. Reyes had let us into the band room before dashing off to the staff room for his second cup of morning coffee. "Yeah, I did," she said. "But I don't get it. Why did I have to spend my whole weekend watching Crown Tiger videos on YouTube?"

I grinned. "Because I realized that we have to appeal to our target audience: fans of Crown Tiger. How can we appeal to the fans if we're not even familiar with what they like?"

The whole weekend I had only one thought in my head: *What Would Valerie Do?* As far as I was concerned, there was only one person who could beat Valerie at her own sales, and that was Valerie herself. I tried to think of everything she would do to prepare for my Monday sale, including messaging Kristy Lo to spread the word.

I'll be there! Kristy said, with a starry-eyed emoji.

Pauline lined up the hair dyes on the music stands. "I guess that makes sense," she said. "At the very least, you definitely got my dad excited that I was watching K-pop music videos. He's been encouraging me to listen to Korean music for years."

I laughed as I fished the postcards out of my backpack. *Hmm, how would Valerie set these up? Laid flat or propped up?* "Your dad gets really excited when you show an interest in Korean stuff, huh?"

She smiled wryly. "Yeah. It's more of a recent thing. My dad was born in America himself. He grew up really westernized, and so did my brothers and I. I don't think he even really realized that he wanted his kids to be connected to his cultural heritage until my grandparents passed away a few years ago."

"Oh really?" I realized I didn't actually know that much about Pauline's family or how she felt about being half-Korean. "What changed after your grandparents passed away?"

"Well, when they were around, I used to speak Korean with them and watch whatever Korean TV shows they were watching. I learned a lot about the culture through them. But after they were gone, it's like I kind of lost my connection to my Korean side, if that makes sense. I tried to keep it up, but it was hard. It was like my Koreanness passed away with them. Does that make sense?"

I winced. "Yeah, it does. And I'm sorry. That sounds hard."

She smiled. "Thanks. It just isn't the same without them, you know? After they were gone, I think my dad just became really conscious about wanting me and my younger brothers to stay connected to our heritage. But I don't know. The older I get, the further I feel from it, and it's hard to force an interest in something, even if it is a part of your identity. Like the Crown Tiger videos are cool, but they aren't something I would watch on my own time or anything. Same with K-dramas."

She finished lining up the hair dyes, stepping back to survey her work. "What do you think?"

"I think that makes sense," I said. "But Korean culture is more than just K-pop and K-dramas. Maybe there's a way for you to connect with your heritage in other ways, especially if you feel like it's still important to you and you just don't know how to bridge the gap."

She laughed. "I meant, what do you think about the hair-dye setup? Does it look okay?"

"Oh." I grinned sheepishly, rubbing the back of my head. "Yeah. It looks good." I surveyed the postcards and decided to prop them up against the whiteboard so people could see them as soon as they walked in. But Pauline's words kept coming back to me.

"Hey," I said, thinking of something. "What about the haenyeo?"

"The Korean divers that Charlie was talking about?" she said.

I nodded. "Yeah. I also learned a bit about them in school when I lived in Korea. I feel like that could be interesting to you, since you love under the sea. Could be worth checking out?"

"I *was* interested when Charlie brought it up," she said thoughtfully. "Maybe I'll check it out. Thanks, Wes."

I smiled just as the door to the band room burst open. Kristy entered with a huge crowd of friends behind her.

"Good morning, Wes!" she said, beaming. "I'm ready to shop! What've you got for us?"

"Good morning, Kristy," I said. My heart rate picked up and the palms of my hands grew sweaty. Was this going to work? "Can I interest you in some Crown Tiger hair dyes? Brand-new. And, um, for only an extra two dollars, you can get one of these vintage signed postcards. Your favorite member is Shiyoon, right?" I held up a postcard of him in a fedora and swanky black vest. "Here's one from his *Lonely Nights* era."

"Oh my God," Kristy said, gasping. "The *Lonely Nights* era is one of my *favorites*. Did you see their music video for 'Call Me Tomorrow'?"

I nodded. I had, in fact, watched it ten times over the weekend, including the behind-the-scenes making-of video and every live performance. My research was thorough. "Yep." I held up a box of blue hair dye. "If you want hair to match Jun from 'Call Me Tomorrow,' this color could look great on you."

"Did you say Jun?" one of Kristy's friends said, already pulling out her wallet. "Jun is my husband. I want that one! With his post-card, please!"

The next half an hour went by in a blur. Pauline and I could barely keep up with people's orders as more and more students filled the band room. By the time the first bell rang, we were almost completely sold out.

I stood there in shock, looking at the nearly empty music stands as Pauline joined Mr. Reyes, who was back with his coffee, at his desk to go through a recap of our sales. Wow. I couldn't believe it had worked. We were making sales. We were nearly *selling out*.

"You really know how to clear out, huh?" a voice said.

I looked up from the music stands to see Lisa Carol standing before me, hugging her clarinet case. Other band students were starting to trickle into class as well.

I smiled at Lisa, feeling proud of myself. "Thank you. Only one box of hair dye left if you want to finish us off."

She picked up the box of pink dye, turning it over in her hands. "It is cute. I've always wanted to try a pink streak," she said. "But I was planning on buying a new emulsion from V&C today. Sorry, Wes."

"Ah." I nodded, pretending to know what the word "emulsion" meant. "Well, that's . . ." I was going to say "okay," but I stopped myself. *What Would Valerie Do?* She'd find a way to make this sale, I was sure of it. "What if I gave you a discount? Fifteen percent off if you shop with me instead of V&C."

She raised her eyebrows. "Seriously? You'll give me a discount if I don't shop with Valerie?"

"Um, yep," I said. And because it felt a little weird to bribe her so explicitly like this, I added, "Don't tell anyone, of course. It's just between you and me."

It wasn't the best tactic, and, as ruthless as Valerie was, I wasn't sure if it was one she would have used. But still, it worked. Lisa grinned, pulling out her leather wallet. "Well, I can't say no to that." She paid, taking my last hair dye. It was official. We'd completely sold out today.

"By the way, Wes, I'm having a party at my house next Saturday night. All the seniors are invited." She touched my elbow lightly. "Will I see you there?"

Alarm bells went off in my head. *Flirting. Flirting. Okay, Wes, time to flirt back. You just cleared out your sales. You can do this simple flirting thing. Put your new confidence to the test.*

"Sure, I'll be there." I clapped my hands together and gave her a double thumbs-up. "Can't wait."

Wow. Double thumbs-up? That was not what I wanted at all. But to Lisa's credit, she laughed, pleased at my answer.

"Great. See you there."

"Great," I said in relief. "See you."

As Lisa walked away, I quickly thumbed through the cash box. My smile faded as I did some calculations in my head. We might have cleared out, but after all the discounts and Pauline's cut, I wasn't left with as much money as I'd hoped. I was still short of being able to fix my sax, and after all my earnings went to repairs, I'd still have $0 for the December application deadline. And, after I spent that, I still had to earn $1,500 by May to pay for enrollment and housing deposits.

This was overwhelming. It was like after I paid one expense, another was right on its heels. If only there were a way I could get more products to sell, or if I had another way to . . .

A thought came to me. I looked down at my palm, remembering the way it had felt to have Valerie's hand in mine. The way it had felt to make a deal. There'd been an uneasiness to it, no doubt, but there was also something thrilling about taking a risk.

Slowly, the thought unfurled into an idea. A very big, very risky idea. I closed the cash box and tried to shake it from my mind. It was ridiculous what I was thinking. It would never work. But something Pauline had said came back to me, sticking to me like a tune on loop in my head. *Smart or not, you only grow by taking risks, right?*

For the rest of the day, this idea was all I could think about. Maybe it wasn't just business strategies that I'd learned from Valerie at the Halloween Market. I thought of her lipstick pressed against my shirt as she made me her walking advertisement.

Maybe there was a way I could make my competition work for me like she had made me work for her.

Saturday / November 16

Lisa Carol's party was already well underway by the time I got there. It looked like everyone from our senior class had actually shown up. Pop music was blasting, and people ran around with red plastic cups filled with beer. I suddenly felt outrageously nerdy in my cardigan with elbow patches. *That's not what you wear to a party.* What was I thinking?

"Wes! I'm so glad you could make it!" Lisa bounded toward me, wearing a pretty white dress, her curly red hair in a high ponytail. "Can I get you a drink?"

A drink? *Oh man.* I get the worst Asian flush when I drink. I basically turn into a walking tomato. *I should say no. I'll definitely say no.*

"Sure," I said.

What is it with my inability to say no to anything?

"Great! Be right back." She beamed and disappeared into the crowd. I watched her go, my stomach sinking.

I looked around the packed living room. Lisa had said that all the seniors would be here. There was one senior in particular I was hoping to see. Would she be here?

I'd been avoiding Valerie at school for the past couple of weeks, while I mulled over my idea and discussed the details with Pauline. Anytime I would see Valerie coming down the hallway, I would turn around and walk the other way. I wasn't ready to see her until I knew exactly what I wanted to say. I thought I had a good idea of it by now, but suddenly, being here with the very real possibility of seeing her face-to-face, I wasn't so sure. Something about her. She knew how to make a guy nervous just by standing next to him.

Ugh. I needed some air. Or maybe just a second to myself. I jogged up the stairs to the bathroom, but it was locked. I stood outside, bouncing from foot to foot, digging through my pocket for my earphones. I would go into the bathroom and listen to one song to calm me down, and then I would come out again and look for Valerie and say what I had planned to say. A short, three-minute song. That wasn't too long to hide in the bathroom, right?

The bathroom door swung open just as I untangled my earphones from my pocket. I looked up to see the very person I had been trying to avoid.

"Oh," Valerie said. "Hi."

I opened my mouth, but no sound came out. There it was. That something. What was it about this girl that caught me completely off guard? Other than the fact that she was totally intimidating, of course. Was it the way her eyes looked like they could see right through you? Or the knowledge that she was as cunning as she was smart? Or was it the fact that in all her sharpness, her lips still looked soft enough to disorient a guy?

"You all right?" she asked.

I managed to nod. "Yep. Totally chill." *Totally chill?* I

immediately wanted to slap myself in the forehead. Why was I such a dork?

A trace of a smile flashed across her lips. "Okay, then."

We just stared at each other for a good ten seconds. Her cheeks grew pink and I wondered if she was thinking the same thing I was, how the air between us grew more electric every time we were together. Suddenly, the past couple of weeks of trying to dodge her in the halls felt like a missed opportunity. She made me nervous, true, but now that she was here in front of me, there was so much I wanted to say. I wanted to ask if she had heard about my sales and what she thought about it, if I was doing a good job, if the lipstick she was wearing was the same one she had used to write on my shirt. There were so many things I wanted to know about her. She made me curious.

But instead I took a deep breath and said the thing I had been rehearsing to myself for almost two weeks.

"Valerie, I was wondering if you might be interested in another bet," I said.

"A bet?" Her eyebrows lifted in surprise, and she glanced at my chest like she was remembering Halloween. Her eyes slowly trailed back up to mine and she grinned. "Why? You want to do some more free advertising for me?"

This girl. I nearly choked on my words, but somehow I managed to get them out. "I was thinking something a little bigger than that. An all-or-nothing bet. We keep track of how much we made throughout the school year, and whoever makes the most wins."

"Wins what?" she asked, looking intrigued.

I swallowed hard. No going back now. "All the other person's earnings from the year, starting now."

Yep. It was risky. If I didn't know it before, I definitely knew it now, by the way Valerie's eyes widened in shock. But as much as I'd gone back and forth on the idea, I knew it was a risk I had to take. It was worth it. With Valerie's money, not only would I not have to worry about paying my school fees by May, but I might even be able to put some aside for the rest of the semester's tuition due in August. According to Kristy Lo, who I had casually had a conversation with to see what she knew about Valerie's business, V&C K-BEAUTY had made around two thousand dollars last year. Apparently, that was a record breaker for any student business at Crescent Brook. With my money, Valerie's money, and some financial aid applications, I might really be able to make this happen.

"Are you serious?" she said. "No. No way."

Not unexpected. When I'd told Pauline my idea, she had predicted Valerie would say this. "That's a big ask," Pauline had said. "What makes you think Valerie will agree?" But I'd seen the look in Valerie's eyes when we were in the haunted house. She wouldn't back down from a little competition.

I straightened up, looking down at her from my full height. "Why? Are you scared you'll lose?"

"Me? Lose?" she scoffed, quickly masking her initial shock. "Are you forgetting who swept who at the Halloween Market?"

"Then why not? If you're so sure you're the better business—"

"I *am* the better business," she said, scowling. "There's no comparison. I just think it would be wildly unfair for me to take such a bet against you when you're so obviously at a disadvantage."

"I'll take my chances." I was oddly satisfied watching her get flustered. It was cute. "I need to make more money, and more money fast, and I'm guessing that you're in the same boat."

That was a guess, but judging by the way she pressed her lips together, it looked like I wasn't far from the truth. "What makes you so sure you'll win?"

"I'm not," I admitted. "But I think I can put up a good fight. Better than I did on Halloween. Give me a chance to redeem myself."

She looked at me for a long time. I held my breath, certain she would say no and tell me to get lost. But then she nodded once, decisively, and said, "Fine. What's the timeline for this bet? Whoever makes the most money by when?"

"I was thinking prom." Prom was on the first day of May, right when my enrollment and housing deposits would be due.

I could see her doing quick calculations in her head. "Prom works." She nodded a few times like she was very satisfied with this timeline. "Yeah. That works really well. We'll have to judge this by seventy percent of the total profits. Charlie and I split things seventy-thirty, and I can't gamble his earnings."

"Fair." I'd discussed this with Pauline, too. Conveniently, we also split things seventy-thirty, so her cut was safe from the bet. It was just me on the line.

"Spreadsheets," Valerie said, snapping her fingers. "Do you have one? I'm going to need to see a spreadsheet of your earnings when we tally up the bet so I know you're not lying."

The bet had been my idea, but I was amazed at how quickly Valerie was making it hers. Her mind moved fast, leaving no bases uncovered.

"Spreadsheets," I said. "Done. And no making up numbers, either." I stuck my hand out. "Deal?"

She scoffed. "Like I need to make up numbers to beat you. Fine." She grabbed my hand and shook. "Deal."

I didn't let go right away. *Wow. We're really doing this.* And suddenly it hit me. The true weight of the risk. And the fact that I was still holding her hand. I let go quickly, all the bravado I had been putting up seeping away. "Okay. Well. May the best business win."

Now I was the one who was flustered. The part I had rehearsed was over, and I didn't know what to do with myself anymore.

So I did the only thing I could think to do. I pushed past her into the bathroom and locked the door.

CHAPTER SEVEN

VALERIE

Saturday / November 16

I blinked, staring at the bathroom door where Wes had disappeared, my heart pounding in my ears. He was a weird one. I still wasn't entirely sure what to make of him or the way my stomach flipped whenever he was near. I pressed the back of my hand against my warming cheek. I didn't see him very much around school, but when I did, I couldn't shake the image of him kneeling down and untangling my stockings from the haunted-house lights. But enough about that. What the hell had I just agreed to?

It wasn't like me to make such a big decision on the spot, but it had been near impossible to resist. If I could double my income by May, that would mean I could take Halmeoni to Paris this summer. This was almost too good to be true. Wes was basically offering me free money! How could I turn him down? Besides, I was 99 percent sure that I had this bet in the bag.

Well. Maybe 90 percent.

The truth was that V&C sales hadn't been so great since Halloween. We'd been down numbers, and from what I'd been hearing, Wes had made somewhat of a comeback over the past couple of weeks. It was probably a fluke. No need to worry.

I quickly moved down the stairs, searching for Charlie. If it weren't for him, I wouldn't even be at this party. Parties weren't really my thing. Too many people, and I never knew what I should be doing. Small talk? Dancing? Standing by the houseplants, nursing my drink? Nope, no thank you, and please spare me. But apparently Charlie felt like he'd made a pretty big fool of himself to Pauline on Halloween, and he'd been waiting for a non-school setting to try to make up for it. I was just there for moral support.

As I made my way through the living room filled with dancing classmates, the music switched from an electronic techno beat to an upbeat K-pop song, and everyone went nuts.

"I love Crown Tiger!" someone shouted.

I tensed at the name. It's not that I hate K-pop. I listen to it sometimes, including Crown Tiger. They have good songs. A nice mix of soft ballads and hype dance numbers. Even Halmeoni likes their music. But ever since Wes had started selling their beauty products, I'd been boycotting them. Some might have called it petty, but what can I say? I'm the queen of petty.

"You've met the new guy, Wes Jung, right?" a girl was saying as I stepped through the mirrored French doors that led into the kitchen, making sure to shut the doors behind me to muffle the music. "Do you think he's dating anyone? He's so cute."

"I don't think so, but Lisa Carol has her eye on him for sure," her friend said, sipping from a red plastic cup. "I don't think he's interested, though. From what I hear, he's only into music and his new K-pop beauty business."

"That's been going super well, huh? Each time I've gone, he's sold out before the first bell rings."

"Ooh, are you a Crown Tiger fan too?"

"Nah. I just go to see Wes's face."

The two girls giggled, and I felt a prick of uncertainty. My confidence dipped to 85 percent. I yanked the fridge door open so hard the bottles clattered inside. The two girls glanced my way before skittering out of the kitchen to continue their conversation elsewhere.

Heat bubbled up inside my stomach as I grabbed a bottle of beer and popped the cap off. It was fine. Everything was fine. I was still mostly positive I could win this. I mentally brought up the image of my Moleskine notebook. It would feel so good to hit my five-thousand-dollar goal. I might even exceed my goal with Wes's money, which meant Halmeoni and I could stay in a nicer hotel. It was, in fact, a good thing that Wes's business was doing well. The more money he made, the more money I would take from him, because no matter how well he was doing, I knew I could do better.

I took a sip from my bottle and grimaced. Yuck. I don't even like the taste of beer. I'd just grabbed it to distract myself from those girls. I was considering draining the rest of it down the sink when Pauline stepped into the kitchen, her eyes searching the room like she was looking for someone.

"Hey, Valerie," she said, her gaze falling on me. As always, she was wearing a sea-inspired outfit. Today was a gray rib-knit turtle-neck sweater tucked into a high-waisted skirt patterned with jelly-fish. The jellyfish skirt was kind of cute, actually. Vintage. I wonder if she'd thrifted it. "Have you seen Charlie? Lisa said he was looking for me."

"He's around here somewhere," I said, rolling the unwanted beer bottle between my palms. Maybe I could hide it behind the toaster. Leave it for the Carols to find in the morning.

"Thanks," Pauline said. She started to leave but hesitated by the door, turning to look back at me. "Could I ask you a question? I mean, I know I technically just did, but another actual question?"

I raised an eyebrow. I could count on one hand the number of times Pauline and I had talked. We'd never really had much reason to. She'd never even come by my locker to shop. "Sure."

She leaned against the kitchen counter, pondering her question. "About Charlie. We haven't spoken in a while, until he started talking to me again at the market. Wes seems to think he might like me." She cocked her head to the side, looking at me curiously. "Is that true?"

I nearly choked on my beer in surprise. God, why was I still drinking this? I put it down on the counter and wiped my mouth with the back of my hand.

He's been in love with you ever since you partnered together for that aquarium field trip! I wanted to say. Sophomore year had been a tough one for Charlie. It was the year his dad said he was going to move back to America, but he ended up taking a promotion at his job in Korea instead. It was when the beauty packages started, though I was fairly certain that Charlie would have rather had his dad back. Apparently, he'd confided some of these things to Pauline while they were eating lunch in front of the otter tank.

"She just listens so well," he kept saying afterward. "I felt so much less alone talking to her. And she's so much fun, too! Did you know she's basically a science genius? She's definitely smarter than me, but she acts like my opinions matter and I have good ideas. Me! Good ideas!"

"Why would you feel alone when you have me and your mom around?" I'd asked. "And since when did you have so many opinions about the aquarium, anyway?"

"It's not *about* the aquarium, Val. It's about the way she really sees me."

I hadn't gotten it then and I didn't really get it now, but still, I was tempted to recount all of this to Pauline. But it wasn't my place to share Charlie's confession, even if I did know the origin story by heart from the number of times he'd recited it to me. So I simply shrugged and said, "If you want to know, you should ask him."

"Right. Go straight to the source," she said, nodding thoughtfully. "That makes sense. Thanks, Valerie."

She smiled and started to leave, when a niggling thought at the back of my mind made me say, "Wait. I have a question for you, too."

She turned, her hand resting against the French doors. I could see through the mirrored doors into the living room, where people were dancing, the muted sound of Crown Tiger booming against the glass. Annoyance swelled inside me like a balloon about to burst.

"Why are you helping Wes with his K-beauty business when you've never even visited V&C K-BEAUTY?" I asked, my voice more accusatory than I meant it to be. "I remember every single customer who shops with us, and you've never come once. I just thought you weren't into K-beauty, which is fine, but now you're Wes's business partner? Why?"

A flicker of surprise crossed her face. "Oh. I didn't realize you were that bothered by it."

"I mean, of course I notice," I said impatiently. "People are either customers or non-customers. You've always been a non-customer." And now she fell into the third category of people: competition.

She searched my face for so long I started to feel uncomfortable. I was beginning to regret asking when she finally spoke.

"You're right," she said. "I'm not into beauty products. Not because I'm not curious about them, but because I have eczema. A lot of products make me flare up, so I stick to the skin-care routine my dermatologist has me on."

"Oh." My cheeks warmed in embarrassment. How had I never known that before? Her skin looked fine to me right now, but now that she mentioned it, I did remember instances when her skin looked a bit more flaky, red, and irritated than usual. I always wondered in those moments why she didn't come to our store and buy a moisturizer.

"As for why I'm helping Wes, it's because my dad wanted me to get involved in a Korean-related activity before letting me volunteer at the aquarium. Wes's business seemed like a good opportunity. He was just starting out and he needed help. And he sees me as a friend." She smiled faintly, her eyes not leaving mine. "Not just as a customer or non-customer. That's why I felt like I could approach him."

A knot twisted in my stomach. "Oh," I said again, not sure what else to say. It was strange having my own words said back to me. It felt totally fine to think of people as customers or non-customers in my own head, but having someone else say it out loud hit differently. Like maybe it wasn't such a normal way to think about people after all. I awkwardly took a swig of the beer I didn't want, just to have something to do. It burned down my throat.

"Anyway, I should probably go find Charlie now." Pauline pushed the doors open, letting Crown Tiger's music come blasting into the kitchen full force. "See you."

The doors bounced shut. I watched her go, feeling like a total jerk.

Through the doors, I spotted Wes standing in the living room, looking around for something or someone. Lisa Carol immediately bounded toward him, double-fisting drinks. One for him, one for her. She smiled brightly at him and he smiled back, taking the drink as she led him over to a group of her friends.

Apparently, Wes Jung wasn't just the most popular business anymore. He was also the most popular guy. Was it because of what Pauline had said? Because he was approachable? Unlike me, apparently. Was that why his business was doing better than mine lately? Was it going to keep getting better?

Confidence: 80 percent.

I scowled. *Forget moral support. Charlie's a big boy. He can handle this himself. I've had enough of this party.*

Going home, I texted him. And then, because I felt bad for leaving early, I added, Sorry. Let me know how it goes with P.

I drained my bottle of nearly full beer in the sink and let myself out the back door.

Lucky for me, it wasn't too far from Lisa Carol's house to mine, and the night was surprisingly warm for November. I popped a grape Hi-Chew in my mouth as I walked. I needed all the help focusing I could get. I couldn't get cocky. I had to up my game to guarantee my win against Wes.

Focus. Focus. Focus.

Verdict after five grape Hi-Chews: fruity breath, but no new ideas. *Oh, Hi-Chews, how could you fail me?*

I walked through the front door of my house, toeing off my shoes. It was still early in the evening. I could hear the clink and clatter of metal chopsticks against rice bowls in the kitchen. The smell of doenjang jjigae filled the air. My mouth watered. Korean soybean-paste stew is one of my favorites, and I hadn't had any food at the party. Looked like coming home early was a good idea for more reasons than one.

I poked my head into the kitchen, where Umma and Appa were sitting at the table, eating dinner. "I'm home," I said.

"Valerie, long time no see!" Appa said. He was still in his dress shirt and pants, his tie loose around his neck like he'd just gotten back from a house showing. He was clean-shaven as always, keeping up his polished image for his real estate clients. "I haven't seen your face in ages. How's my daughter doing?"

"Good," I said. "Where's Halmeoni and Samantha?"

"Samantha had a group project meeting, so she'll be coming tomorrow instead. And Halmeoni's in her room, resting. She ate earlier," Umma said. "Did you eat yet? I made your favorite jjigae."

I smiled. Things might have been tense with Umma sometimes, but she'd always had an uncanny sense for preparing my favorite foods when I most needed them. "I haven't eaten yet. I'll get some rice."

As I headed for the kitchen cupboards to pull out another rice bowl, Umma gave me a once-over, her eyebrows creasing together.

"Valerie, what are you wearing? Are you still shopping for old clothes worn by other people?"

"It's called thrifting, Umma." I tugged self-consciously at my vintage eighties vest, trying to let her comment slide off my back. I loved this vest. It was one of my best thrift-store finds.

Umma shook her head, looking at Appa over her chopsticks. "Your daughter is always digging through garbage for clothes."

"If it's her style, what's wrong with it?" Appa said. I felt a swell of gratitude for him.

Umma sighed. "Did we immigrate all the way here just so she can wear other people's clothes? No, we did not."

Appa looked chagrined. "I suppose you're right. Valerie, do you need yongdon to go shopping?" He was already reaching for his wallet. "I can give you allowance if you want."

"It's fine, Appa," I sighed, scooping rice into my bowl from the rice cooker. I just really wanted them to drop it now. But Umma was still going.

"Why don't we go shopping together sometime, Valerie? We'll get you some nice, brand-new blouses. And some practical shoes too."

I tried not to cringe. Shopping with Umma was about as much fun as staring at the spinning rainbow wheel on a frozen MacBook screen. She was very picky and had a specific style she envisioned for me—a.k.a. not my style at all.

"It's time you think about your future, Valerie," she said. "And start dressing for it. When I was just a little older than you, I was already applying for office jobs to help support your halmeoni. You think anyone would have taken me seriously if I didn't dress like a professional? It will be fun! We can upgrade your wardrobe together."

"Yeah, but I'm not applying for any office jobs right now, Umma," I said. "Or anytime soon."

"Didn't you say you want to be a businesswoman?" she pressed. "I know you're playing pretend right now with that makeup club of yours, but one day if you want to do it for real, you'll have to dress the part."

Playing pretend? Heat flushed my cheeks as my fingers tightened around the rice scooper. I couldn't believe she'd just said that.

"I didn't know you wanted to be a businesswoman, Valerie," Appa said. "What a cute dream for you!"

There it was again. *Cute.* Any semblance of warmth I had been feeling toward them earlier immediately vanished. I wished I had never told Umma about V&C K-BEAUTY or wanting to go into business. I wished I had never told her anything at all.

"Say, isn't Samantha taking that business elective in school right now?" Appa said.

"She is," Umma said proudly. "She got an A on her last test."

Suddenly I didn't have an appetite anymore. I fumed, dumping the rice I'd scooped back into the rice cooker and dropping the bowl on the counter with a clatter, making both my parents jump in their seats.

"Be careful with those bowls, Valerie," Umma said, startled. "And why did you stop scooping your rice?"

"I'm not hungry anymore," I said, walking out of the kitchen. My voice came out all tight, like I was going to cry at any second. I hated that.

As I left, I heard Appa whisper to Umma, "Did we say something wrong?"

I ran up the stairs, my stomach grumbling with hunger. But better to starve than to sit at the table listening to Umma and Appa critique me all night. *It's fine. Whatever. I'll just eat Hi-Chews for dinner.*

Before I could disappear into my room, Halmeoni emerged from hers in her Pompompurin nightgown, a concerned look on her face. "I thought I heard your voice," she said. "What's wrong?"

"It's nothing," I said. "I don't want to talk about it."

"Hmm." She put her hands on either side of my face, squinting her eyes and surveying me closely. She released me and nodded once decisively. "All right. Put your shoes back on. We're going out."

"Huh?" I stared as Halmeoni disappeared back into her room, reappearing in a pair of jogging pants and a puffy purple down jacket. "Where are we going?"

"For a walk." She zipped her jacket up to her chin. "Let's go, my girl."

She tiptoed down the stairs and I followed suit, too curious not to. She pressed her fingers to her lips as she passed by the kitchen, not making a sound. *Ah. She doesn't want Umma and Appa to know she's leaving the house. Umma would flip if she knew Halmeoni was going out at this hour.* Luckily, they didn't look up from their dinner as we snuck by unnoticed, slipping on our shoes and letting the door click shut softly behind us.

"Ahh, it feels so good to be outside!" Halmeoni said, looking mighty pleased with herself. "Your parents have been keeping me locked up at home all day. You know, I was hoping you would come home early so we could sneak out together."

"You don't have to do this for me, Halmeoni," I said, smiling in spite of myself. "I know you're only doing this because I'm sad."

"What are you talking about? Didn't you hear me? I'm doing this because I want to go out." She gave me a stern look. "Now, I don't want to hear another word like that out of your mouth. Got it?"

I laughed. "Okay. Fine. Where are we going?"

Her eyes twinkled. "Hmm. Where should we go? Oh! How about the strip mall?"

It was only a short walk to the nearest strip mall, but at Halmeoni's pace it took us double the time to get there. She used to be a swift walker, pumping her arms as she zoomed down the sidewalks of our neighborhood, but even I had to admit she wasn't as fast as before. Her arms didn't swing by her sides the way they used to. It was probably because Umma kept such a tight watch on Halmeoni these days. If Halmeoni had been able to get out more, I was sure her muscles would loosen up again. But the walk was still nice, and I didn't mind slowing down to match her pace, our arms linked together, making our shadows merge into one under the streetlamps.

The strip mall is pretty run of the mill. There's a dollar store, a shawarma restaurant, a laundromat, a bagel bar, and an arcade that's been there for as long as I can remember. It has all the classic arcade games, like *Street Fighter* and *Bubble Bobble*, and a row of sticker-picture machines that I used to be obsessed with when I was a kid. Halmeoni would take me and Charlie to the arcade all the time on weekends when Sunhee Eemo was working and Umma was driving Samantha around to all her tutoring sessions.

"Remember this place?" Halmeoni said, peering through the arcade window. She gasped, pointing at the sticker-picture machines in the corner. "Look, Valerie, they still have those sticker machines! When's the last time we took a photo in one?"

"I don't know," I said with a laugh. "Maybe five, six years ago? Those machines must be ancient by now."

"Let's take one now," Halmeoni said, already walking into the arcade. She held the door open, ushering me in. "I just got my hair dyed. I want to see how young I look!"

Nostalgia washed over me as I walked into the arcade. It smelled exactly the same as I remembered it: a faint citrusy scent like peeled mandarin oranges. A crowd of middle school kids gathered around the *DDR* machine, cheering as two boys battled it out on the dance floor, while another group of kids duked it out at the air-hockey table. The sound of music, laughter, and video-game voices announcing "Three, two, one, fight!" pulsed in my ears, dimming only when Halmeoni and I stepped into a sticker-picture machine, pulling the curtain shut behind us.

Sticker-picture machines are like photo booths, except way cooler. You can choose different backgrounds and decorate your photos on the computer screen before they print out on sticker paper. Halmeoni picked a series of pastel-colored backgrounds for our four different poses. The camera lights flashed with each pose.

We made peace signs.

Flash.

Finger hearts.

Flash.

Fish faces.

Flash.

I reached over, wrapping my arms around her in a giant hug. She smiled the biggest smile. Just before the lights went off, I thought: *The wrinkles around her eyes are beautiful.*

Flash.

"How should I decorate?" I asked, tapping the drawing pen against the screen.

"Give yourself a crown," Halmeoni instructed. "Because you are my princess." She patted my cheek and I warmed up all over.

"How about for you, then?"

"A bigger crown, obviously, because I am the queen," she said with a grin.

I finished decorating, scribbling *Valerie Hearts Halmeoni* in cursive on one of the photos. The machine printed out two copies, one for me and one for Halmeoni.

"Aigoo, look at this silly halmeoni taking photos like a young person," she laughed, looking at the sheet of sticker pictures. "I don't really look so young, do I? Maybe I should stop taking these."

I grabbed her hand and squeezed. "Never. You look perfect." I beamed at the sticker pictures, tucking them safely into the pocket of my vest. "And these are perfect too. Thank you, Halmeoni."

By the time we walked back home and tiptoed into the house, Umma and Appa were upstairs in their room. From the sounds of it, it seemed like they hadn't noticed we were gone. Good on Halmeoni for leaving her bedroom door closed with the lights on inside. They probably thought she was still resting in her room.

Halmeoni was glowing the whole time as we went into the kitchen. She hummed along to a song inside her head as she reheated the doenjang jjigae for me. I watched her simple movements, my heart aching. She'd had such a good time just walking to the strip mall. It would be so wonderful if she could explore beyond our city.

I felt a sudden surge of determination. I would beat Wes, and I *would* take her to Paris this summer. And when I accomplished that, we'd see what Umma and Appa had to say about my business. *They won't think it's so cute when I pull off something this epic.*

I was going to one-up my competition. I just had to figure out how.

CHAPTER EIGHT

WES

Saturday / November 16

As it turned out, the cardigan with elbow patches was a bad idea not just because it wasn't cool party wear, but because I had not been able to stop sweating since making the bet with Valerie. I desperately wanted to take it off but wasn't sure what to do with it if I did. Hold it slung over my arm like a butler taking coats? Tie it around my waist like Dad does with his windbreaker when he hikes? Or try to leave it on the back of the couch where two kids that I recognized from my English class were currently making out? Um. I glanced around the living room. Maybe I could find a coat hanger around here somewhere.

"There you are, Wes!" Lisa appeared by my side, holding two bottles of beer. "I've been looking for you."

She handed me a bottle with a cheerful grin. I took it and smiled back, though inwardly I was already dreading the flush.

"Come hang out with us," Lisa said, leading me over to a couple of girls hanging out on the staircase, laughing and sipping from red cups. There was Natalie Castillo, with a pair of white headphones hand-painted with flowers looped around her neck, and Kristy Lo's friend who had called Jun her husband. She had made good use of the hair dye: pops of electric blue peeked out from her strands of black hair. A true fan. "We were just talking about your Crown Tiger merch."

"Wes!" Natalie shifted over, making room for me on the stairs. "Come sit!"

"Thanks," I said. "Cool headphones."

She grinned. "Thanks. I painted them myself. It's my latest DIY." She gestured to Kristy's friend. "You know Mimi, right? We're friends from art club."

"Kind of." I turned to Mimi. "I've seen you at my sales before, right?"

Mimi grinned back and stuck out her hand. Her nails were decorated with nail art that looked like juice boxes. "Yep. Nice to formally meet you. I'm Mimi Takenouchi."

I shook her hand, my memory flashing back to holding Valerie's hand just moments ago. "I'm—"

"Wes Jung, duh. Everyone knows you." Mimi laughed. "Everyone's been talking about your Crown Tiger beauty business. You're even more popular than V&C K-BEAUTY, and no one's had a better business than them since they started."

My stomach flipped at the mention of Valerie's business. It shouldn't have surprised me that people associated us, but hearing our names together out loud made my cheeks feel warm. It reminded me that while we may have been in indirect competition before, we were very much in direct competition now.

I took a sip of beer. "That's cool," I said, trying to sound casual. "I don't know about more popular, though. They've been around for a lot longer, and Valerie really knows her stuff when it comes to business." Um, what was I doing? Was I *trying* to help Valerie win the bet? "Obviously, though, she doesn't have the same products that I do," I added quickly. "Woo! Go, Crown Tiger, am I right?"

Wow. It would be great if my social skills could show up right about now. I tugged awkwardly at the collar of my cardigan, seriously overheating.

Lisa giggled. "Don't worry, Wes. She may have been around longer, but your products are definitely better." She winked. "And don't worry. I won't shop with V&C as long as you keep giving me that discount."

"Wait, wait, what discount?" Natalie said, perking up. "I want in on this!"

Oh great. I stared at Natalie and Mimi, who were looking back at me with expectant eyes, and then glanced up at Lisa. She slapped a hand over her mouth, her cheeks flushing.

"Oh my God, sorry, Wes. That was supposed to be our secret." She glanced at her beer bottle and lowered her hand from her mouth, biting her lip apologetically. "I'm a little buzzed."

"Soooo?" Mimi said, leaning forward. "What's this special secret discount? And don't worry. We won't tell anyone." She held up her red cup. "This is just punch with, like, the tiniest amount of alcohol. I'm one hundred percent sober."

"And this is just water," Natalie chimed in. "I'm designated driver."

"Um . . ." It had felt okay to give one person a discount to stop shopping with Valerie. But three people? I mean, maybe it was fine, even if my conscience was sending me signals that it wasn't the fairest way to run a business. Especially now that we were officially in competition. Would this be considered sabotage?

"Pleeeease, Wes?" Natalie said, rubbing her hands together. "I really want to keep shopping with you, but my parents are putting a limit on my spending. Again. I could really use a discount."

She and Mimi looked at me with puppy-dog eyes. Argh. Why was it so hard to say no to people?

"Okay, sure," I said. They cheered. "But please don't tell anyone else. I don't want to make this a big thing."

Natalie mimed zipping her lips and throwing away the key while Mimi nodded eagerly.

"Of course, of course. And TBH, I'm totally willing to drop V&C for Crown Tiger. No remorse," Mimi said. "Besides, Valerie's kind of stuck-up. I'd way rather give my money to you."

I blinked, caught off guard by her comment. In the background, a group of people were organizing a drinking game, shouting and grabbing people to join. "Oh. Well, no need to make it personal, right? Valerie seems nice."

I knew "nice" wasn't exactly the right word to describe Valerie, and the way Natalie, Mimi, and Lisa were exchanging glances, they knew it too. Still, I had to say something. I didn't know why I felt such a strong need to defend a girl who had betrayed me in a haunted house, defaced my shirt with lipstick, and become my actual archrival as of tonight, but I did. There was just something about her. She wasn't *nice*, but I got the sense that there was more to her than just "stuck-up."

"You're new around here, Wes, but it's kind of true," Lisa said. "We've all tried to hang out with her before, but she's not interested in making friends. She only has time for you if you're related to her business or just flat-out related to her. That's why her cousin is her only friend."

"Speaking of her cousin . . ." Natalie giggled, pointing across the living room.

Apparently, the drinking game was being spearheaded by Charlie himself. He had a big group of people standing excitedly in a circle as he hopped back and forth, explaining the rules.

"Okay okay okay, everyone, this is a popular Korean drinking game!" he yelled, bouncing eagerly from one foot to the other. "Rules are simple. You say a number from one to five while showing a different number with your hand. For example, I say three and hold up two fingers." He held up two fingers to demonstrate. "Then the person on my right says the number of fingers I'm holding up while showing a different number on their hand. So JL here would say . . ."

"Two!" the guy with dreadlocks next to Charlie shouted, while holding up four fingers.

"And so on and so forth around the circle," Charlie said. "If you mess up and say the wrong number or hold up the same amount of fingers as the number you say, you gotta take a shot! Sounds easy, but I swear"—he shook his head, all serious—"it's harder than you think when we go fast. I'll start! One!"

The group hollered as they went around in the circle at lightning speed, screaming with laughter whenever someone messed up and said five while holding up five fingers.

"Charlie always teaches us the best drinking games," Lisa said, grinning. "I love having him at my parties."

"It's not just parties or drinking games, either," Natalie said. "Remember the junior camping trip? He had everyone in stitches playing games around the fireplace. He said he learns them from Korean TV shows."

"He's the best," Mimi agreed. "Totally opposite of Valerie. But he's such a lightweight. You know what happens when he has more than one drink."

"Oh yes," Lisa and Natalie said, nodding their heads.

This was another thing about being the new kid. There were common facts that friends and classmates knew about one another, things they'd picked up over the years without even realizing they were picking them up. They were just by-products of growing up together, and I suddenly felt a wave of loneliness, like I was always on the outside looking in.

"What happens?" I asked.

"You'll see pretty soon," Mimi said.

The game had pared down to two players for a lightning round, Charlie and JL. They went back and forth, shouting and holding up fingers while everyone watched.

"Three!"

"One!"

"Five!"

"Two!" Charlie yelled, throwing up two fingers. He looked down at his hand like he couldn't believe what he was seeing and cried out in agony. Everyone cheered, shouting, "Shot, shot, shot, shot!" while JL gave a deep victory bow.

Out of the corner of my eye, I saw Pauline leaning against the wall by the couch, patiently watching the game with an amused smile on her face. I quickly excused myself from the group and headed over to join Pauline. I had to update her on the bet.

"Hey, where've you been all night?" I asked.

"Looking for Charlie," she said, nodding at the circle of people. "I found him. But he seemed busy."

I chuckled. "Yeah. Hey, listen, I talked to Valerie today and—"

"Valerie?" Charlie's voice said. I nearly jumped out of my skin. He was standing right behind me, eyebrows raised. *When did he get here?* "Are you giving my cousin a hard time again? Because if you are . . ." He held up a fist right in front of my nose.

Uh-oh. Was this what the girls were talking about when Charlie drank too much? Did he start picking fights? I suddenly had a mental picture of Charlie's fist slamming into my glasses. I could see the headline now: NEW GUY GETS PUNCHED AT PARTY. HE WAS WEARING ELBOW PATCHES.

Charlie's fist turned into a finger wagging in my face. "You'll be in serious trouble." He laughed, slapping me good-heartedly on the shoulder. I laughed along awkwardly.

His eyes shifted over to Pauline and he smiled, smoothing out his hair only to make it stick up more in the back. "Hey, Pauline. How's it going?"

"Hey, Charlie," she said. "I was actually hoping to talk to you about something, but . . ." She suppressed a smile as he tried, unsuccessfully, to fix his hair. "Maybe next time."

"Next time? Why? I was meaning to talk to you, too, actually," he said.

She shook her head. "I should get going."

"You're leaving? Right now?" Charlie looked devastated. "What about our talk?"

"I feel like now is probably not the right time."

He sighed. "It's never the right time. I don't understand why people always have to leave so suddenly." To my shock, his eyes began to grow misty. He looked up at the ceiling, furiously trying to blink back tears.

"Are you okay?" Pauline asked gently as he covered his eyes with his hands.

"Yeah, no, I'm totally fine," he said, his voice an octave higher than usual. "Um, maybe you're right. You should just go."

Pauline glanced at him, his eyes still covered, and then at me. I shot her a bewildered look, but she simply smiled a small smile and shrugged like she wasn't surprised by this at all.

"Okay. Bye, Charlie," she said. She turned to me. "Make sure he doesn't drive, okay? And text me what you wanted to tell me about Valerie."

She waved and headed out the door. Charlie waited for a moment and then he said, "Is she gone?"

"Yes," I said.

He lowered his hands, revealing teary red eyes. "She didn't see me crying, did she?"

Considering the fact that she'd been standing right in front of him, I was pretty sure she knew exactly what was happening. But there was no need to upset him more than he already was. "No, I don't think she did."

"I don't believe you," he sighed. He paused and gave me a long, steady look, his eyes still watery. "Can I tell you a secret, Wes?"

Was he going to confide in me about Pauline? I nodded slowly. "Sure. Go ahead."

"To be honest, I don't give a damn about K-beauty," he said instead, surprising me. "I really don't. But to Valerie, that business is her life. That's why I help her with it, because I know how much it means to her. I know you've got your own business thing going on, but I meant it when I said you'll be in trouble if you give her a hard time. Don't take V&C away from her. Okay? Just don't." His voice cracked at the end, and he rolled his eyes up to the ceiling again, pressing his hands against his face. "Damn it."

I opened my mouth, unsure what to say. Before I could think of anything, JL came over, patting Charlie on the back.

"Always the life of the party until he drinks too much and cries," JL sighed. He glanced at me. "You all right, Wes?"

"Yeah," I said, surprised he knew my name. We didn't have any classes together. "You're JL, right?"

"Yeah. Jason Leonard, but everyone calls me JL." He gave me

a friendly palm slap. "I've heard about your business. Song Song here told me about it."

Song Song? "I'm guessing that's Charlie?"

He grinned. "Yeah, we all have nicknames on the basketball team. Hey, you got some height. You should think about joining."

"Thanks. Maybe," I said, smiling, though I knew I probably wouldn't. Sports were fun, but playing competitively wasn't really my thing. Besides, with this new bet against Valerie, one competition was more than enough for me.

"Ugh, what's wrong with me?" Charlie said, still trying to blink back tears. One escaped and rolled down his face.

I turned to Jason, lowering my voice. "Is he going to be okay?"

"Who, Song Song? Don't worry. He does this every time. Put a little alcohol in him and his feelings start spilling out everywhere. I'll drive him home." He guided Charlie toward the door. "Come on, buddy, let's go."

I watched them as they disappeared through the door, feeling a bit wistful at the inside jokes and nicknames everyone seemed to share. It was probably time I headed home too. I had a lot to think about.

That night, I sat at my computer with my headphones on, listening to my Best of Louis Armstrong playlist and staring at the spreadsheet on my screen. I'd had one going to track my sales and income even before Valerie had suggested it. After my most recent sale this week, I had officially logged $375 earned, after Pauline's cut. It wasn't enough to repad my saxophone, but Pauline had generously loaned me the difference after she saw me stressing about it. "I'll just take the amount you owe me out of our next sale on top of my cut," she'd said when I tried to refuse. "It's more urgent for you than it is for me."

Thanks to her, I'd been able to drop off my sax for repairs. But it also meant I owed her money. And I had to make enough for applications.

I opened a fresh spreadsheet page to track everything from now until prom. The timeline of the bet. I logged in everything I needed to apply to Toblie School of Music:

$110 by December 1 for the application.

$1,000 for the enrollment deposit by May 1, along with $500 for the housing deposit.

The rest of the semester's tuition due by August 1 which was . . . a lot.

I had time to think about that, though. One hurdle at a time. I just had to win this bet. If I lost, I wouldn't even be able to jump the May hurdle. Not to mention, the bet began now, which meant that if I earned and spent money on my application fee, I'd technically have to owe that money back to Valerie. I hoped she was okay with taking an IOU.

No. I can't think like that. I have to believe that I can really win this.

I went onto Google and typed in: *Tips for running a small business.*

What Would Valerie Do? was a good place to start, but I needed more help. I spent the night reading articles, taking notes, and making sale ideas. Somewhere between trying to stay awake and reading about knowing your audience and social-media platforms, I ended up on V&C K-BEAUTY's Instagram page.

It was well curated, full of high-quality close-ups of beauty products and even some quick tutorials of Valerie demonstrating the order of products to use for a nighttime skin-care routine.

My stomach sank. When it came to Instagram, there was definitely no way I could compete against Valerie. My own personal account only had two photos: one of my saxophone with my reflection caught weirdly in the frame, and another of a sunset that I thought looked nice, creatively captioned with the hashtag *#sunset*.

I really hope Pauline is better at this stuff than I am.

I scrolled through V&C K-BEAUTY's follower list and paused on the handle @vkwonishere. Valerie's personal account? I tapped on it.

It was private.

The only thing I could see was her profile picture: her smiling next to someone who had to be her grandma, her arms wrapped around the old woman's shoulders. I couldn't help but grin slightly at that photo.

I knew she'd have a pretty smile.

It was strange. Valerie had been at this school for years, but from the way her classmates talked about her, I got the feeling that she might be on the outside of a lot of things, just like me. My finger hovered over the request-to-follow button. But no. I shouldn't. I shook my head and turned off my phone. *What I should do is stop thinking about this and go to bed.* Tomorrow I'd talk business with Pauline and go pick up my saxophone.

For now I slept, my dreams full of music, spreadsheets, and Korean drinking games.

CHAPTER NINE

VALERIE

Sunday / November 17

I woke up the next morning to a series of texts from Charlie, each one more urgent than the last.

Charlie: So yesterday's conversation with Pauline was a disaster. I'm pretty sure she saw me cry. How do I fix this?!

Charlie: Scratch that. There's no fixing this, is there? It's over for me.

Charlie: Hello? Are you awake? Where'd you go yesterday anyway? Maybe if you stuck around you would have stopped me from making a total FOOL of myself.

Charlie: Valerie??

Charlie: I'm going to church today. Mom needs a ride and also since you're not answering, maybe I'll try talking to Jesus.

Charlie: TEXT ME.

I rolled out of bed and got dressed, feeling more than a little guilty about ditching Charlie at the party last night. How was I supposed to know that his talk with Pauline would end up in an epic fail if I wasn't there to supervise him? Well, okay. Maybe I should've known. I'd make it up to him and go meet him in person at True Vine Presbyterian Church.

Sunhee Eemo is a pretty devout Christian, and she goes to a local Korean church whenever she isn't working at the soondubu restaurant, which isn't very often. She almost always works Sundays. But whenever she does go, Charlie drives her and attends the English Ministry youth service while he's there. I'd been a couple times with them for Easter and Christmas.

I arrived at church just as the service was ending. People were mingling and chatting over bags of chips and cheese-caramel popcorn mix. I spotted Charlie standing at the snack table, talking to a guy in a gray beanie who looked vaguely familiar.

"Yo, Valerie!" Charlie said, catching my eye and waving me over. "Look who I found! Remember Taemin Park?"

"Oh, hey," I said "Whoa. It's been forever."

So that was why he looked familiar. Taemin Park was one of Charlie's youth-group friends from when they were kids. His dad was the senior pastor for the Korean adults. Taemin had a bit of a reputation for being a rebellious pastor's kid. Rumor had it that his last escapade had involved crashing his dad's car into their neighbor's fence. Supposedly, he was still paying his dad back for the damage. And his neighbor, too.

"What's up, Valerie?" Taemin said, grinning. His dimples were just as deep as I remembered.

"I was just asking Taemin how he's been," Charlie said brightly.

It seemed like running into Taemin was distracting him from his woes about Pauline. This was good. Maybe I had less damage control to do than I thought. "It's been a while since I've seen him here."

"Yeah, what's the devil doing at church?" I asked.

Charlie stepped on my foot and I yelped.

"She didn't mean that," he said as I rubbed my foot.

Taemin laughed. "Nah, it's cool, bro. It really has been a while. I didn't think anyone would miss me, though." He put his hand over his heart. "I'm touched."

I was pretty sure that most people *didn't* miss Taemin. From what I knew, he was kind of a lone wolf, but not by choice. A lot of people kept their distance because of his impulsive reputation.

"Anyway, I'm here 'cause Pastor Richard kept calling me up to have bingsu," he said. "You've met PR, right? The new EM youth pastor? He wants to catch up. And, to be honest with you, he's trying to help me turn over a new leaf. You know, helping others, becoming a better person, all that Jesus stuff."

"I didn't realize you were interested in turning over any leaves," I said.

"Yeah, well, it's time for a change," Taemin said. "Besides, my dad said if I don't get my act together, he's going to make me work at the church for no pay this summer." He made a face. "I figure I'd rather be disciplined by PR than by the church ajummas. Could you imagine a whole summer of hearing their jansori? It would be death by nagging."

"Good for you, man," Charlie said in admiration. "That's great."

"Yeah." Taemin grinned. "Besides, you know your boy can't say no to bingsu."

"You always did love shaved ice," Charlie said. "We should ball sometime—it's been a while."

"That'd be cool," Taemin said, brightening. "We'll have to find a time we're both free! I work a lot."

"Where do you work?" I asked.

"At Roseman Hotel. I'm a bellboy and I work events."

"Ritzy," I said.

"Gotta get that bread." He grinned toothily. "Charlie was telling me you guys are selling K-beauty products at school. Let me know if you need a hookup with some more beauty products. I know a guy who sells some real good stuff." He leaned in, dropping his voice to a whisper. "Real fake, that is, but it looks exactly like all the best brands. It's basically the same thing."

I made a face. "No thanks. V&C doesn't do knockoffs. How do you even know someone who deals fake brands of beauty products anyway?"

"The hotel," he said easily. "Man, the rich folks I meet there. They do all kinds of interesting stuff."

"And they just tell you all this?"

"Nah. You have no idea how much gossip I hear just standing around or moving bags for people. It's amazing what you can learn from people just by being near them. They wouldn't know a spy if they saw one."

I rolled my eyes. "I thought you were turning over a new leaf."

"And part of that is helping others, remember? I was offering

147

you assistance." He nodded at Pastor Richard across the room. "My free bingsu awaits. See you later, guys. Charlie, call me up about basketball. You have my number, yeah?"

They fist-bumped. "Sure thing, bro," Charlie said. He watched as Taemin walked away, a broad smile on his face. "Man, I missed that guy. Great to see he's doing well."

"Yeah," I said. A sudden idea was forming in my head, turning over what Taemin had said. *It's amazing what you can learn from people just by being around them. They wouldn't know a spy if they saw one.* I pulled a green-apple Hi-Chew out of my bag, my brainstorming flavor, and unwrapped it, thinking carefully. This could be exactly the advantage I needed in my bet against Wes.

"Uh-oh," Charlie said. "Green apple. What are you thinking about?"

"Can I have Taemin's phone number?" I asked, watching as he left the building with Pastor Richard. I reached for my phone and popped open a new text message. "You think he would be interested in an unconventional job?"

Snow Bunny was one of the most popular bingsu cafés in town. Their mascot was a bunny skiing down a bowl of shaved ice, and one wall of the shop had a giant mural of said bunny wearing ski goggles and hitting the slopes. Taemin had asked me to meet him here after his meeting with Pastor Richard. I spotted him sitting in a corner booth as I entered the café, the bell on the door announcing my arrival.

"Hey! Perfect timing," he said, waving. "PR just left. Where's Charlie?"

"He had to run some errands with his mom," I said. Just as well that he wasn't here in person. When I'd told him about my bet with Wes and what I had in mind to ask Taemin, he thought I was out of my mind. "Taemin is never going to say yes to that," he'd said. But you never know what people will say yes to until you ask. Case in point: yesterday's bet.

"Well, I'm very curious about this business proposition you have for me," Taemin said. "Shall we get a bowl of bingsu to begin our discussion?"

"Didn't you *just* have one?" I asked, eyeing the empty bowl on the table.

"Yes, but when you're interviewing someone for a job, it's customary to offer them a drink," he said. "Or, in my case, a matcha shaved ice."

I sighed. "Fine." I'd consider this a business expense.

Ten minutes later, we were sharing a bowl of matcha-flavored shaved ice topped with mochi, sweet red bean, and two heaping scoops of green-tea ice cream.

"So," Taemin said, popping a piece of mochi into his mouth, "how can I help you?"

I sat up straight, folding my hands on the table. "I'd like to hire you for a one-time spy job. There's a boy at my school named Wes Jung. He runs a competing K-beauty business, and we have a bet going to see who can raise the most money by prom. If you can help me figure out what he's selling for the next week or two, I can strategize my sales to beat him. What do you say?"

He let out a low whistle. "That's a pretty sneaky strategy. Why me, though? Why don't you just get someone from your school to ask him?"

"There isn't really anyone at school I can ask," I said truthfully. "And definitely not without seeming suspicious. You're the perfect fit."

He laughed. "Do you always rope random people you haven't seen in years into working for you?"

"You call it random; I call it networking."

"Hmm." He took a bite of ice cream and rolled his eyes up to the ceiling, thinking. When he looked at me again, his lips were quirked up in a smile. "What's in it for me?"

Valid. I had been preparing for this question the whole way here. "You said earlier that PR was helping you turn over a new leaf, right? And that helping people was part of that? I'm giving you an opportunity to help me, which is really giving you a chance to help yourself."

His brow furrowed as he followed along with my logic. "Huh?"

I sighed. "Look, Taemin. My business is really important to me. And so is this bet. If you can help me get a leg up on Wes even a little bit, it would mean a lot. You have no idea how much I have to lose."

It was weird being this candid with someone, but somehow it helped that it was someone I didn't know so well. Sometimes it's easier to tell strangers the truth than it is to tell the people closest to you. I was confident that I would beat Wes, but a small part of me had kept wavering since last night. If I lost against him, not only would I would lose my money, my opportunity to prove myself to Umma, and any hope of taking Halmeoni to Paris, but I was terrified that it would hurt my pride to the point of no recovery. What would it say about me if the business I'd so painstakingly crafted over the years could be easily dethroned by a newbie who'd just happened to stumble onto the scene? How could I ever take myself seriously again? If V&C failed, I failed. I needed to play every advantage I could get.

"You don't say this kind of stuff to people a lot, do you?" Taemin said.

I pressed my lips together and shook my head.

He surveyed me carefully and sighed. "Okay. I'll help you."

My eyes widened. "Really?"

"Yeah. PR said that part of turning over a new leaf was to be more mindful of others and thoughtful in my actions. So"—he waved a hand in my general direction—"your whole spiel about helping me help you? I get it. This means a lot to you, and helping you out with this small thing is something I can do for you."

I let out a breath of gratitude. "Thank you. Oh, and I'll pay you for your time of course. In one bingsu."

A wide grin spread across his face, his dimples deepening. "Well, why didn't you say so? You're one year older than me, right? Nuna? Can I call you Nuna?" He patted my hand. "You can trust me. I'm a master at getting info from people. Just call my name whenever you feel like buying me a bingsu. You have my number."

After my meeting with Taemin, I felt way lighter about my bet with Wes. My confidence was back up to 99 percent, which was exactly where I liked it to be. I unwrapped a mango Hi-Chew to celebrate as I walked to the grocery store where Umma, Appa, and Halmeoni went shopping every Sunday afternoon around this time. It was only twenty minutes away from Snow Bunny, and if I timed it right, I could sneak a bag of Hi-Chews in the cart and catch a ride home.

I paused outside the mirrored grocery store windows to straighten my outfit—high-waisted mustard-yellow pants with a cream crop sweater and a small-brim bucket hat—before entering through the sliding automatic doors.

Aha. There were Umma and Appa, picking spinach in the vegetable aisle. I quickly let them know I was there before making my way to the candy aisle.

"Try to find Halmeoni if you can!" Umma called after me. "She's probably in the cereal aisle."

Hi-Chews . . . Hi-Chews . . . Hi-Chews . . . bingo. I grabbed a bag of mixed flavors and jogged over to the cereal aisle to find Halmeoni.

Only to find Wes standing there instead, holding a box of Honey Nut Cheerios.

I froze, staring at him. Was that really him or was I just imagining he was here because I'd been thinking of him all day? Thinking of the bet with him, I mean. Not thinking of him. Obviously.

He looked up and stared directly at me. His eyes widened in shock, the cereal box nearly falling out of his hands. "Valerie? What are you doing here?"

"Shopping with my family," I said blankly. "What are you doing here?"

"I was, um, in the area to pick up my saxophone from the repair store across the street," he said. "My dad asked me to get some groceries for him while I was out here."

I nodded. "All right, then."

Well, this was awkward, seeing Wes right after hiring someone to spy on him. I should have seen it coming. I always ran into someone from school here. Sunday was a popular grocery day. In fact, around this time I usually saw—

"Valerie! Wes!"

Kristy Lo came rolling down the aisle with a shopping cart, her hair bright violet and tied up in a braided bun. "What are you two doing together?"

"We're not together," I said quickly as Wes mumbled, "Cereal, getting cereal."

"So funny to see you! I just saw Ethan Phan with his parents too. Did you hear he and his boyfriend broke up?" She shook her head. "So sad. I gave Ethan my Ben & Jerry's coupon to help him mend his sorrows."

"Ethan Phan is the one with the pottery business at school, right?" Wes said.

Kristy nodded. "Yep. Though the pottery studio was where he and his ex met. I'm not sure if he'll want to go back there anytime soon."

"Speaking of business, Kristy, will I see you at V&C tomorrow?" I asked. "I'm stocking a new package of deep-restoration vitamin-C face masks."

Her face lit up. "Oh my God, Valerie, *yes.* That's exactly what I need. My face has been feeling so dry these days." She pressed the back of her hand against her cheek and shook her head. "It's like the desert."

"Um, Kristy, are you sure you don't want to shop with me instead?" Wes jumped in. "I have limited samples of Crown Tiger's new perfume line. I could save Shiyoon's perfume for you if you want."

Kristy gasped, her hand moving from her face to her heart. "What? Those are impossible to get here."

I shot him a look out of the corner of my eye. *What does he think he's doing right now? Is he really trying to one-up me while I'm standing right here? As if I'm going to let that happen.*

"What about the deep-restoration vitamin for your face, Kristy?" I asked. "It's perfect for the fall, and all the beauty vloggers are using them these days."

"Face masks are cool, but Crown Tiger is really like deep restoration for the soul," Wes said.

Cheesy AF, but Kristy was nodding like this really spoke to her. "True, true. That's what Crown Tiger does."

"You have to be careful with perfume sometimes, though," I said. "It can irritate your skin, especially if you're having trouble with dryness."

"But this perfume is really low scent," Wes said quickly, glancing at me. "Especially Shiyoon's. His fragrance is violet. Besides, would you rather have a face mask that you throw out after one use or the scent of Crown Tiger that you can carry with you all day?"

"Please, you know the effects of a face mask are way more beneficial than perfume. We're talking long-lasting steps toward glowing skin over smelling like violets for a day."

"Some people happen to love violets."

"Well, some people happen to love vitamin C!"

"Um, Valerie? Wes?" Kristy looked back and forth between the two of us. "I'm still here, you know."

Oh. Somewhere in the middle of our conversation, we had turned to face each other instead of Kristy. I cleared my throat and quickly turned back to Kristy as Wes adjusted his glasses, his cheeks pink.

"Anyway," Kristy said, "I really do want both. I'll have to think about it. See you two at school tomorrow?"

"Yep, see you," I said as Wes waved and mumbled, "Bye, Kristy."

She smiled brightly and waved back, rolling away with her shopping cart.

Wes and I glared at each other.

"You totally overreacted," I said. "'Deep restoration for the soul'? Really?"

"Me? What about you?" he said. "Trying to discredit my perfume by saying it's irritating."

"I didn't say it's irritating; I said it *can* be irritating for dry skin."

"We all know what you were insinuating."

I folded my arms across my chest. God, he was infuriating. Before I could snap back, a very familiar voice called down the cereal aisle.

"Valerie!" Halmeoni was walking toward me in her daisy-print pants, waving her hands. "Your mom said I would find you here."

Oh my God. What was it with everyone showing up in the cereal aisle today? I ran to Halmeoni and grabbed her hand.

"You found me! Okay, let's go."

She glanced behind me, where Wes was standing, and patted my hand excitedly, nodding in his direction. "Who's your handsome friend?"

Before I could say anything—*Friend? No friend here; I don't know who you're talking about*—Wes stepped forward and bowed politely. "Annyeonghaseyo. My name is Wes Jung. I'm classmates with Valerie."

"Omo, so you're Korean, too!" she said, doubly pleased. She stepped back to look at him more closely. "Wow, you're so tall. Your parents must feed you well."

He laughed. "Yes, and I'm not a picky eater, which probably helps."

"Oh, that's a good quality. Good eaters are the best," Halmeoni said, beaming right back.

Uh-oh. There's no faster way to bond with Halmeoni than to say you like food. I had to put a stop to this, stat.

"Come on, Halmeoni, we should get going." I linked my arm through hers and started steering her away. "Quick, before Umma gets mad."

"So nice to meet you, Wes!" she said. "Come over sometime!"

"Come over sometime"? Oh, Halmeoni, no.

Wes grinned, all good humor as he bowed goodbye. "Get home safely, Halmeoni."

Annoying. Why did he have to be so sweet to Halmeoni? Now

she was going to think he was just a nice boy who should come over to eat, when really he was the enemy of all enemies.

"Your friend seems very nice," she said, patting my arm as we walked away.

"We're not friends."

She gave me an amused smile. "Okay, my girl. Whatever you say."

I glanced over my shoulder to see Wes leaning against the cereal aisle, watching us leave with that good-humored grin still on his face.

Yeah. Definitely not friends.

CHAPTER TEN

WES

Sunday / December 1

The aquarium was decked out in strings of holiday lights and hanging snowflake decorations. I wrapped my scarf around my neck as I stepped out into the outdoor aquarium area, the frosty air nipping at my cheeks. Pauline was narrating the sea-otter show, and we'd decided to meet here after her volunteer shift to talk business plans. Though, to be honest, I was definitely more interested in seeing some sea otters. I needed something to help me de-stress. Life had been a bit overwhelming lately, to say the least.

I sat down on a bench by the sea-otter tank and rubbed my forehead, as if that would help smooth out all the thoughts in my head. Honestly, my mind these days was like an orchestra of out-of-tune instruments, all competing to be heard over the others. My parents were at the forefront of that, nudging me to study harder, to keep my grades sharp, to get my college applications ready. Not that I was going to apply to the schools they wanted me to. I just hadn't figured out a way to tell them that yet.

Then there was the business and the sales I was trying to keep up with, constantly asking Mom for new merch and digging through her office for old stuff when she didn't have any. Not to mention my own saxophone practices and music-school applications. My stomach did a flip when I thought about the application I had secretly sent out yesterday to Toblie School of Music. I had managed to raise enough money to both pay Pauline back for what she'd loaned me and to apply to one school, which left me with equal parts relief and horror. Relief that I'd gotten it in and horror that I was really doing this behind my parents' backs. What would they do when they found out? I got anxious every time I thought about it. That, and the fact that I didn't apply to any backup schools. The only person I'd told outside school was Uncle Hojin, who I'd still been emailing with here and there. He was thrilled. If only I could feel certain that my parents would feel the same.

And then, of course, there was Valerie. And the bet. I was constantly going back and forth on whether that had been the right move or not, especially after our run-in at the grocery store a few weeks ago. She was tough competition, and seeing her with her grandma had made things harder in a way I hadn't expected. It made her more human than rival, and I already had enough trouble thinking straight when it came to Valerie.

I didn't have time to doubt, though. I had to win this. After I had sent in my application to Toblie, I'd gone through the class list for the first-year jazz program, and my heart had ached so bad with wanting. I wished I could be there right now, learning music theory and playing in ensembles with other people who loved music as much as I do.

"Is this seat taken?"

I startled out of my thoughts, looking up to see a guy around my age standing next to my bench, holding a paper cup of hot chocolate in his hand. He was wearing a white hoodie with the hood up over his head and a puffy black North Face vest. I slid over on the bench to make room for him.

"Thanks," he said gratefully. "I'm Taemin Park, by the way."

I smiled in recognition of the Korean name. "Wes Jung."

"Yo, no way," Taemin said, pointing at me with his hot chocolate. "I've heard of you. Aren't you the guy who sells Crown Tiger beauty products at Crescent Brook?"

What the—? I gaped at him. "How'd you know that?"

"I've heard the rumors," Taemin said. "I'm a junior at North Hill Academy. You know, the school your school is always losing to in basketball?"

"Sorry." I laughed, though in my head I was still turning over the fact that people outside our school knew about my business. Strange. A terrifying thought seized my brain. *What if Mom and Dad find out? Shit. Let's hope my reputation doesn't reach that far.* "I'm new here."

"Where you from?" Taemin asked.

Ah. The "where are you from?" question. Always difficult for me to answer. Do I share where I was born? Where I lived the longest? Where I felt most comfortable before being uprooted yet again? I settled on my default answer.

"I was born in Seoul, but I moved around a lot."

"Wow, so you have lots of homes," Taemin said.

I smiled politely, though what I really wanted to say was, *Lots of cities, but not that many homes.* A specific place never came to my mind when I thought of the word "home." The only thing that came close was my saxophone, and that wasn't even a place.

"I bet none of the places you've lived before has an aquarium as nice as this one," Taemin said. "This place is the bomb. First time here?"

"Yeah. I'm actually here to meet a friend. She's about to narrate the sea-otter show."

His eyes widened. "Dude. I *love* sea otters. Perfect timing."

"Are you hanging out here by yourself?" I asked, taking a quick glance behind him to see if any of his friends or family would be joining. Not wanting to sound judgmental, I hastily added, "It's fine if you are, of course."

"Yep, just me. I'm actually here to try and convince the aquarium to hire me part-time as a magician. My youth pastor thinks I should do more volunteering." He shrugged. "No dice, though. The aquarium just doesn't appreciate my talent. Wanna see a card trick?" He chugged the rest of his hot chocolate and crumpled the cup in his hand before pulling out a deck of cards from the pocket of his vest. He fanned the deck out in front of me. "Pick a card."

I laughed. There was an easygoing manner to Taemin that made him fun to talk to. I slid a card out from the middle of the deck. "Now look at it, but don't tell me what it is," he said. He covered his eyes with a theatrical sweep of his hand. "I promise I'm not peeking."

I glanced at the card. A joker. Huh. I wondered if he'd forgotten to take those out. "Okay, I'm ready."

He uncovered his eyes and patted the deck. "Put it back anywhere, my friend."

I slipped the card back and watched as he shuffled the deck several times, slicing it this way and that. Finally, he stopped, the deck facedown in his palm. He flipped over the card on top.

"Is this your card?"

A joker stared back at me.

"Wow, yeah!" I said, totally impressed. "How'd you do that?"

He grinned. "A magician never reveals his secrets."

Just then, Pauline stepped out by the sea-otter tank, dressed in her red volunteer vest with a wireless microphone attached to the side of her face. "Welcome to the sea-otter show, everybody," she said. "Please join me in welcoming our trainers and otters!"

Taemin burst into applause along with the rest of the audience. Pauline introduced the otter trainer, Eileen, and all the otters: Kenny, Benjamin, and Mister Ottermelon. She did a great job narrating as the otters held hands, spun in circles in the water, and were fed by Eileen. "All these otter friends have been rehabilitated at the aquarium after being found onshore with injuries," Pauline said. "Though they've been deemed unable to be released back into the wild, we do our very best here at the aquarium to make them feel safe and at home."

Fifteen minutes of sea-otter tricks and feedings later, the show came to an end. "Thanks for coming, everyone!" Pauline said. "Eileen will be available for further questions."

"Man, that was awesome," Taemin said as Pauline approached us after the show. He stood up to shake her hand. "Excellent narration. You should do audiobooks."

"Thank you," Pauline said, looking somewhat bewildered. She glanced at me and then back at Taemin. "And you are . . . ?"

"Taemin Park. Sea-otter fan and aspiring aquarium magician."

"The aquarium doesn't have any magicians," Pauline said.

"Not yet they don't." He held out the deck of cards. "Pick a card."

She pulled one out, an amused smile on her face. She raised her eyebrows. "Wait, but this is a joker."

"A joker?" I said at the same time Taemin sighed, "You're not supposed to *tell* me that."

"Can we see the rest of the deck?" I asked, realization dawning on me.

Taemin pressed his lips together in a sheepish smile. "Okay. You caught me." He flipped the deck over to reveal that every single card was, in fact, a joker. "Maybe not my best trick."

"I can't believe I fell for that," I groaned.

Taemin and Pauline laughed, and I couldn't help but join in, feeling some of my earlier stress lift from my shoulders. It felt good to just laugh about something and put a pause on the dissonance in my head.

"So, are you ready for our planning lunch?" Pauline asked me.

"Yeah." I turned to Taemin, not quite ready to say goodbye to someone who felt like a potential new friend. With everything on my mind, making new friends hadn't really happened yet outside of Pauline. I was struck by a sudden sense of boldness. If I was trying to grow in confidence, why not in making new friends, too? "Do you want to join us? You're here on your own, right? We have some business stuff to talk about, which might be boring for you, but you're welcome to eat with us if you want."

Taemin perked up, a smile spreading across his face, revealing deep dimples. "Really? I would love to join you." He tucked the deck of jokers back into his pocket. "Lead the way."

Monday / December 2

By the time Monday morning rolled around, my mind was back in overthinking mode. There was no way Toblie would have gotten back to me by now. Callbacks for auditions weren't even until the new year. But for some reason, logic didn't stop me from checking my email every chance I got. The only thing that was in my inbox, though, was a list of college websites that Dad had sent me. *When you get a chance!* he wrote.

Between that and the imagined terror of my parents somehow stumbling into my email and seeing *"Your application to Toblie School of Music has been successfully submitted"* and the many notes from Uncle Hojin suggesting audition songs, I almost didn't notice when the first bell rang and over half the tinted-foundation mini bottles I'd gotten from Mom were still left over on the music stands.

"Huh," Pauline said, considering the cash box. "We didn't do so well today. Maybe the worst sales day we've had since Halloween."

"That's so weird," I said. I picked up one of the bottles designed with Namkyu's tiger, the silver one eating a corn dog. "I thought these would sell really well."

So well that I hadn't even brought anything extra. No postcards or key chains or bonus items to make a package deal. Had that been my mistake? Or maybe foundation wasn't as popular as I thought. What the hell did I know about foundation anyway? Maybe it wasn't even what I thought it was.

"You use this on your face, right?" I asked.

Pauline nodded. "Yeah. Listen, I have to head to class, but why don't you ask Kristy Lo what's up?" She nodded to the band-room door, where Kristy was walking in with her flute case tucked under her arm. "If anyone will know what's going on, it'll be Kristy."

"Right." I quickly packed up the leftover foundation bottles as more band kids filed in for class. I'd have to get to Kristy quick before Mr. Reyes started rehearsals. We were performing at a district-wide band festival next week, and he was keen to have us master the theme from *Star Wars* by then.

"Good morning, Kristy," I said, shuffling awkwardly over to the flute section with my backpack full of foundation in tow. "I, um, didn't see you this morning."

"Hi, Wes!" she said. She smiled brightly and then her face dropped into a pout. "I know—I'm bummed I missed your sale. But I saw on Valerie's Instagram last night that she restocked all her foundations, primers, *and* concealers! All her products look freaking amazing, too. Want to see?"

I was still trying to wrap my head around everything Kristy was saying—primers? Concealers? Huh? Was that all stuff to put on your face too?—when she stuck her phone in front of my face, playing an Instagram video on V&C K-BEAUTY's page of Valerie holding up different bottles of beauty products against her hand and sampling the products. My heart did a weird lurch when I saw her face on the screen. I cleared my throat, trying to ignore the sudden heat crawling up my skin.

"She would make a great beauty guru," Kristy said, turning her phone off. "She should make YouTube videos or something. Anyway, I'm saving my allowance to go shopping with Valerie today after school." She smiled apologetically. "Sorry, Wes. Your foundation is super cute, but I want to try the one that Valerie's selling."

"I understand," I said, just as the second bell rang. I hurried to my seat to tune my saxophone, turning over this new information in my mind.

What a weird coincidence that Valerie was promoting foundation the same week I was selling it. I sighed. Talk about terrible timing. Not to mention, it brought up the whole social-media concern again. Pauline and I had attempted to set up an Instagram account for our business, but neither of us was social media–savvy enough to keep it up or even know how to make good posts. There were so many other things to juggle that we were constantly forgetting about it too.

Things weren't looking good for me. Had I made a huge mistake in betting against Valerie?

Monday / December 9

The bad luck continued.

Today I brought the same foundation from last week, along with some Crown Tiger postcards from their Italy travel series and the leftover stock of lip balm from Halloween. Yeah, the lip balm was stuff people had seen before, but I was hoping enough time had passed that maybe they would be in need of a new one. Lip balms only lasted so long, right?

And maybe that would have been the case. But I never found out, because that very same day, Valerie announced that she was launching a brand-new line of lip balms that was apparently all the rage in Korea. Oh, and she was continuing her foundation sale.

Argh. Of all the times.

It didn't help that we had to cut our sales short because of my field trip to the band festival. Before the first bell rang, all the band kids were required to meet in the school parking lot, wearing white collared shirts tucked into black pants, instruments in hand. Maybe it was for the best. I could use a full day of playing music to take my mind off my dismal sales and my growing regret at having bet against Valerie.

The district-wide band festival gathered school bands from all over the city at the Florence Lennon Convention Center, where we played for a panel of judges and anyone from the neighborhood who wanted to watch. It was basically a free event where we could practice playing in front of an audience. The judges were mostly there to give feedback rather than to run an actual competition.

Which was truly fine by me. One competition in my life was enough.

When we weren't playing, we were hanging out in the convention center's multipurpose room with all the other students, waiting for our call time. I'd been to school band festivals before, and these in-between times were always the worst. I never knew who to sit with or what to do. Everyone always seemed so settled in their friend groups, and I felt awkward orbiting them, with nothing to say even if they were nice enough to invite me. Lisa Carol smiled and waved me over to join her and her friends, but I politely smiled back and gestured to my saxophone like, *Whoops, sorry, I already made plans,* before retreating to a corner to practice. I probably should have said yes—to making new friends and growing in confidence and all that—but today I didn't have it in me to be social in such a big group.

Just as I was about to start up on some scales, I happened to glance up and make eye contact with a familiar face across the room, a boy eating a bag of Sour Patch Kids and wearing a NORTH HILL ACADEMY BAND sweater. What the. Was that . . . ?

"Yo!" Taemin's eyes widened as he recognized me. He bounded across the room, his face splitting into a huge grin as he high-fived me. "Wes! I should've known you would be at this festival. You said you play saxophone, right?"

"Yeah," I said, shocked. We'd been texting here and there since the aquarium, but I hadn't even thought to ask him if his school would be part of the festival. "I didn't know you were in band too. What do you play?"

"Trumpet. But I suck. They wouldn't even let me join the marching band because I kept messing up formation." He rolled his eyes. "Sticklers. Whatever. Anyway, how's it going, man?"

"It's going okay. Could be better," I said truthfully.

"Girl troubles?" Taemin asked.

I raised my eyebrows and he clapped a sympathetic hand on my shoulder.

"I can tell. Call it a sixth sense, if you will. So, tell me about her. What's the problem?"

"It's, um, kind of complicated." I chewed my lip, trying to figure out where to begin. "Her name is Valerie."

A flash of recognition crossed his face and I looked at him curiously. "Do you know her?" I asked.

"Depends," he said. "Do you mean Valerie Kwon? Cousins with Charlie Song?"

My mouth dropped open. "Yes! That's her."

"Yeah, I know her. Charlie and I are buddies from church."

"Whoa. Small world."

"Koreans know Koreans," Taemin said, shrugging nonchalantly. "So what's the deal with Valerie? Do you love her or something?"

My face burned instantly. "What? No! That's not—no. No, I don't."

He laughed. "I'm just kidding, bro."

I laughed too, but it came out as more of a wheeze. "It's just that she runs a K-beauty business in school," I said, quickly changing the subject. "You've probably heard of it if you know Charlie?" He nodded slowly, and I continued. "We kind of have this bet going to see who earns more money with their business by prom. I thought I stood a chance against her, but these past couple of weeks it's like she knows exactly what my sales are going to be."

"What do you mean?" he asked.

"For example, remember that day we had lunch at the aquarium? Pauline and I were talking about how we were going to sell Crown Tiger foundation the next day and lip balm the week after that. But then last week, Valerie announced that she's going to have a fifty-percent-off sale on her foundation. And then today she comes out with a brand-new line of lip balm! Man, I can't seem to get a leg up." I glanced at Taemin, who suddenly looked a bit pale. "Hey, are you okay?"

"Huh? Oh yeah." He smiled sheepishly. "I just got spooked for a second there. Sounds like she has a sixth sense too."

"Right?" I sighed. "I don't know what to do."

"Don't worry, bro," he said, patting me on the arm. "Her sixth sense probably won't last forever. In fact, it was probably only good for a couple weeks. These things are like that."

"I don't know . . . Ugh. I never should have made this bet against her. What was I thinking?"

"Out of curiosity, what *were* you thinking?" Taemin asked. "Why would you make a bet like that?"

I looked down at my saxophone, my somber reflection staring back at me. "I just thought, I don't know, that I had a chance. I'm trying to save up money to go to music school. I managed to pull together enough to apply to my top choice, but . . ." My mind flashed to the spreadsheet on my computer. "There are a lot of other expenses coming up in May. And then a tuition deposit after that. Not to mention, auditions are in February, which is this added mental stress. The closer all these deadlines get, the more panicked I feel that I won't be ready for them. But I need to be. I have to get in."

"Wow, you really want to go to music school, huh?" Taemin said.

I nodded. "Yeah. I just wish my parents were more supportive. Especially my dad. He's really against it, so I'm kind of trying to secretly fund myself right now." The secret part was starting to weigh on me. I didn't like lying to my parents, and I would have to tell them sooner than later that I wasn't going to apply to the schools they wanted me to. It was all getting to be a little too much.

Taemin fell silent. Worried I'd overshared and made things weird, I smiled lightly and nudged him in the elbow. "Hey, why do you look so guilty? It's not like you're the one stopping me from going to music school."

"Yeah, ha-ha, true," he said meekly. "It's just, yeah, I know how dads can be. That sucks."

He paused for a long time like he was going back and forth about something in his mind, chewing his lip. And then he straightened up, clapping a hand on my shoulder and looking me in the eye like he had made a decision about something. "Listen, Wes, you're a good guy. If there's anything I can do to help you, let me know."

"Thanks," I said, smiling, not quite sure why he felt so much empathy for me. He must be a really sensitive guy. "But I'm not sure what you can . . ." I trailed off, a sudden idea flashing into my head. But no. This was definitely not a good idea.

"What?" Taemin said.

"What?" I said back.

"You're looking at me like I'm a ghost that just crawled out of your TV or something."

"Uh. It's just . . . You said you're friends with Charlie and Valerie, right? I guess I was just wondering if maybe you would be interested in, uh, helping me out by letting me know what they're up to with their business these days?"

He blinked. "Like a spy?"

Oh God. That sounded so bad. "No, no, not like a spy. More like a . . ." More like a what? There was really no other way to put it. "Okay, yeah, kind of like a spy. But it would just be a one-time thing. I just need to know what they're planning on selling next so I can finally get my momentum back. I'll pay you back in some way, of course."

It looked like he was rolling the idea over in his mind, considering it from all angles. "Okay, I'll do it."

"Really?"

"Yeah. I'll help you even out the playing field again. It's the least I can do after I . . . promised my pastor I'd try to be a better person." He smiled brightly. "Don't worry about it. Just treat me to a bingsu to pay me back."

"Bingsu? As in shaved ice?"

"Yeah. I can never say no to bingsu."

"Okay," I said. "Deal."

I swallowed back the guilt poking at me from the inside as we shook hands. This was fine, right? I wasn't really hiring a spy to discover anything secret. I just needed to get myself back in the game. Level out the playing field, as Taemin said. It was an oddly accurate choice of words, but it definitely summed things up. I was losing ground fast, and I had to catch up.

Music school depended on it.

Monday / December 16

"Valerie is doing a big sale on moisturizers this Monday. We're talking hydro gels, water creams, and brand names with the word 'glow' in them. If I were you, I'd sell something so amazing, it'll distract everyone from her products. Do you have anything like that?"

I turned over Taemin's advice in my head as I looked at the clock on Monday morning. He'd called me over the weekend with this tip on V&C, and after watching a dozen K-pop unboxing videos, I'd finally had an idea.

What was better than a great deal? A great *limited-edition* deal.

Me: Hey Kristy, you definitely don't want to miss my sale today. I'm selling limited-edition Crown Tiger makeup pouches. They don't sell these in Korea anymore and I only have a few, so spread the word . . .

Kristy: OMG! Thanks Wes! I'LL BE THERE!!

Thank God I'd found these pouches in Umma's office. Each one was made of a durable canvas material with a colorful zipper that matched the color of the cartoon tiger on the pouch. It was true that I only had a limited supply. And a Google search showed me that they weren't being sold anywhere else. They must be discontinued. Thus, limited edition.

The band room doors burst open as Kristy ran in, followed by a crowd of Crown Tiger fans I hadn't seen in weeks.

"Wes, Wes!" Amelia Perry cried, already reaching into her bag for her wallet. "I heard you have *limited-edition* makeup pouches? I want the one with KP on it!"

"No way, KP's *my* bias!" someone else shouted. "Wes, save that one for me! I'll pay double!"

Bless you, Taemin Park. Things are finally looking up.

Something I'd learned about the PNW: It rains. A lot.

I pulled the hood of my jacket over my head as I jogged out to the parking lot after school, my glasses already getting speckled with rainwater. Sometimes it will literally come out of nowhere on an otherwise non-rainy day like today. I inwardly thanked my parents for letting me use the second car as I ducked into the driver's seat. Man. I'd lived in a lot of cities, and I'd never seen it rain as much as it did here. Still, whatever the weather looked like, nothing could bring down my mood from today's sale. I was feeling on top of the world.

I dried off my glasses on the hem of my sweater before switching on the windshield wipers and pulling out of the parking lot. I squinted through the rain as I spotted a familiar figure walking down the sidewalk, hugging a cardboard box to her chest, getting totally soaked.

Valerie.

For a second, I hesitated. I could just drive by. I mean, we weren't exactly friends. But we weren't strangers, either, and it felt weird to just pretend I didn't see her.

I slowed down and rolled open the passenger-seat window.

"Hey! Valerie! Do you want a ride?"

She startled, looking over at me. Maybe it was the wrong timing, but I was struck by how pretty she looked, rain plastering her hair against the sides of her face. I had the sudden temptation to smooth out her hair and pull the wet strands away from her cheeks.

"No, I'm good," she said. And then she kept on walking, her boots slapping against the wet concrete.

I inched the car forward, keeping pace with her. "Are you sure? Where's Charlie?"

"Basketball tournament," she said, her eyes fixed in front of her. "And yep, I'm sure. Bye."

"Okay, well, this is my last offer if you change your—"

Riiiip. The bottom of Valerie's cardboard box tore open, completely waterlogged. Bottles and round tubs of moisturizer came tumbling out, rolling along the sidewalk as Valerie gasped. "Oh my God!" she cried, desperately trying to grab them all before they got away.

It hit me suddenly that a good sale day for me meant a bad one for her. These must be all the products she couldn't sell today. Without thinking, I pulled over and threw open the car door, grabbing as many beauty products as I could until we had them all secured, our arms laden with moisturizers as we stood in the middle of the sidewalk, staring at each other through the downpour.

"You sure you don't want that ride?" I asked.

She gritted her teeth. "Fine," she said finally, yanking the passenger side car door open. She climbed in with her beauty products. "But I'll pay you back for this somehow."

"You don't have to," I said, passing her the beauty products in my arms through her window before getting back into the driver's seat. I took off my glasses and wiped them down yet again. She stared at me the whole time as I put the glasses back on my face.

"What?" I said self-consciously.

"So you really need them? They're not just for fashion?"

I laughed, caught off guard at her question. "Yeah. Of course I need them. I think I'm almost legally blind."

"Just curious," she said, sitting back in her seat and looking forward. She cleared her throat. "And you're wrong, by the way. I do have to pay you back."

"It's really fine. It's just a ride. Where do you live?"

"Just go straight and then a left at the next traffic light. And no. I have to." Her voice was firm. "I don't want to have to owe you anything."

I smiled in spite of myself and she glanced at me. "What?" she said.

"Nothing. It's just that you talk about everything like a business. How you have to pay me back otherwise you'll owe me. It's like everything has a cost."

"Everything *does* have a cost. Everything has to be earned."

"Not everything. Sometimes people do things just to be nice. It's not always a transaction."

"'Just to be nice,'" she repeated, rolling her eyes. "That's a soft way to think. You can't always be nice to get what you want. Sometimes you have to be ambitious and fight to prove that you're worth what you think you are. Take a right here."

I turned right, suddenly feeling defensive. "Yeah, that's true, but sometimes you have to recognize that people are people and not just customers you do business with. There isn't always a price tag or a black-and-white answer for why people do what they do. It's a bit narrow-minded to think like that, isn't it?"

She turned to face me sharply, narrowing her eyes. "Are you talking about me?"

"Well, are you talking about *me*?"

We fell into heated silence. I didn't know what it was about this girl that made me clap back in ways I would never have with anyone else.

Valerie pointed to a town house up ahead. "This is me."

I pulled up to her house and cut the engine. Now it was really quiet, so all we could hear was the sound of the rain dancing across the car roof like fingers on piano keys. Neither of us moved. I sighed, turning in my seat to face her.

"I'm sorry if I offended you," I said. Speaking my mind was one thing, but I didn't want to end the car ride like this, not when I knew she already had a shitty day.

"Why are you sorry?" she said, her voice softer as well. "You just said what you think."

Her words made me pause. *Why* am *I always sorry for saying what I think? Because I hate it when people are mad at me. Because being sorry is easier than standing by what I really mean.* But maybe she was right. Maybe I didn't have to be so sorry all the time.

"I'll take you up on your offer," I said. "To pay me back. A favor for a favor. Since it's so important to you."

A hint of a smile flashed across her face. "You make it sound like you're doing me a favor by accepting my favor."

I shrugged, smiling back. "I'll think of a way to make it work for me." I fumbled for my phone, holding it out to her. "Your number? So I can text you when I'm ready to cash in my favor."

"It better not be something that'll make me regret this car ride," she said, but she took my phone and punched in her number all the same. She was definitely smiling now, even though she was trying to pretend like she wasn't. She passed it back without a word before gathering her beauty products in her arms and stepping out of the car. She paused before closing the door, looking carefully at me. "Thank you," she said finally. "For being nice."

She slammed the door shut before I could respond. I watched as she made her way into the house, staring after her until she disappeared inside.

I looked down at my phone. Valerie Kwon's phone number shone back at me, and a smile spread across my lips.

CHAPTER ELEVEN

VALERIE

Saturday / December 21

He texted me that weekend, the first day of winter break. I was in the kitchen with Halmeoni, peeling the skin off the goguma she had roasted for us. Our love for sweet potatoes is unparalleled. Halmeoni is always telling me, "Manhi muguh, manhi muguh!" *Eat a lot, eat a lot!* It's because she buys so many boxes of sweet potatoes from H-Mart and no one else in our family likes them as much as we do. She doesn't want it to go to waste, and I am happy to oblige.

Wes: Hi Valerie, it's Wes. I thought of a way you can repay your favor. Would you be able to meet me at my house sometime during winter break?

Meet him at his house? I almost choked on a piece of sweet potato when his next message came in.

Wes: Sorry I just read back on what I wrote and I hope that didn't sound weird or creepy?? I was hoping you could actually help me with some social media stuff.

As I read the rest of his message, Halmeoni raised her eyebrows at me. "What's wrong?" she asked. "You look serious."

"It's Wes Jung," I said. "He wants me to come over to his house during break."

Halmeoni's eyebrows rose higher, nearly disappearing into her hairline.

"It's not like that, Halmeoni," I said quickly. "Don't think anything weird."

"I wasn't thinking anything." A smile quirked her lips up. "But if I were to think something, I'd say it's good for a girl your age to go out and make new friends. Maybe even date a little, hmm?"

I opened my mouth but closed it again when I couldn't think of anything to say. Instead I took a giant bite of goguma, my cheeks flushing.

She laughed. "Is it good?"

"Mm-hmm," I said through the smoky sweet-potato flavor, nodding my head.

The corners of her eyes wrinkled in a deeper smile. She reached across the table and patted my hand. "Manhi muguh, my Valerie."

Friday / December 27

The heater was broken in Charlie's car again. I was bundled up in a beanie and a red checkered blanket scarf, but I forgot my gloves at home and my fingers were freezing. I buried them in my scarf to keep them warm. Charlie was wearing three sweaters.

"Are you sure you can't come in with me?" I asked, shooting

Charlie a hopeful look. The closer the day got, the more nervous I became about going over to Wes's house alone. I wasn't even sure what I was nervous about. I just never really knew what to expect around him.

"Sorry, Val," he said. "My mom wants me to help her with a bunch of errands today. Including getting the car fixed. My dad always says he'll do it next time he visits, but who knows when that'll be."

There was an unmistakable edge to his voice. Charlie's dad was always promising to visit, but then he would get caught up in work and not be able to come after all. That meant a lot of the maintenance work around the house fell on Charlie.

"Besides, I'm already missing my basketball game today to help my mom *and* drive you to Wes's house," he pointed out, his voice still frosty. "That counts for something, doesn't it?"

I glanced at him. Things had been a little off with us ever since I abandoned him at Lisa Carol's party. This wasn't the first time since then that he'd been colder to me, even though I'd apologized. "Hey, what's going on? Are you mad at me or something?"

He sighed as he made a left turn onto a wider street, where the houses were more spread apart and everyone had a front yard. "I'm not mad. I'm just a little hurt that you made that bet with Wes without consulting me about it first."

I stared at him, surprised. "What? You're upset about that? How come you didn't say anything until now?"

"I don't know. I guess I didn't want to make a big deal out of it," he said. "But to be honest, it's been bothering me."

"I'm only betting my share though," I said. "I made sure to protect your cut from the bet."

"I know, I know. And you're entitled to do whatever you want with your earnings. But it's not just a personal decision that affects you. It's a business decision that's affected how we run things. You've been asking a lot more of me recently. More meetings, more rides, more help with sales. Which is fine when I'm able to, but sometimes I'm not, and I feel bad about that, because suddenly you have so much riding on this. I just wish you had talked to me about it. We're supposed to be business partners."

I fell silent. "I'm sorry," I said finally, looking down at my bundled hands. "I didn't think about it like that." In fact, I hadn't really thought of Charlie at all other than protecting his 30 percent. I felt bad now that I hadn't thought beyond the money. "If I could go back and do things differently, I would have asked you what you thought first."

He sighed. "Okay."

I touched his arm lightly. "Really."

He glanced at me, his voice softer now. "Okay."

We pulled up to Wes's house, both peering out the window at the same time to get a first look. I had to admit, I was curious about where Wes lived.

It was a nice house with a spacious driveway. Definitely a modern design, with floor-to-ceiling tinted glass windows and a flat, sloped rooftop that made it look like the house was wearing a graduation cap. With its double garage and stone wall accents, it looked like a home straight out of one of Appa's real estate catalogs.

"I'll be here to pick you up after," Charlie said. "I'll text you when I'm on my way."

"Thanks for the ride," I said, stepping out of the car.

As I walked up the driveway, Charlie honked and rolled down the passenger window.

"Val!" He flashed me a thumbs-up. "Good luck!"

I smiled feebly and rang the doorbell. The door opened almost immediately, startling me.

"Whoa," I said.

Wes stood before me, dressed in a pair of jeans and a heather-gray sweater. It was a simple outfit, but he looked way more stylish in it than anyone should, like he'd just stepped out of a winter-wear magazine for men. His eyes widened behind his glasses. "Hi. Sorry, did I freak you out? I wasn't waiting by the door or anything, I swear. I just happened to be close by when you rang . . ."

His voice trailed off like he had no idea how to finish his thought.

"It's fine," I said. "You didn't scare me."

I glanced behind my shoulder, where Charlie was still waiting. He waved through the window.

Wes smiled hesitantly and waved back. "Um, thanks for coming." He stepped aside, inviting me in.

Warmth enveloped me as I entered the house, slipping out of my boots and into a pair of slippers that Wes offered me. I looked around at the open-concept living room. It was spotless and minimal, stylish but also somewhat bare, like it was missing something. I glanced at the walls. Frames were hung up, but none of them held photos of Wes and his family. Instead they looked like the stock photos that came with the frames: sunsets and ocean waves and writing in the sand. It felt more like I was in a display home instead of an actual home.

"Can I get you a drink?" Wes asked. "Water? Tea?"

"Tea would be nice," I said, curious to see the rest of his house.

He led me to the kitchen, where a row of tea canisters was set out on the jade marble island along with snacks. Lots of snacks. I spotted my favorite sweet-potato sticks as well as rows of Pepero boxes, shrimp crackers, and chocolate biscuits in the shape of mushrooms.

"Wow, did your mom do an H-Mart run this morning or something?" I asked.

"No," Wes said. "I did."

"You got all this ready?" I said, surprised.

"It's no big deal," he said. "Just common manners when you have someone over."

Huh. For a guy cashing in a favor, he was definitely a considerate host. At this rate, I'd have to pay him back again for being so hospitable. I gasped, my eyes falling on a bag of Hi-Chews I'd never seen before. "What are *these*?"

Wes rubbed the back of his head, making his hair stick up funny. "I noticed you holding a bag of the originals that time at the grocery store. So I got the tropical bag for us to try. Have you had them before?"

Wow. I couldn't help but be impressed. I inspected the flavors inside. "Mango I've had. But kiwi and pineapple I've never seen before. I can't wait to try these."

He smiled, a look of relief passing his face. It was strangely disarming to see how pleased he was to see me happy. "What kind of tea do you want? These are from my mom's collection. She gets a lot of tea gifts."

I surveyed the tea selection. Wes was right. There were tea bags from all over the world to choose from. I selected a genmaicha green tea from Japan.

"Your mom must be popular if she gets so many gifts," I said, leaning against the jade counter as Wes prepared the tea. "Are these from Crown Tiger?" I know, I know. I was boycotting Crown Tiger out of pettiness, but I couldn't help but be curious about his mom's job. I didn't know anyone else who worked in the Korean entertainment industry.

"Some of them might be," he said, setting a mug of genmaicha in front of me. "But to be honest, I don't know exactly what she does or who she meets all the time. I just know that her job is the reason we move around so much."

"Where have you lived?" I asked, wrapping my hands around the mug. My fingers were finally starting to thaw out from the freezing car ride. As much as Wes consumed my thoughts these days (because of the bet, of course), I realized I didn't actually know that much about him.

"Born in Seoul. Then we moved to Tokyo. Then back to Seoul for a bit when I was in middle school. Then to LA, and finally here." He counted the places off on his fingers, reciting them like he had been asked this question a million times. Which, to be fair, he probably had been.

"What was your least favorite place?"

For a second he looked taken aback, and then he laughed. "Most people ask me what my favorite place was, not my least favorite."

I shrugged, sipping my tea. It was perfectly steeped, just the right mix of bitter and nutty. "I'm just curious."

Wes considered this carefully, as if weighing my question very seriously. "That second time in Seoul was tough," he finally said. "I went to an international school in Tokyo, so when I moved back to Korea, my Korean was way behind the other kids'. My parents tried sending me to public school for a bit, but I was teased mercilessly. Everyone would ask me, 'If you're Korean, why can't you speak it?' Eventually, I did get better, but I ended up moving to America pretty soon after."

"Huh. That's interesting," I said, swirling my tea bag around. "And weird. You'd think as a Korean person you'd feel like you belonged the most in Korea."

"Yeah . . . I mean, maybe that's the case if you're *Korean* Korean. But when you're a third-culture kid like me, it gets a bit more complicated."

I cocked my head to the side. "'Third-culture kid'? That's when you move around to a lot of different places when you're a kid, right?"

He nodded. "Yeah. The more exact definition is when a kid grows up outside of their parents' culture for a lot of their early years, which, as you said, usually involves moving around to a bunch of foreign countries."

"Thanks, Wikipedia," I joked.

He laughed. "Sorry. I answer this question a lot."

"What else do you say about it?"

"Hmm." He drummed his fingers on the counter. "I say that it can mean being exposed to a lot of different cultures but not really being 'from' anywhere." He got a wistful look in his eyes.

"What?" I said.

"Huh?"

"That look in your eyes. What are you thinking?"

He hesitated and then shrugged. "I was just thinking that I wish I could just say I'm Korean American like you. I feel like it would be way simpler. But I don't think I can really say that and feel honest about it. I was born in Korea. I lived in Tokyo for the most consecutive years. I may have gone to American schools for most of my life, but I haven't actually lived in America that long. I don't think I can even name all the states."

I laughed. "Honestly? I always forget a couple too." I rested my chin in my hand, mulling over what he'd said.

"What?" he said.

"Huh?"

"Now *you* have that look in your eyes. Like you're thinking something you want to say."

I pressed my lips together and ran my finger around the rim of the teacup. I didn't open up about these things much, but he was right. I did have thoughts I wanted to share. "It's not as simple being Korean American, either," I said finally. "What you said about not really being 'from' anywhere? I kind of get that, even though I was born here and never left."

He leaned back on the counter, thinking this over. "If you were born here and never left, why would you feel like you don't belong here?"

"No, I do. Most of the time. There are just moments, you know, little things like strangers asking me where I'm from or why my English is so good or yelling 'ni hao' to me on the streets. Or going to the movie theater in the city I grew up in but not seeing anyone on the screen who looks like me." I shrugged. "It feels more like home than Korea, though. The few times I've been, I felt way too American to fit in. I don't even know what it is—my hair? My style? The way I talk? I don't know. It's everything. It's like you said. If you're not Korean Korean, where do you fit as a Korean person in the world?"

Whoa. Where did all that come from? I immediately stopped talking and took another sip of tea. Somehow I'd gotten caught up in the smell of genmaicha and Wes's attentive gaze, like he was soaking up every word I was saying, like he really wanted to listen. I rarely talked about stuff like this, even though I low-key felt it all the time. I guess that's what happens when you keep things bottled up. You overshare to a boy who's supposed to be your enemy.

"Anyway," I said, clearing my throat before Wes could continue the conversation, "I came here to pay you a favor, so let's get started, shall we?"

"Ah, right." He looked a little regretful that we were changing topics. "That's probably a good idea."

"You said in your text that you needed help with your social media?" Honestly, I had been pretty surprised that this was the favor he was asking for. I thought he was going to ask me to do something way more embarrassing, like dress up as a Crown Tiger mascot at school. After all, I'd made him walk around the school with lipstick writing on his shirt. God, now that I thought about it, I couldn't believe I'd really done that. Despite everything between us, he'd consistently offered me kindness, and I had definitely done anything but.

He nodded. "Specifically Instagram. I set up an account for my business, but, um, I have no idea how to keep it going. I've read articles and I've attempted, but I think I need some one-on-one coaching."

"A good way to start is by taking photos of your products. After all, Instagram is all about the photos." I considered the things I thought about when I was taking photos for V&C's Instagram account. "Natural lighting is always nice. Where do you have the most natural light in the house?"

"I get pretty good light in my room," Wes said. Then, as if realizing what he might be suggesting by this, he quickly said, "But, I mean, there's light in the whole house. We don't have to go to my room."

"No, it's okay. We can go," I said, my cheeks warming. What did he think I was thinking when he said that? To be honest, though, I was genuinely curious about what Wes's room looked like. I grabbed the bag of tropical Hi-Chews to snack on later, and I followed him out of the kitchen and up the stairs.

His room was nothing like the rest of the house. It felt actually lived in. There were black-and-white posters of famous saxophone players lining the walls and a vinyl-record player in the corner of the room. His saxophone case lay open on the floor, sheets of music spread out on the bed like he had been playing right before I got here. A row of succulents lined the windowsill.

"Sorry for the mess," he said, gathering the sheet music.

"It's way cleaner than my room," I said. I pointed to the saxophone in the case. "So. Is this your passion?"

He nodded. "Is it obvious?"

I gestured to the posters on the wall and grinned. "Kind of."

He smiled. "I've played since I was a kid. My uncle Hojin in Korea taught me everything I know. I've been in love with it ever since."

My stomach fluttered weirdly when he said the words "in love." I kept my face casual. "Oh yeah?"

"Yeah. It's been the one thing in my life that's never changed. I know there's a lot of uncertainty in pursuing music, but to me, it feels more uncertain to have anything besides music at the center of my life. I feel like I would just float away if I didn't have my saxophone to ground me." He paused like he was trying to decide whether to share more or not. "Actually, the reason I even have this K-pop beauty business is to raise money for music school. My parents aren't so supportive of the idea, so if I want to go, I need to figure out a way to get myself there."

I found myself nodding along. I could understand that. That feeling of something you love being the only thing to tether you when you're on the verge of floating away. I wondered what Wes's parents were like. "What would they want you to do instead?" I asked.

"Be a doctor."

I laughed. "How very stereotypically Asian." I sat cross-legged on the floor. Something in my mind nudged me to get started on the social-media stuff, to leave the personal conversations behind. It wasn't like I'd come here to chat. But curiosity won over logic, and I heard myself saying, "Are you very good? If you're very good, your parents have to at least acknowledge that."

"I think I'm not bad," he said.

I snorted. "That means you're very good."

"No, no," he laughed. He bit his lip, glancing at me. "I can show you a video if you want? It's a song I've been practicing for my music school auditions. Uncle Hojin recommended it to me."

The way he asked, part shyness and part excitement to show me what he'd been working on, did strange things to my heart. It made me feel drawn to him in ways I hadn't expected. He wanted to invite me in, to show me his world. A part of me suspected that he would have offered to play his song for me live on the spot but was too self-conscious to ask.

Move the conversation along, Valerie, I told myself. *This is not why you're here.*

"Okay, yeah," I said instead. "I'd like to see the video."

He scrolled through his phone and hit play on a video before passing it to me. He sat down on the floor across from me as the music filled the room. It wasn't a song I recognized, but I was immediately captivated. The song went from upbeat and intricate to slow and moving, showcasing his whole range, every note clear and resounding. I couldn't take my eyes off his face. It was undeniable that he was in his element, that this was his passion. God. He was so hot.

The sudden thought made my cheeks warm again. *What am I thinking? We're still in competition, and I'm sitting here getting all soft for my enemy because of a measly video?* Thank God he wasn't playing for me in person. I would have really hated myself then.

The clip ended, and I looked up from his phone to see he had been watching me the whole time, gauging my reaction.

I cleared my throat, passing the phone back. "See, I was right. You are very good."

Oh, the way his face lit up. "Really?"

"Really. I think your parents will definitely come around one day. And if they don't, it shouldn't stop you. You've got something that not everyone gets in their lifetime. Why give that up for someone else?"

He stared at me with a deep, intense gaze. *Damn those eyes of his. They really are beautiful.* "Like what you said in the car about fighting to prove that you're worth what you think you are," he said quietly.

"Yeah. Exactly." Hearing my own words spoken back to me in that way made me feel suddenly vulnerable, like I had exposed a part of myself that I hadn't meant to reveal. But now that it was out there, I felt oddly comforted by the fact that he could relate.

"Anyway," I said, clapping my hands, reminding myself that having a heart-to-heart with Wes was not the reason I was here today. "Social media, right? Let's get started."

For the next hour, we set up his products in nice photogenic spots around his room. I taught him how to shoot from different angles, how to use props in his photos, how to highlight the product so it looked its very best. In the back of my mind, I was tempted to store away all the information on what I was seeing here and use it to strategize my own sales later.

But a twinge of guilt stopped me. Wes was undeniably kind, and I was here because I owed him a favor. I could have the decency to not spy on him when I was paying a debt. For today, I would focus solely on helping him.

"You need to follow some people so they know you're out there and they can follow you back," I said as he pulled up his Instagram account. "In the case of our school, there's only one person you really need to follow." I did a search for @k.lo.gram. "Kristy Lo. Once you follow her, she'll follow back and bring the rest of our grade with her."

"Wow," Wes said. "That's power."

"That's Kristy."

He cleared his throat. "Can I follow your Instagram?"

"I mean, you could," I said. "It's VCKBEAUTY. But we are still competitors, you know."

"No, I mean, um, a personal account. Not business-related."

My stomach did a strange flip at this new knowledge that Wes wanted to follow my personal account. "Oh. Sure," I said. "It's vkwonishere."

"Okay cool. I'm wesplaysmusic. I'll follow you?"

"Okay," I said. "Sure. But, um, just warning you. It's just a bunch of pictures of my grandma. And food."

He laughed. "That's okay." He looked curiously at me, his knees almost touching mine from where we were sitting cross-legged on the floor, the winter light from the window slanting across our hands. "Sounds like you and your grandma are pretty close?"

"Yeah." I smiled, feeling more comfortable talking about Halmeoni. "She's the best. Do you have any grandparents here?"

He shook his head. "My grandparents on my dad's side both passed away before I was born. And my grandparents on my mom's side are still in Korea. They used to watch me when we lived there, but I haven't seen them since we moved the second time."

"Same with my dad's parents," I said. "And my grandpa on my mom's side died a year before Halmeoni immigrated with my mom and my aunt. They were all supposed to come together . . . but I guess things don't always go the way you hope. I wish I got to meet him. Halmeoni says I remind her of him a lot."

My face flushed when I realized how much I was sharing again. Seriously, what was up with me today? But Wes didn't seem to mind. If anything, he seemed pleased to be having a more personal conversation. And to be really honest, I was enjoying it too. I found myself carefully storing away everything he said like they were all things I wanted to remember for a long time.

"Your grandma seems really cool," he said with a smile. "I could tell, even from our short encounter at the grocery store."

I got a little teary thinking about Halmeoni, so all I could do was nod, swallowing the lump in my throat. What would it have been like if she lived far away in Korea and we could never see each other? I thought of her alone at night, her face aglow with the light from the television screen. And then I thought of the opposite: me and her together, free in Paris. The dream. Why did I keep losing sight of it when I was sitting here with Wes? *Come on, Valerie. Get your head on straight.*

"Are you hungry?" Wes asked suddenly. "Do you want to try the Hi-Chews?"

How did he know I needed a distraction? If there was one thing I could say with certainty, it was that Wes was good at reading people. I nodded gratefully.

He ripped open the bag and took out two kiwis. We both tried them at the same time. His face lit up while I grimaced.

"Yuck," I said. "I am not feeling that one."

"Oh, really?" His face froze as if he wasn't sure how to respond to that.

I laughed. "It's okay if you like it. You're allowed to speak your mind, remember?"

"Okay." He smiled. "I can't lie. I like kiwi a lot. But I like pineapple more, so I think this one will be even better."

He passed me a pineapple. I popped it in my mouth. The tropical flavor burst with brightness on my tongue. "Oh my God. This might be my new favorite one. I'll have to put it on the roster."

"Roster?" Wes said.

Now it was my turn to freeze. *Oh shit.* I'd never told anyone about my Hi-Chew moods, other than Halmeoni and Charlie. It was so ridiculous. But Wes was looking at me with such curiosity, I wasn't sure how to backtrack out of this one.

"It's just this thing—I eat different flavors for different moods.

So I eat grape to focus on a task, green apple to think or brainstorm, strawberry to calm down. Stuff like that."

It sounded so awkward saying it out loud, but he nodded seriously, like this made 100 percent sense. "What will pineapple be?"

I grinned, appreciating that he asked me in a way that felt genuine instead of making fun of me. "Hmm. It has kind of the same vibe as mango, which is what I eat to celebrate good things. But it's also a little sweeter, and definitely more of a bright flavor."

"Maybe it can be what you eat when you're feeling like everything is just right with the world." He smiled and it was truly the purest thing I'd ever seen. "Hopeful and right. Like when everything is as it should be."

My heart thrummed inside my chest. "I like that."

We sat there, knees touching, pineapple Hi-Chews on our tongues. There were so many disarming things about Wes. He was kind. Somewhat awkward and surprisingly perceptive. And he took me seriously. He looked at me like I was someone he could learn something from. He made me feel like I was seen. Suddenly, Charlie's words from sophomore year came back to me: *It's not about the aquarium, Val. It's about the way she really sees me.* For the first time in my life, I finally understood what he meant.

My phone pinged, making us both jump. I glanced at my screen. "Charlie's on his way. I should get ready to go."

"Oh, okay," Wes said. Was it just me or did he look a bit disappointed? "I'll walk you to the door."

As we stepped outside, I felt something cold land on my nose. I looked up at the sky, pulling my red blanket scarf around my shoulders. "Oh wow," I said. "It's snowing."

"It's not just any snow," Wes said, his cheeks pink despite the coldness. "It's the first snow of the winter." He glanced at me. "Do you know what that means?"

I blinked. "That it's going to be a cold winter?"

He rubbed his elbows, pressing his lips together and looking up at the sky. "Um. Yeah, that's it."

I raised my eyebrows, amused. "You're a terrible liar."

A smile cracked across his lips, his eyes still on the falling snow. "So I've heard."

A car honked as Charlie rolled into the driveway. He waved at me from the car.

"Thanks again for all the snacks. And the tea," I said. "I guess I'll see you at school?"

"Yeah." He hesitated like he wanted to say something more, but he settled on "Thanks for all your help today."

I nodded and headed for the car, feeling a little wistful.

"Hey, Valerie," Wes called out.

I turned around.

"You're really good at this stuff. The whole business thing. I really mean it when I say thanks."

My stomach flipped.

"I was just paying you back for the ride," I said, keeping a cool face. The snow was falling fast now, clinging to Wes's hair, making him look like a figurine in a snow globe. I wanted to watch the snow settle on his shoulders, building like the mountains that reminded me of home.

I snapped out of my trance and got into the car, buckling my seat belt. The heater was going strong, and Charlie was down to one sweater.

"How warm is it in this car? Toasty, eh?" he said as he pulled out of the driveway.

"Hey," I said. "Do you know what's so interesting about the first snow?"

"First snow? That's the Korean myth, right? That if you're outside with someone you like when it first starts snowing, you'll fall in love." He laughed. "Koreans, so romantic. Anyway, how'd it go today? It looks like you survived?"

I looked into the rearview mirror, where Wes was watching the car drive away, his hands in his pockets, cheeks still pink with cold.

"Yeah," I said. I settled into the warmth of the car, smiling. "I guess I did."

CHAPTER TWELVE

WES

Friday / December 27

Did you get home safe?

I stared at the unsent text on my phone. To send or not to send? Was it too eager? Kind of creepy? I didn't want Valerie to think I was some kind of stalker or something who needed to know her every move. But it *was* starting to snow pretty hard. It was totally reasonable to ask if she'd gotten home safe in this weather. Decision made. I hit send.

Before I had time to regret anything, the front door opened with the sound of stamping feet. I looked up from my spot on the couch to see Dad walk in, shivering under his coat.

"Ah, Wes, you're home?" he said. "Good, good. It's snowing a lot out there."

The snow was piling higher on the windowsills. I guess Valerie didn't know about the first-snow myth. She would probably think it was ridiculous anyway. *Does she even believe in myths?* I realized with a lurch in my stomach that there were so many things I didn't know about her. So many things I wanted to know.

"What were you up to today, son?" Dad asked, shaking the snow from his coat. "Final application deadlines for our college picks close in a few days. Let me know if you want me to read over anything before you send them in."

Oh. I opened my mouth trying to think of something to say. Maybe this was the moment to confess: *Actually Dad, I'm not going to apply to the schools you suggested. I've already applied to a school. A music school.* Instead I said, "Um, sure. Thanks. Maybe later?"

What? Was that really the best I could come up with? I mentally slapped myself in the forehead. *Come on, Wes.*

Dad nodded. "Later sounds good. How about after dinner?"

By "later" I meant more like way later. Like the never kind of later. But I found myself nodding, not wanting to let him down. "Yeah, that could work."

What is wrong with me? I kept my smile up until Dad walked out of the living room, and then I slumped deeper into the couch with a sigh.

My phone pinged with an incoming text message, and I immediately sat back up, grabbing my phone.

Valerie responded with one thing: a thumbs-up emoji.

Straight to the point. So like Valerie. I laughed and sent a thumbs-up emoji back and held my phone against my chest.

The smile slipped off my face as I remembered my conversation with Dad. What would Valerie have done in that situation? I didn't have to ask to know that she would have said something better than "Sure, maybe later." She probably would have spoken up for herself and said what she was really thinking.

"Wes, what do you feel like eating tonight?" Dad asked, walking back into the living room with a bunch of takeout menus in his hand. "Sushi? Pizza?"

I was about to say, *Anything is good,* but I stopped myself before the words came out. "How about pizza?" I said. "Um . . . can we get Hawaiian?"

"Sure," Dad said without even looking up from the menu. "I'll order one large Hawaiian and one large pepperoni, then."

He walked out of the room again and I let myself exhale slowly. Choosing what to eat for dinner might not have been much, but it was a start to saying what I really wanted. Maybe eventually I could move up from speaking up about pizza toppings to bigger things like my future.

I glanced back down at my phone and smiled.

Friday / January 17

By the time winter break ended, I was more than ready to go back to school. There were three reasons for this that I realized within the first two weeks back.

Reason one:

Ever since Hawaiian pizza night, I've been running out of ways to avoid talking about colleges with Dad. I got out of going over applications with him that night by saying I had a headache and never bringing it up again. Was it weird to want to go to school to avoid talking about future school?

Maybe. In any case, I was relieved to have an excuse to get out of the house. Especially after I got an email from Toblie School of Music inviting me to come in for an audition in February.

Holy shit. Cue panic.

I was three days back in school when the email came. Toblie was my dream school. World renowned, famous for their jazz program, and only a two-hour drive away. Perfect distance for my in-person audition.

It was exciting, but it reminded me that I had to tell my parents about this soon. The longer I waited, the more nauseous I felt at the idea of bringing it up. It was like this pressure inside my chest that was building, building, building. But another more fearful part of me wondered if it was better not to say anything until I knew for sure I was accepted. No point in telling them if I didn't even get in, right? Though I wasn't sure how I would explain the part about having not applied to any of the schools he chose for me either. Dad was under the impression that I had applied to all of them by the deadline, but really, I had applied to none of them. Maybe I should have as a plan B, but I couldn't bring myself to do it.

I would tell them.

Soon.

But not yet.

Reason two:

Mr. Reyes let me use the band room to practice after school when there weren't any rehearsals. It felt good to practice in a space that was outside my room, outside my house, and outside Dad knocking on my door, saying, "Are you still playing the saxophone, Wes? Shouldn't we be studying instead?"

"You're sounding really good, Wes," Mr. Reyes said during one of my practices, a week back into school. The socks that peeked out from the cuff of his pants were striped like a candy cane. "Say, I was wondering. The Senior Showcase isn't until the end of the year, but would you be interested in playing a saxophone solo during one of our numbers? Of course, you'll have to try out like all the other kids during class, but I feel like you would really nail it."

"Really, Mr. Reyes?" I gaped at him. "That would be awesome."

He laughed. "Why do you look so shocked, Wes? You're clearly very talented, and you put in a lot of hard work."

"I guess I've just never had so many people tell me that before," I said slowly. I thought back to that day with Valerie. She'd said I was *very* good. It was the first time I'd heard it from someone who wasn't an instructor.

"Well, whether people tell you or not, it doesn't change the facts. You are an excellent saxophonist," Mr. Reyes said. He smiled warmly. "But I am very glad you have people in your life to affirm that for you. Musicians don't grow in a vacuum, right?"

Which led me to reason three:

Friday at lunch at the end of the second week back, I was browsing in the library for my history essay. As I pulled a book off the shelf, I spotted Valerie through the empty spot in the shelf. Caught off guard, I dropped the book with a thump. Valerie looked up as Ms. Reeves, the librarian, put a finger to her lips and hissed, "Shhh."

I raised my hand in apology, fumbling to grab the book from the floor. When I straightened up again, Valerie was peering through the shelf, staring at me through the space where the book had been.

"Hi," she whispered.

"Hi," I whispered back.

"Having trouble?"

I laughed and then cast a quick glance toward Ms. Reeves. "A little."

She nodded toward the common area where all the study tables were. "Are you studying?"

"Ah . . ." I scanned the tables. That had been the plan, but most of them were full, and the ones that weren't had backpacks on the seats to save a spot. Exam season had students squeezing for space to study even during lunch. "No room, I don't think."

She paused and then motioned for me to follow her. She led me to a table where two seats were saved with a backpack on one and a jacket slung over the other.

"You can sit with me," she said.

"Aren't both these seats saved?" I asked.

She shrugged. "Nah. I just put my jacket there so no one would sit next to me. But you can take it if you want." She cleared her throat. "I'm only offering because it would be rude of me not to when I know you need one. Don't sit here if you don't want to."

"No, no," I said, quickly taking a seat. "I want to." I smiled. "Thank you."

She grunted back, but I could see the small smile on her lips as she sat down next to me with her stack of books. She arranged the stacks around her like a half-curved wall. Then she pulled out a notebook from her backpack and started writing with one hand, scrolling through her phone and punching in Google search after Google search with the other, the books untouched next to her.

"What are you working on?" I whispered.

She hesitated and then whispered, "Business stuff." She showed me the list of jargon on her notebook page. I had no clue what any of it meant. "These are ingredients that I'm not familiar with in some of the products I'll be selling next month. So I'm researching what they are."

I whistled softly. "That's dedication."

"It's important to me to know what I'm selling and where it comes from."

My level of respect for her rose even higher. She put so much thought into her business. Sitting here with her like this, I could almost pretend that we weren't still locked in an all-or-nothing bet. Almost. It was always there, floating around in the back of my mind. But for now I pushed it away.

"What are the books for, then?" I asked, noticing all the random titles. *A–Z Encyclopedia. Alice in Wonderland with Commentary and Essays. Fundamentals of Physics.*

"It's so people won't look at me while I work," she said. "Call it a book barrier, if you will."

My chest warmed. She made book barriers and pretended to save seats so people would walk past her, but she let me sit next to her. Did that mean something? It felt like it did.

"Cool," I said, unable to keep a smile from spreading across my face. "I'll let you get back to it."

She smiled back before returning to her notebook.

Of all the reasons I was happy to be back at school, the third one was maybe my favorite of all.

Saturday / February 1

"Our sales are way down. Do you even want to win this bet against Valerie, Wes?"

Pauline, Taemin, and I sat around a table at the aquarium café for our business meeting. He joined us every now and then when he was around the aquarium, still hoping for a job as a magician.

"Yes," I answered. And I really, really did. But I also wanted to spend more time with Valerie. Of course, there was also music school to think about. Now that I had a real audition coming up, I had to be mentally prepared, not distracted.

"Do you have a strategy?" Taemin asked.

A strategy? I should definitely be thinking of one. But all I could think about was Valerie's smile, which was even prettier than I'd first imagined it. I didn't want to be in competition with her anymore. I wanted to be more than that.

"I don't know—maybe we should call off the bet," I blurted out.

Pauline raised an eyebrow. "Why?"

The back of my neck grew sweaty. "Why? Because, um . . ."

Why? That was a good question. *Because I don't want to be her rival anymore? Because I think I might be falling in love with her?*

The thought came into my head before I could stop it, striking me silent. *Was* I falling for her?

I sighed, shaking my head. "No, forget I said that. I'm just stressing." Did I really want to call off the bet? I wasn't totally sure. A part of me did. But a part of me wanted the future I had been dreaming of, and I didn't want to let that go.

Understanding dawned on Pauline's face like she was putting two and two together. "You and Valerie seem to be pretty friendly these days," she observed, as if reading my thoughts.

Taemin looked back and forth between me and Pauline. "Wait. Is there something going on between you and Valerie?"

Maybe. Yes. I hope so? I wanted to say. But the words lodged somewhere in my throat. I wasn't ready to speak the truth out loud yet, to confess, especially to Taemin or even Pauline. If I was feeling something for Valerie, I would want to tell her about it first.

"No. Absolutely not," I said instead, inwardly cringing at my own dishonesty.

"Do you not want to go to music school anymore?" Taemin asked. "I thought it was important to you."

"It is important to me." *Important enough to keep competing with Valerie?*

Taemin frowned thoughtfully and then looked at me in sympathy, nodding his head. "I think I see what's going on."

I swallowed. "You do?"

"Yeah. You're caving under your dad's pressure, right? He doesn't want you to go to music school, so you're having second thoughts. Dude, I totally get that, but you need to grow a spine. Take more risks. Don't be a pushover when you've come so far!"

His words jabbed at me, hitting me right where it hurt. He had no idea how hard I'd been trying to do exactly those things for months now. To grow a spine. Take more risks. Not be a pushover.

"That's not it. I'm not caving under my dad."

"Yes, you are. I can tell."

"No, I'm not."

"Yes, you are."

"No, I'm really not."

"Then why are you getting friendly with Valerie like Pauline said? It's not because you've already given up on music school to appease your parents?"

"No!" I said, louder and angrier than I meant to. "No. I mean, yeah, we've been getting closer. But that's just so I can learn more about her business. You know, get the inside scoop on things. Like what you did for us before. She even showed me some of her business notes at the library the other day, so I'm making good progress in strategizing how to beat her. I just need more time to figure out this business stuff."

Ugh. What was that? I had no idea why I'd said all those things, and I felt gross even having those words come out of my mouth. I just wanted to get Taemin off my back. Pauline frowned at my obvious lie, but Taemin's eyes widened; he was buying every word.

"You've been getting closer to her so you can spy on her business?" he said. "That's . . . wow. Didn't see that coming."

Pauline sighed. "All right, Wes. Whatever you say. But you

should make a decision about your business soon. Lisa, Mimi, and Natalie were asking me if their discount with you still applies if they don't shop with V&C. I think they want to buy from Valerie again if you're not going to keep things up."

Taemin's eyes got even wider. "Whoa. You gave discounts to people to make them stop shopping with Valerie?" He chewed his lip. "Didn't see that coming either."

"Same," I muttered to myself. This was seriously stressful.

Pauline rose from the table. "I should get going. My volunteer shift starts soon and I'm leading a new info session." Her eyes lit up. "Actually, Wes, I was meaning to tell you. You know haenyeo? The female divers in Jeju? I did some reading on them, and they really are the coolest. I'm doing an info session on scuba divers and I got permission to include a section on divers of the world, so I'm going to share about them today."

"What! Pauline, that's awesome," I said, feeling simultaneously happy for her and relieved that the subject had changed.

"Yeah. My dad's really excited about it." She smiled. "I should probably thank Charlie at some point, huh? I would've never known about them if it wasn't for him. If we ever talk again, that is." Right. After the awkward encounter at Lisa's party a couple months ago, Charlie seemed to be steering totally clear of Pauline. "Anyway, I'll talk to you guys later."

"I'll come with you. I want to learn about these female divers," Taemin said. He downed his hot chocolate and stood to leave, glancing back at me with a strange expression, like he wasn't totally sure what to make of all the things I'd just said. Honestly, I couldn't blame him. I barely had any idea what I'd just said either. "Talk to you later, Wes," he said, before bounding after Pauline. "Any chance you need a magician at your info session?"

I watched them go and breathed out a sigh of relief, grateful to be alone to sift through my thoughts. My heart raced.

Am I in love with Valerie Kwon?

Friday / February 14

Just like they did for Halloween, Crescent Brook High went all out for Valentine's Day. The entire school was decked out in pink and red streamers, and all the teachers coordinated to dress up in T-shirts printed with candy hearts, except the hearts said things like ME + MATH; EYES ON ME, NOT ON UR SCREEN; and BE MINE-DFUL OF OTHERS. They were very pleased with themselves.

The senior student council was hosting a huge rose sale in the cafeteria during lunch. I walked by their table, where Kristy waved me down, her hair back to pink for the occasion.

"Wes, Wes! Care to send a rose?" she said. "All proceeds go toward prom!"

A rose? My mind immediately flashed to Valerie. It was weird how often and quickly I thought of her now. When had this happened to me? One day she was just my rival. Now she was my rival who I wanted to buy a rose for?

"You can buy one and give it to them yourself, or you can choose the option where we deliver it for you," Kristy said. "If you choose the second option, you can make it anonymous. You just have to tell us what their last class of the day is."

I blanked. I had no idea what Valerie's class schedule was. We didn't have any classes together. That would mean I'd have to go with option one and give it to her in person. I tried to imagine doing that without erupting into flames. It was difficult to picture.

"Hey, Charlie!" Kristy said, waving at someone behind me. "Want to buy a rose?"

Charlie appeared beside me, surveying the single stemmed red roses laid out on the table. "I'm not sure. Maybe."

"Is it for Pauline?" I asked.

He turned sharply toward me, his mouth dropping open like he was about to protest. "What? No. Psh. That's ridiculous." Then he sighed, his shoulders sagging like the fight was deflating out of him. "Is it that obvious?"

"Pretty obvious," I said, wincing on his behalf.

Things between Charlie and me had cooled off a lot since Lisa's party. He'd apologized to me in calculus class for crying at the party. I'd said it was nothing to be sorry for. I asked if he knew about the bet. He sighed and said that was between me and Valerie, and he was staying out of it. Since then, we'd kind of reached this mutual understanding. He didn't even bug me in class anymore. Okay, well, sometimes he still did, but I suspected it was just for his own amusement at this point.

I wonder if he knows about me and Valerie.

Whatever there is between us.

Does she talk to him about me?

I was so lost in my thoughts that I didn't even realize Charlie was still talking.

"... made a total fool of myself and have been avoiding her ever since. Now it's been months and I still haven't said anything."

"I think you should send her a rose," I said, piecing together what I had missed. "If there's anything I know about Pauline, it's that she's a pretty straightforward person. She likes facts. And honesty. And besides," I added, recalling what she had told me about their relationship, "she has a higher opinion of you than you think."

Charlie perked up. "Really?"

I nodded. "Really."

"Okay, then. Honesty? I can be honest." He shook out his arms, jumping in place like he was psyching himself up. "Give me a rose for delivery, Kristy. I'll attach a note, too."

"Great," Kristy beamed. She turned to me. "And you, Wes?"

"Um, I'll take one too," I said as Charlie got to work writing his note. "To go."

"Ooh. In-person delivery, huh?" She wiggled her eyebrows. "Who's the lucky person?"

My face heated up. "No one."

"Okay, okay, keeping it a secret, that's cool. I can respect the mystery. That'll be a dollar."

I fished out a dollar as Kristy handed me a red rose wrapped in cellophane and tied with a gold ribbon.

"Thanks," I mumbled. "Good luck, man," I added to Charlie, who flashed me a thumbs-up.

As I walked down the hall, I felt eyes watching me, zeroing in on the rose in my hand. I didn't know if I was imagining things or not, but I could have sworn I was hearing whispers wherever I went. *Oh God.* I couldn't walk around like this all day. I had to hide this somewhere.

I rushed to my locker and slid the rose inside, slamming it shut.

For the rest of the day, all I could think about was the rose inside my locker. Was it wilting? Didn't flowers need sunshine and water? And fresh air? Oh my God. What if I gave Valerie a dead rose? My palms were starting to sweat at the very thought.

As soon as the last bell rang, I booked it for my locker. I let out a sigh of relief when I saw that the rose was still there, healthy and vibrant as ever. I carefully took it out and closed my locker. And then I opened my locker and put it back in, slamming the door shut.

I'll give her the rose. I won't give her the rose. I'll give her the rose. I won't—

"Why do you keep opening and closing your locker like that?"

Pauline stared at me as she opened her own locker, shooting me a concerned look. She was holding a rose in her hand. "Do you have issues with your lock or something?"

"I got a rose for Valerie, but I don't know if she'll hate it or not."

"Ah." Pauline nodded. "Well, you better decide fast. I just had English with her, and last I saw, she was headed for her locker. She'll probably leave soon."

Damn it. If I was going to act, I'd have to do it now. I opened my locker and gingerly took out the rose. I glanced at the one in Pauline's hand.

"From Charlie?" I asked.

She smiled and nodded. "Yeah. I'll tell you about it later. Good luck with Valerie."

"Right. Thanks."

The hallways had mostly cleared of students, and for a second I was worried that she would be gone. I speed walked to her locker, passing by teachers tidying up their classrooms, a storage room with the door left ajar, and a couple of freshmen giggling over their Valentine's cards.

And then I saw her. Down the hall. She was standing at her locker, wearing a red dress, her hair in a bun on top of her head, held up with a heart-printed scrunchie.

I watched her for a second, my heart pounding in my chest. Then, as if sensing my stare, she looked up and stared straight at me.

We looked at each other. And then I did what anyone would do if Valerie Kwon was staring at them with her piercing eyes.

I ducked into the storage room, held open by a shoe, and hid.

CHAPTER THIRTEEN

VALERIE

Friday / February 14

Um, okay. That was weird. I blinked, staring at the spot where Wes had disappeared. I closed my locker and walked to the storage room.

I opened the door and stepped inside, kicking aside a random shoe on the floor and looking around. The storage room was filled mostly with stuff for the theater students. Amelia Perry's domain. Costumes from the school's latest production of *The Wizard of Oz* hung on coatracks; feather boas draped over boxes of glitter and face paint slotted neatly into the shelves. The door clicked shut behind me as I turned on the lights, a row of bare bulbs hanging from the ceiling flickering to life.

"Wes?" I called out.

There was a pause and then a shuffle, and then Wes poked his head out from behind a coatrack of old Shakespeare costumes. "Oh, hey, Valerie," he said, trying very hard to sound casual and failing miserably at it. "What are you doing here?"

I raised my eyebrow, folding my arms across my chest. "Really?"

He smiled sheepishly. I rolled my eyes and laughed. When had I become someone who laughed so easily?

"Come on, let's get out of here and talk outside," I said. I reached for the doorknob, but to my surprise, the door didn't open. I jiggled it again, turning it to the left and then to the right, a dawning realization creeping up my back.

I cleared my throat. "Wes, you wouldn't happen to have a key, would you?"

"A key?" Wes came up beside me, his hands clasped behind his back. "No, but there was a shoe keeping the door open, wasn't there?"

A shoe? I looked down at the old boot I had kicked aside when I walked into the room.

"You mean that shoe?" I said.

His eyes followed my gaze. He nodded grimly. "That'll be the one."

We stared at the shoe and then at each other, and then we burst out laughing.

"My bad," I said. "I'll call Charlie and ask him to find the janitor or something."

It wasn't until Charlie's phone rang straight to voicemail that I remembered he was at basketball practice. He never checked his phone when he was playing ball. I left him a message and then a text for good measure.

"He'll probably come after practice," I said. I was suddenly aware of how close Wes and I were standing and how very alone we were in this storage room. Just the two of us. My palms felt way too clammy. I wiped them against my dress, cursing myself for leaving my fanny pack of strawberry Hi-Chews inside my locker. "Maybe I'll try calling someone else—"

"Wait."

Wes looked just as nervous as me, like he was trying to decide whether or not he should bungee jump off a cliff into the ocean. He took a deep breath and smiled, a warm smile that sent tingles up and down my arms. "I, um, got something for you."

He carefully brought out a single long-stemmed red rose from behind his back. Every thought in my mind immediately stilled except for one: *He got me a rose.*

Not just any rose. A Valentine's Day rose.

"This is for me?" My voice came out with an edge of suspicion, even though what I was feeling was more disbelief. He got flowers? For me?

He nodded shyly. "Yeah." And then a crease between his eyebrows. A look of uncertainty. "Do you hate it?"

"No!" I said too loudly. I cleared my throat and tried again. "No. I like it. It's just, um . . . I've never gotten flowers before. From anyone. So I don't know exactly how to respond or what to even do with my face. Like, am I glaring at you right now? I feel like I'm glaring."

"Yeah, you're glaring a little," he laughed.

I laughed too and covered my eyes with one hand. God, talk about oversharing. He'd caught me so off guard, I didn't even know what I was saying anymore. All I knew was that my heart was racing inside my chest and no amount of Hi-Chews would be able to calm it down. And the weirdest part? I wasn't even sure if I'd want to calm my heart down if I could. The way I was feeling right now was unlike anything I'd ever felt before, and I didn't think I wanted it to go away.

There was a pause between us, a moment where I could almost feel Wes mustering up his courage, deciding again whether or not he should jump off the cliff. He reached out and gently touched my hand, lowering it from my eyes so we were staring directly at each other. His fingers wrapped around mine, our palms pressed lightly together. My breath caught.

He's your enemy, I reminded myself. *Don't forget about the bet.* But for some reason, all I could think about was what it would be like to kiss him on those lips, to have him kiss me back.

He held the rose between us. "Happy Valentine's Day, Valerie," he said.

And then he leaned in.

Or maybe I leaned in.

I don't know who did first, but when his eyelids closed behind his glasses, I know mine did too. Our lips pressed together, hands held, bodies close, the smell of rose petals and storage-room paint caught between us. My whole body hummed with the nearness of him.

Our kiss started light and soft and then grew deeper, his hand that held the rose moving to press against the small of my back. It was intoxicating. I never wanted it to end. I would move into this storage room, start V&C K-BEAUTY 2.0 in here. This was where I lived now.

The doorknob rattled and we sprang apart just as the door

swung open, revealing Charlie and Amelia Perry holding the storage-room key on the other side.

Amelia raised an eyebrow at us, looking back and forth between me and Wes. "What are you two doing in here?"

"I, um, left my backpack here," Wes said. "I came to get it."

"Really?" Amelia said, craning her neck to look behind him. "Where is it, then?

He froze and then laughed, running his hand through the back of his hair. "Oh, whoops. I guess it's not in here after all."

Wow, he was truly a terrible liar. We shuffled out of the storage room, my lips still tingling, replaying the kiss over and over again in my head. I wanted to sing, to dance, to shout, *What! Just! Happened!!!!* But mostly I wanted to kiss him again.

Instead I turned to Charlie, hoping my cheeks weren't as flushed as they felt. "Thanks for coming to get us."

"No problem," he said, his grin a little too knowing for my liking. "Basketball practice got canceled last minute, so I was able to see your message. Lucky for you, Amelia was at theater rehearsal with her storage-room key."

"Which I should get back to. The stage calls my name," Amelia said. She gave a pointed look to Wes as she skipped down the hall. "Hope you find your backpack, Wes."

"Thanks," he said, blushing.

"Anyway, Val, I'm heading out now if you want a ride home," Charlie said.

I nodded. "Sure. Let's go."

"Oh, and Wes?" Charlie held up a fist. "Thanks for the talk earlier. You give good advice. Can I get your number in case I want to text you for more help?"

"Sure, man," Wes said. He looked surprised and just a little dazed, but he quickly returned the fist bump and gave Charlie his number. Then he turned to me and cleared his throat, holding out the rose. "Don't forget this."

If my cheeks weren't warm before, they definitely were now. I glanced at Charlie, but he just grinned, looking away to give us a moment of privacy. I took the rose from Wes, careful not to bend the stem.

"Thank you," I said, feeling suddenly shy around him. This was a new feeling. Everything with Wes felt new.

"You're welcome," he said.

I turned to leave, following Charlie down the hallway. As I walked, I couldn't help but sneak a look back at Wes. He was staring at the storage room, touching his lips with two fingers, a smile spreading across his face.

My heart sang.

I was in trouble.

"Halmeoni, Halmeoni, Halmeoni!"

I tossed my backpack onto the living room couch and raced up the stairs as soon as I got home. Halmeoni was resting in her floor bed when I burst into her room.

"Guess what happened today?" I said. I paused, taking in how tired she looked. "Are you okay?"

"Yes, yes, I just had some trouble sleeping last night, so I thought

I'd try to squeeze in a nap," she said, sitting up. She patted the blanket for me to sit down. "But I'd much rather talk to you. Tell me what happened." Her eyes grew huge. "Let me guess. You won the lottery."

"What? No, that's ridiculous," I laughed.

"Ah. Well, your halmeoni can dream, can't she? Okay, tell me. What is it?"

I had been so excited to tell Halmeoni about the kiss, but as I looked at her now, I was filled with so much affection. For her, for her Pompompurin nightgown, for first kisses, for moments that I knew I would never forget. No words could express that, and for now I didn't even want to try. I just wanted to feel it. There was always tomorrow for stories.

"Nothing," I said simply. I lay down, resting my head in her lap. "I just wanted to say hi."

"What? Silly girl," Halmeoni said, swatting my leg. "What is it? Tell me!"

I tilted my face up toward her and smiled. "Just that I did what you said. I made a new friend."

A big smile broke out across her face, and she patted my cheeks with both hands like I was the flour dough she used to make sujebi, her favorite hand-torn noodle soup. "Did you now? Aigoo, jalhaesseo. You did good. See how much more fun life is when you let people in? Halmeoni knows what is best."

I beamed, letting both the moment and her wrinkled hands hold me close. "Are you sure you're okay, Halmeoni? I don't want to interrupt your nap."

"After hearing this good news? I'm not even tired anymore."

Later that night, I dug out the bag of tropical Hi-Chews Wes had given me and unwrapped a pineapple one. I held it to my lips and paused. Wes said that pineapple was for when things were hopeful and right, like when everything was what it was meant to be. But were things right? What did kissing Wes mean for the bet? For Paris?

I hesitated and then put the Hi-Chew in my mouth because, despite it all, if ever there were a pineapple Hi-Chew kind of day, it was definitely today.

Saturday / February 15

Ding!

I woke up to the sound of my phone pinging with a message. Groggy, I fumbled for the phone on my nightstand, immediately sitting up in bed when I saw the name on the screen.

Wes: Hi, good morning! I have an audition with Toblie School of Music tomorrow so I'll be practicing all day today, but I was wondering if you wanted to hang out on Monday?

A dot-dot-dot appeared on the screen, disappearing and then reappearing several times before another message appeared.

Wes: Wish I could see you sooner.

I couldn't stop the smile from spreading across my face. Wes wanted to hang out on Monday. It was a holiday, so we had no school. Was this a date? And he had an audition! I quickly replied, wishing him luck and saying yes yes yes to the hangout.

I flopped back down, staring up at the ceiling with my phone against my chest. So it hadn't been a dream. I pressed my fingers lightly against my lips, remembering what it had felt like to kiss Wes. The sparks, the warmth, the feeling of wanting to do it again and again and again.

A feeling of uneasiness interrupted my state of bliss. I kissed Wes. What did this mean for the bet? Was the bet still on, even?

I looked at the photos on the wall next to my bed. It was a random collage of life snapshots, aesthetic K-beauty products, and color palettes, but my eye went immediately to the sticker photos that Halmeoni and I had taken together just a few months ago. If I called off the bet, that meant no Paris this summer. And if not this summer, maybe it would be never.

But maybe, I thought hopefully, maybe it could be one day. Halmeoni was healthy this year. She could be healthy enough next year too or the year after. I could work it around college somehow. Just because nothing was certain didn't mean I had to jump to the worst conclusion.

And what about Umma? I closed my eyes and sighed. If I didn't have Paris, I'd have nothing to prove to her that I could do big, meaningful things like Samantha. But Wes's words came back to me, steady and strong: *You're really good at this stuff. The whole business thing. I really mean it when I say thanks.*

Was it worth it to give up on someone who saw something in me just to try to prove something to someone who didn't?

The answer was painful, but clear. I had to call off the bet. There was no way we could keep going. Not after that kiss. We couldn't go back to how we used to be. Competing. Spying. Being rivals.

That reminded me. I still hadn't paid Taemin back for spying on Wes for me that one time. A wave of fresh guilt washed over me. Another thing I had done against Wes when he was nothing but kind to me. I chewed my lip as I raised my phone again, texting Taemin.

Me: Hey! You free today? I owe you a bingsu.

His response came a couple minutes later.

Taemin: Finally. I can meet u at Snow Bunny in 2 hours?

Me: See you there.

I rolled out of bed with a fresh wave of determination. Meeting Taemin felt symbolic in a way. Treating him to bingsu would be my final action regarding the bet, and after that I would tell Wes that it was over. I would call the bet off and we would have a fresh start.

Spurred by my resolve, I quickly started getting ready. I pulled on a chunky knit sweater and grabbed my purse, shoving my wallet, bus pass, lip balm, and emergency Hi-Chews inside.

Halmeoni was still sleeping when I went downstairs, but Umma and Samantha were busy in the kitchen as always. It looked like a kimbap factory in here. The table was laid out with dried rectangular seaweed sheets, a giant bowl of steaming rice, and trays of eggs, spinach, sausages, and danmuji all sliced into long strips to fit into the kimbap rolls.

"You're up early," Samantha said, looking up from the kimbap she was rolling. "I don't think I've ever seen you in this morning light before."

"Meeting a friend," I said. I was too giddy to be fazed by

Samantha today. "You're here cooking extra early too."

"Umma asked me to come over to help her make kimbap," Samantha said.

She'd called Samantha instead of asking me when I was right upstairs? And Samantha came running to help? For kimbap? There really was no topping my older sister. Normally, this might have bothered me, but today I decided to shrug it off, reaching for a piece of sliced kimbap instead. "Can I have one before I go?"

Umma slapped my hand away. "Yah! This is for Appa's work meeting later," she said. "If you want one, you can have an end piece."

"I like the end pieces," I retorted, even though it was a lie. No one likes the end pieces. They're always falling apart and too big to fit in your mouth in one go. But I grabbed it anyway and shoved it in my mouth, losing a piece of spinach on the way. "Mmm. So yummy."

"Is it?" Umma said, looking pleased with herself.

"Yes. Samantha, you should try one. That piece in the middle looks good." I specifically pointed at a piece with a particularly large slice of danmuji. I knew for a fact that Samantha hated that yellow radish. She always avoided it when we went out to eat jjajangmyeon, which was wild because black bean noodles with danmuji is basically the best combo ever.

"Yes, yes, Samantha, you should try one too." Umma picked up the piece and held it out for Samantha to eat. "You try it too and tell me what you think."

Samantha eyed the danmuji inside the roll and pursed her lips.

If I were her, I would just take the radish out even if it would make Umma upset. But of course, Samantha is Samantha, so she opened her mouth and ate the kimbap without a word.

"So good," she said, smiling tightly. She forced herself to swallow and then reached for her water. "By the way, Valerie, how did all your school applications go?" she asked, her eyes sparking with revenge. *How dare she.* She knew that Umma would jump on a chance to nag me about my grades if she started talking about applications. "Deadline was in January, right?"

"Yep," I said. I'd been trying not to think about it since I sent in my applications to my top-choice business programs. Ms. Jackson had written me a glowing recommendation, and my personal essay was strong. But still, unwanted doubt settled in my bones. What if I didn't get in?

"What are you going to do if you don't get in?" Samantha asked, like she was reading my thoughts.

Umma glanced up from the kimbap rolling. "You said your grades have been good lately, Valerie. Have they not been good?"

I scowled. "They've been good. I will get in."

"I'm just saying, it's always good to have a plan B," Samantha said. "I'm just looking out for you, since you seem kind of spacey these days. You have to keep your focus up until the end of the school year, you know. Even if those schools accept you in the spring, it's conditional acceptance based off your performance for the rest of the year."

"Okay, Admissions FAQ," I said, rolling my eyes, not liking how nervous her words made me. Did I seem spacey lately? I guess maybe I hadn't been as focused since the new year started. There'd just been a lot going on.

Speaking of. I glanced at the kitchen clock. I had to get a move on if I wanted to be on time.

Umma opened her mouth to say something more on the topic of my grades, but I quickly interjected.

"Have fun rolling kimbap," I said. "Sorry I can't help. Oh, and Umma, you should put extra danmuji in the rolls. Appa loves danmuji."

Umma clapped her hands together. "You're right! Here, Samantha, I'm going to make a double danmuji roll. You tell me how it tastes, okay?"

Samantha glared at me. *You're dead,* she mouthed. I blew her a kiss as I grabbed another end piece and ran out of the kitchen.

When I arrived at Snow Bunny, Taemin was already sitting in the corner booth, the same one where we'd had our first meeting. I carried a bowl of bingsu over to our spot, this time the classic patbingsu: just shaved ice with red bean and a few pieces of rice cake on top. My personal favorite. Taemin waited for me, his knee bouncing up and down under the table.

"Didn't your mom tell you it's a bad habit to shake your leg like that?" I asked, putting the bingsu down.

"Yes," he said. "All the time. But since when were you my mom?"

I rolled my eyes, sitting down across from him. He grinned at me, his dimples flashing.

"Thanks, Nuna," he said, digging into the red bean.

"It was long overdue," I said with a smile. "Enjoy."

He raised his eyebrows as he took a bite of ice cream. "You're in a good mood today. I don't think I've ever seen you like this before."

"Really?" I rested my chin on my palm. "I guess I'm just happy today."

"You have a new namjachingu or something?" Taemin said, drizzling a mini pitcher of condensed milk over the ice.

Namjachingu? I wasn't totally sure how to answer that. Was Wes my boyfriend now? If he wasn't yet, would he be soon? I chewed my lip, distracted by how the music in the café kept cutting in and out as the bingsu cashier tried to settle on a playlist.

"Seeing as you're not answering right away, it must be true," Taemin said. He grinned cheekily, pointing his silver spoon at me. "Wow, I'm happy for you. Who is it? He's not someone from church, is he? Do I know him?"

"He's not from church," I said, my cheeks warming. "Stop guessing. Shut up and eat your bingsu."

"Oh, so then it is someone I know!" Taemin said gleefully. Suddenly the smiled faded from his face. "It's not Wes, is it?"

My heart skipped a beat at the sound of his name being dropped so casually. *Who am I?* When I hesitated, Taemin lowered his spoon and folded his hands on the table, looking at me with a serious expression.

"Why are you staring at me like that?" I asked.

"Listen, Nuna, I feel like I need to tell you something. I wasn't going to tell you this, but seeing how happy you are right now, I feel like you have a right to know."

"Um? Okay?"

"This isn't easy for me to say, but as Pastor Richard says, sometimes you need to tell the hard truth to help people."

I rolled my eyes. "Okay, already. Spit it out."

Taemin took a deep breath. "Wes is getting closer to you just to get insider info on your business."

I stared at him. A song started, then stopped again. The inside of the café was eerily quiet without the music. "What do you mean?"

"That's what he said. We hang out at the aquarium sometimes, and he said that you two have been getting closer so he can get insider information on you and win the bet you have going on."

"No way," I said, doubt in my voice. "He said that?"

He couldn't have. Wes wouldn't do something like that. Taemin had to have heard wrong.

"Almost word for word," Taemin said. "He also said you showed him your business notes at the library. Listen, it's probably not my place to say, but you should be more careful about who you show your personal notes to. You're practically throwing your business in his lap."

I swallowed hard. He told Taemin about my notebook? And he said he was getting insider info on me? Okay. Deep breath. Just because someone says something it doesn't mean they always mean it.

"Since when do you guys hang out, anyway?" I asked, trying to ignore the storm of confusion growing inside me.

He paused, not answering right away. He poked at a piece of rice cake with his spoon, rolling it around the red bean.

"Taemin?" I said, narrowing my eyes.

"Okay, okay, I'm sorry," he said. "I may have told him what you were planning to sell one time and we became friends. I wasn't planning to, I swear! But he told me his whole story about wanting to go to music school and I felt really bad for spying on him. It felt different, suddenly, knowing him as a person instead of just your rival. And, well, it's not like I really put you in a negative spot. I just kind of evened things out for both of you again. I was trying to do the right thing."

He did what? I scowled at him. "Asshole. You're telling me this now after I paid for your bingsu?"

He smiled apologetically, flashing me a finger heart. "I love you, Nuna." His smile faded. "But you heard what I said, right? You have bigger things to worry about right now."

He was right. As annoying as it was that Taemin had gone double agent on me, I could kind of understand where he was coming from. What I couldn't understand was why Wes would say those things to him. He didn't seem like the kind of person who would go around saying things he didn't mean. Besides, he was a terrible liar. Was he really just getting closer to me to sabotage my business?

An awful thought crept into my mind. Maybe everything he had been doing lately—the rose, the kiss, wanting to spend more time together—was to distract me from my business so he could steal my customers. Maybe he was only trying to get close to me to learn more about V&C so he could rip off my strategies.

Maybe, at the end of the day, what mattered most to him was what it had always been about: winning the bet.

No, no. This was Wes we were talking about. Wes Jung. The boy who got me Hi-Chews and talked to me about family and identity and things I never talked about with anyone. The boy who made me feel seen, really seen, like no one had seen me before.

But what if . . . Doubt began to bloom. What if that had all just been a cleverly laid trap to get my guard down so I would lose focus on my own business?

Before I could stop myself, I flashed back to the day of the first snow, sitting on his bedroom floor, helping him with his Instagram account. My stomach turned. I'd *helped* him. Knowingly. When, all this time, he might have been laughing behind my back, playing me like a fool.

Focus. Samantha's words from earlier rang in my ears. *I'm just looking out for you since you seem kind of spacey these days.*

Maybe I had been spacey. Losing my focus over a boy.

Letting my rival in.

My head hurt. I needed time to think about this.

"I'm sorry, Nuna," Taemin said, truly looking apologetic. "I honestly don't think Wes is a bad guy, but I mean, you guys *are* rivals. You have this huge bet going on. He even said—"

He broke off. Dread filled me. "What? What did he say?"

"I mean, it might just be salt in the wound. But, um, do you know girls named Lisa, Natalie, and Mimi?"

I nodded slowly.

"It sounds like he gave them all a discount if they promised not to shop with you anymore," he said hesitantly.

My heart dropped. So that's why I hadn't seen those girls around in months. Wes was bribing them to stay away from my business?

"Nuna?" Taemin said cautiously. "Are you okay?"

"I'm fine." I took a deep breath. I wasn't fine. But I would be. I had to be. "Thanks for telling me about this."

"Really? Because right now, seeing the look on your face, I'm thinking I may have just made a huge mistake."

"No, no." I shook my head. "It's better that I know."

"Does that mean you forgive me for telling Wes about your business?"

I glared at him. "'Forgive' is a strong word."

"Got it," he said. "What are you going to do now?"

Shit. What *was* I going to do? Wes had made me too soft. He'd been distracting me from what was really important: my business and my goals. I thought of Umma and Appa sitting at the kitchen table, talking about how "cute" my business dreams were. Maybe they were right. Maybe it was just a cute pipe dream. Maybe I didn't have what it took to survive in the business world if I didn't even have the foresight to see sabotage coming for me right in front of my face. My fists curled in my lap, my nails biting into my palms. I couldn't believe I'd just let Wes into my life so vulnerably. He was my *rival*. How could I have done this to myself?

"I'm going to do what I said I'd do from the beginning," I said. "I'm going to win."

CHAPTER FOURTEEN

WES

Sunday / February 16

I couldn't get Valerie out of my head all weekend.

I must have replayed our kiss a thousand times over in my mind. I replayed it to the sound of my alarm on Saturday morning. I replayed it as I texted her, deleting and retyping, deleting and retyping, deleting deleting deleting, trying to get the words exactly right.

Me: When can I see you?

Too eager? Definitely too eager.

Me: Hi, what's up?

Too casual? I think too casual.

Me: So should we talk about what happened yesterday or . . .

Well, now that just sounds passive-aggressive.

I settled on good morning. I told her about my audition, asked her to hang out on Monday. She texted back yes and good luck with a thumbs-up emoji.

I replayed our kiss the whole day as I practiced. And then on

Sunday, I replayed it the entire drive to Toblie School of Music. It was probably the only thing that kept me from looking over my shoulder every ten minutes, paranoid that my parents would somehow be following me.

Even at the audition, I thought of her. I thought of her confidence as I walked into the audition room and introduced myself. *You've got something that not everyone gets in their lifetime,* I heard her saying. *You got this.* And I truly believed that I did.

For the audition, I had to perform one song for three faculty members, followed by an interview. As soon as I started playing, I was in my element. It was the best I'd ever played, better than any of my rehearsals or any of the videos I'd recorded, including the one I'd shown Valerie. My saxophone and I were working as one, and I was so glad I hadn't gone with a rental from school. As sentimental as it was, I knew I wanted to go through this experience with the instrument that had carried me through all those moves around the globe and brought me to this moment.

The music portion was exhilarating. The interview portion, however, had my palms sweating again.

You got this, I reminded myself again.

"So, Wes," one of the faculty members said, leaning forward in her seat. She was a stylish woman wearing purple glasses and a head wrap. "We'd like to hear more about why you want to study at Toblie School of Music."

For a moment my brain froze. And then the words came easily. "For all my life, music is the one thing that has ever truly felt like home. I feel like at Toblie, I would not only be able to further my skills as a musician, but expand my home into a community."

The longer we talked, the more at ease I felt. At the end of the interview, all three faculty members shook my hand, but the woman with the glasses gave me an extra-warm smile. "Lovely performance, Wes," she said. "We hope to see you soon." By the time I walked out of the audition, I was on cloud nine. No matter what happened now, I could truly and honestly say I gave it my all.

As I headed for my car, my phone pinged with an incoming text. I grabbed it immediately, thinking it might be Valerie. I was surprised to see it was Charlie instead.

Charlie: Hey man. I need some moral support and I can't get a hold of Valerie.

Charlie: I'm going to tell Pauline how I feel. For real this time. Is she at the aquarium?

Charlie: And um, will you meet me there?

I supposed I could make a pit stop on the way home. I texted him back.

Wes: She'll be at the sea otter tank. See you there in two hours.

Charlie was watching Benjamin the sea otter float idly on his back when I arrived. He had his hair gelled back, and he looked nervous like he might pass out at any moment. When he saw me, he rushed over, greeting me with a fist bump.

"Wes, thanks for coming," he said. "I know we're not that close, but I needed some moral support and I couldn't reach Valerie. And my other friends don't know Pauline as well as you do. How do I look?"

"Fine," I said. "Kind of dehydrated, though. Do you want some water?"

He shook his head. "I'm okay. I know this is sudden, but after I sent her that rose on Valentine's Day, I just kept thinking about what you said. How I should be honest with her. Today I realized I just really need to tell her in person once and for all, and I need to do it now before I chicken out again."

"Again?" I said.

"You don't want to know how many times I've tried to ask her out," he said, sighing. "But today's the day. I'll never be more ready than this moment."

I glanced behind his shoulder. "I hope so, because here she comes."

He froze, slowly turning around as Pauline approached us, wearing her red volunteer vest. "Wes? Charlie? What are you guys doing here?"

"I'm, uh, here to see Mister Ottermelon," I said, stepping toward the otter tank. I pretended to busy myself staring at the otters. I could see Charlie and Pauline reflected in the glass, staring at each other.

Charlie cleared his throat, shoving his hands in his pocket. "Hi. Pauline. Um, did you get the rose I sent you?"

She smiled hesitantly. "I did. Thank you."

He glanced at the sea-otter tank and gestured at Benjamin. "Remember that time we did the aquarium scavenger hunt and had lunch together here? I told you about my dad and how I wished he would come home and you just listened to me. You didn't call me too sensitive or tell me to accept things as they are like other people did. You just listened. And you said that sounds hard. And you offered to share your blueberries."

She laughed. "I do remember that."

He smiled and took a deep breath. "I think that was the moment I realized I liked you. I liked the way you ask questions about the world and how you want to understand things for what they are. You see things differently than other people because you listen, like actually really listen, even when you don't have to. It's just the way you are every day, so you might not even notice, but for me, it's really cool how you do that, and I just . . . I think you're really special."

He paused, looking down at the ground. "I wanted to tell you all of this two years ago. But you suddenly stopped talking to me." He looked up at her, his face open and honest. "I never had the guts to straight up ask you until now, but why? Did I do something wrong?"

Benjamin swam in circles between them. Pauline pressed her fingers against the tank, thinking, confusion furrowing her brow.

"I overheard you telling Valerie that you had a study date with me and inviting her to join," she said. "But after she told you that she didn't want to hang out with me because I wasn't a customer, you bailed on me. And then it seemed like you were the one avoiding me after that, so I started keeping my distance. And then we just . . . naturally drifted."

His mouth dropped open. "What? You think I bailed on you because of what she said? No way. I told you she asked me to help her with some business stuff. I really didn't want to cancel on you, but she needed an extra hand and I didn't want to let her down. Honestly, I was so mad at her about that, but she promised that if I helped her, she would try to get to know you. Even if you weren't a customer." He shook his head. "And then, after that, I wanted to make it up to you by asking you on a real date, but I kept messing up or missing my chance. That was probably why it felt awkward. I swear I wasn't trying to avoid you on purpose. But I guess because of that, the vibe between us got weirder and weirder until . . ."

Silence hung between them. "Until now," Pauline finally said. She hung her head. "Wow. I'm sorry, Charlie. I shouldn't have pushed you away without getting all the facts first, even if I thought I knew what was going on. That was my mistake."

"Wait, so all of this was just a classic case of miscommunication?" he said in disbelief.

"You say that like it's ridiculous," she said with a small smile.

"I mean, it is! One conversation and we could have avoided this whole thing!"

She cocked her head to the side, thoughtful. "Yeah, but it never is just about the one conversation, is it? It's about being brave enough to start it, wise enough to choose the right words, and self-aware enough to know what's going on inside your brain. That's a lot of things that have to line up all at once. It's kind of a miracle that people are able to communicate properly at all."

He gaped at her. "See. This is why I like you. Who even thinks like that?"

She laughed. A comfortable silence hung between them.

"It is still sad, though," she said, "that we lost all those years because of a miscommunication."

"Yeah," Charlie sighed. "I can't believe we could've been together this whole time."

"Well . . . ," she said. "We could've been friends this whole time. To be honest, Charlie, I don't know what I would have said if you'd asked me out two years ago. I liked being friends, but I don't know if I liked you in a romantic way, and I still feel that way now."

"Oh." His face fell with disappointment. "So it really is a jjak sarang."

She raised her eyebrows.

"A one-sided, unrequited love," he said.

"Maybe in the romantic sense," she agreed. "But not in the friendship sense. You were as important a friend to me as I was to you. I mean, you helped me realize that aquatic life was my passion! That's always stuck with me. Besides, why is friendship any less meaningful than a romantic relationship?"

"That is true," he said. He paused for a moment, his face still disappointed. After hyping himself up for this talk for so long, this probably wasn't the exact outcome he was hoping for. But after a few seconds, he managed a grin. "Does that mean we can be friends again? Because I have a cool under-the-sea fact to share with you."

She grinned back. "Yeah. Friends again. And maybe this time we can both be a little more honest."

They laughed, which I took as my cue to turn away from the otters, which I'd completely forgotten to pretend to look at. I felt proud of Charlie for finally speaking up. I rejoined them, glad that the air had cleared between them. Maybe we could all even hang out together. With Valerie, too.

"So why is Wes here again?" Pauline said, glancing at me. "Are you really here for the otters?"

"Yes," I said. "And maybe a little bit of moral support."

"Thanks again," Charlie said, giving me a fist bump. "By the way, I was meaning to ask you, because Valerie won't tell me a thing, but what's going on between you two?"

Now it was my turn to fumble for my words. "Um . . . I'll let you know." *Probably best if I tell people after Valerie and I have had a chance to talk about it for ourselves.* "But I'm thinking about calling off the bet."

"Thank God," Charlie said in relief. "I told her it was a bad idea from the start."

I had been thinking about it during the entire car ride. The audition had gone so well, and I was feeling more confident than ever that I had a shot at getting into Toblie. But I also didn't want to be in competition with Valerie anymore. I felt like I was facing another huge risk. By canceling the bet and pursuing something more with Valerie, I was risking not being able to pay for my spot at Toblie, especially with my sales being so spotty lately. But I'd made my decision. I would find another way to make music school happen, even if it meant deferring my acceptance for another year while I made more money or finally admitting the truth to my parents and begging them to help me.

Music school for me had always meant finding a place to truly be myself, but in a strange twist of fate, Valerie had started to mean that for me too. I couldn't let her go.

Just then, my phone pinged with a text message, and her name lit up my screen.

Valerie: Hey. Can you meet me at the school courtyard tomorrow at noon?

My heart leaped. I would tell her tomorrow then that I wanted to call off the bet. Face-to-face.

Me: Of course. See you there.

Monday / February 17

It was a cold day and the courtyard was deserted. I shivered in my jacket, the zipper pulled all the way up to my nose, wondering why Valerie wanted to meet here, of all places, when school was closed for the holiday. Hopefully this was just a meeting spot and we could hang out somewhere warmer for the rest of the day.

As with all important things, I had practiced what I wanted to say a hundred times. *Let's call off the bet.*

I don't want to fight anymore.

Be my girlfriend?

But no matter how many times I practiced the words in front of my mirror, they never rolled off my tongue the way I wanted them to. And then I decided that some things weren't meant to be practiced and that maybe this was just one of those things where the right exact words would come to me in the moment.

I spotted Valerie walking across the courtyard and my heart

lifted. Her hair hung long and straight down her back, her hands tucked into the pockets of her winter jacket. The urge to touch her was overwhelming. I wanted to run to her, take her in my arms, kiss her again like we had last Friday.

But the vibe was strange. Her face was drawn and serious, her eyes back to being the sharp and piercing gaze I was so familiar with. No warmth. Just business.

"Valerie?" I said as she drew nearer.

"Thanks for meeting me," she said, her voice crisp.

I reached for her, but she didn't pull her hands out of her pockets. My hand fell back down by my side. "What's going on?"

"I wanted to ask you a question." It was so cold out, I could see her breath as she talked. The sharpness in her eyes dimmed, and I saw something else there. Uncertainty, like she was scared to ask me whatever it was that was on her mind. "Did you tell Lisa, Natalie, and Mimi that if they stopped shopping with me, you would give them a discount?"

Whatever I'd been expecting Valerie to say, it wasn't that. I felt like someone had tipped the world over and I was suddenly standing upside down, with blood rushing to my head, drowning out all my thoughts. "What?" It was the wrong thing to say, but the only thing I could manage.

"Did you tell Lisa, Natalie, and Mimi that if they stopped shopping with me, you would give them a discount?" she repeated. Her voice didn't waver, but I could see the pain in her eyes. It hurt her to ask me, and I had made her ask me twice. I had to answer.

"I . . . did," I confessed.

For a split second, she looked devastated. She let out a breath that hung between us in the cold and closed her eyes. "So it was all true. I can't believe this."

"Valerie, I can explain." I took a step toward her, but she opened her eyes and stepped back, stopping me.

"Don't come closer." Her face was closed off again, her voice steel. She was Valerie of September, the day I'd first met her in front of my locker. All business. No wavering. "You fucking bribed them to stay away from my business? How many others did you offer the same deal to? Not that that's even a deal. That's just sabotage. They used to be my loyal customers, and now they won't even stop at my locker."

"Valerie, please," I said, desperate to make her understand. "That was—I didn't mean to—I was just trying to make a sale."

It was the wrong thing to say again. She laughed bitterly, shaking her head. "Well. Good job, Wes Jung. You did what you set out to do. What a way to knock me out of the competition."

"I'm so sorry," I said. I felt like my chest was cracking open. *How do I fix this? How do I say the right thing?* "I'm so, so sorry, Valerie. That wasn't my intention. And it was before—"

She held up a hand, stopping me again. *It was before the kiss,* I wanted to say. *Before I fell for you. Before we were anything but rivals.*

"I don't need any explanations, Wes," she said. "I just wanted to ask you that one question and tell you that from now until the end of the bet, there won't be any sabotaging of each other's businesses. It's a clear game from here. Got it?"

"The bet?" My face fell. She still wanted to do the bet?

"I'm not finished," she continued. "I also wanted to tell you that we shouldn't see each other anymore. If you see me in the hallway, ignore me. Don't call me. Don't text me. Let's not talk again until prom and I cash in my winnings."

I stared at her, at a loss for words. How could someone change so drastically over the weekend? What *happened*?

"You're not even going to give me a chance to explain?" I said. "Or talk about us? What about Friday?"

"That was a mistake," she said, her voice flat. "I got distracted. I lost sight of my goals, but I remembered over the weekend what they are. I want to be the best business in our school. And I'm not going to let anybody stand in my way, especially not you."

"Are you serious?" Anger surged in me now. I couldn't believe how stubborn she was being. "You can't keep treating people like this, Valerie! Like they're either a help or a hindrance to your business life. People are more than that. I'm more than that! When are you going to wake up and get it?" My voice softened. "Please, let's just talk about this."

She looked away and said nothing.

I stared at her in disbelief. "So that's it, then? Is winning really all you care about right now?"

"It's what I've always cared about." She put her hands back into her pockets and turned away. "See you at prom, Wes."

And then she walked away, leaving me to stare after her in the cold.

The bet wasn't over yet, but why did it feel like I had already lost?

CHAPTER FIFTEEN

VALERIE

Friday / April 3

Toners. Face wash. BB cream.

No. No. No.

I scratched my notes out of my notebook with furious crosses of my pen. That wouldn't work. I was trying to think of my feature product for the month, but nothing was clicking. Everything felt old, played out, not interesting enough. I needed a new strategy. Something that would blow Wes out of the water.

Things hadn't been going so well since our falling out in February. The entire month of March had passed by in a blur of schoolwork and business planning. I knew my grades were slipping. Ms. Jackson was more than a little concerned.

"You look exhausted lately, Valerie," she'd said during our last mentor meeting. "I don't want to see you burn out. This is your senior year. You should be having fun, too."

But I didn't have time for fun. My entire March spring break was devoted to content creation. New Instagram posts, new beauty tutorials, new graphics. I stayed up late into the night, texting Charlie at three a.m. with new ideas.

Me: What if we brought back the snail masks?

Me: Are you free tomorrow? Can you come over to film a new video?

Me: I think we should go to IKEA and get new shelving for my locker. It's getting old.

His reply would always come in the morning, and it was the same every time.

Charlie: I gotta help my mom out at the restaurant today, but I'll come over after.

Charlie: But Val, I'm worried about you.

Charlie: Are you sure you're okay? Have you talked to Wes?

My answer was always the same too. Yes, I'm okay. No, I haven't talked to Wes.

Sometimes we saw each other in the halls at school, but we hadn't spoken since that day in the courtyard. He kept to my request: he didn't talk to me, he didn't text me, and he didn't call me. My heart still ached when I thought about him, which I tried not to. I stored all my thoughts of him—from the day at his house to the kiss in the storage room—away in a deep part of my mind. But his words from the courtyard were harder to push away. *You can't keep treating people like this, Valerie! When are you going to wake up and get it?*

He was one to talk. After all, *he* was the one who'd tried to use me to sabotage my business. Hypocrite. Still, I couldn't shake the feeling that maybe there was some truth to his words. They bothered me more than I wanted them to. I tried not to think about it, though. I didn't have time.

He's a distraction, I reminded myself. *Distraction and competition. That's all. Focus on the bet.*

All that mattered now was winning. Not only was my pride on the line, but so was my goal to go to Paris with Halmeoni and to show Umma that I could do this. I could be a smart and savvy businesswoman. I had to show her. I had to show myself.

There was a light *tap-tap-tap* on my bedroom door, and Halmeoni poked her head in.

"Not sleeping?" she said. "It's getting late."

"Just staying up a bit longer," I said, hunched over my desk without looking up. "I want to get this done before I sleep."

Halmeoni lingered in the doorway. "Sleep is important if you want to be well rested."

"I know, Halmeoni," I said, sighing. "I just have to finish this one thing."

She shuffled over to my bed, taking a seat and facing me. "Valerie. Look at me for a moment."

I forced myself to look up from my notebook. She stared at me, hands clasped in her lap, brow furrowed, wrinkles deep with concern.

"I am worried about you," she said. "You haven't been yourself lately. I can hear you late at night working, and when I pass by your room in the morning, I see you always fall asleep with the light on. Are you even sleeping properly anymore? What is going on?"

"It's nothing, Halmeoni." I tried to make my tone sound reassuring, but it came out more as a snap. My nerves were totally on edge these days, even around Halmeoni. "I'm really fine. You know how it is. End of the school year, busy studying for final exams."

She glanced at the closed textbooks on my desk. "Studying is important," she agreed. "But so is your rest."

"Halmeoni, gwaenchanayo. I'm telling you, I'm okay. Now, if anyone should be sleeping, isn't it you? You've still been tossing and turning at night. I can hear you, too, you know. You need to rest."

Halmeoni nodded. "That you are right about. My body has been aching very much lately. I feel so stiff."

I softened, guilt pinching at my heart. I had been so busy the past month and a half, I really hadn't been spending as much time with Halmeoni as I usually did. "We should go see the doctor soon for a checkup."

"You just worry about you," Halmeoni chuckled. "I'm sleeping now, then. Jalja, my girl."

"Jalja, Halmeoni. Sweet dreams."

She shuffled out of my room, the door clicking shut behind her. As soon as she was gone, I grabbed a hoodie and stuffed it under the crack beneath my door so sound wouldn't travel. Then I switched off my lights and turned on the flashlight app on my phone. Just in case I fell asleep while I was working, I didn't want Halmeoni to wake up in the morning and see me sleeping at my desk with my lights on all night.

Just a little longer, Halmeoni. I promise I'll win this bet, show everyone whose business is the best, and then we can celebrate by having the time of our lives in Paris.

I flipped to a new page in my notebook and worked late into the night, without her ever knowing.

Saturday / April 4

"Hey. *Hey.* Wake up. It's almost noon!"

I sat up with a start. I had fallen asleep at my desk. Again.

Samantha looked down at me, eyebrow raised. "You have drool all over your face."

My hand immediately flew up to my chin. Gross. Dried drool.

"What are you doing sleeping at your desk anyway?" Samantha asked.

"None of your business." I tilted my head to the side, stretching my neck. Ugh. I was sore all over. I had to stop doing this.

She held up her hands in defense. "Okay, okay. I just came to get you because Charlie's here to see you. He's waiting for you in Appa's office."

I nodded, massaging my shoulders. "Okay. Tell him I'll be there in a minute."

She examined my face in concern. "Are you okay? You look really on edge."

"Yep. Totally fine."

She opened her mouth like she wanted to say something more

and then closed it again. "Okay," she finally said. "You obviously don't want to talk right now. That's fine. Here." She dropped an envelope on my desk. "This came for you."

As soon as she left my room, I immediately sat up straighter. Oh my God. It was a letter from Sommerson College.

I ripped it open and scanned the first lines.

Dear Ms. Valerie Kwon,
Thank you for applying to Sommerson College. While we were thoroughly impressed by your student-run business, we're afraid we will not be accepting your application at this time. Due to the high volume of applications we receive, we are only able to admit . . .

The words blurred in front of my eyes. I shoved the letter back into the envelope and leaned back in my seat, covering my face with my hands. *Deep breaths. Inhale. Exhale.*

It's fine, I told myself. *There are still more schools I'm waiting to hear back from. Sommerson wasn't even my top choice. It's fine. It's fine it's fine it's fine.*

I opened my desk drawer and buried the letter inside. I didn't have the brain space to think about this right now. Besides, Charlie was waiting for me. I had to get ready.

I stumbled into the bathroom to brush my teeth and wash my face, dabbing on some moisturizer and concealer to hide the dark bags under my eyes while I was at it. I looked like a panda. No wonder everyone was so worried about me.

When I walked into Appa's office, I found Charlie sitting in the spinning leather chair, his fingers drumming restlessly against the desk.

"Val," he said, standing when he saw me. "Hey."

"Hey," I said. "What's up? I thought you were helping out with your mom all day today."

"Yeah, I am. But we got some news this morning that I wanted to tell you in person." He took a deep breath, bouncing his fists against each other. "I don't really know how you're going to take it, but I'm really excited, so just hear me out, okay?"

I raised my eyebrows. "O . . . kay. What is it? You're kind of freaking me out."

"My dad is going to move back from Korea. He's finally coming home."

A smile broke out across his face. He looked like he was trying to hold it back, but he just couldn't help himself. He was excited about this. He'd been wanting his dad to come back for years.

But. My mind stilled, not ready to open up to the meaning behind what Charlie was really saying.

"Coming back?" I said. "Here? As in *here* here? PNW here? When?"

He nodded. "He'll be back by the end of the month. He's been thinking about it for a while, and the timing is finally right. He misses living with us and he knows we miss him. And he's been unhappy living on his own in Korea for so long. He just wasn't sure if he would be able to find a job here that's as good as the one he has there, but a friend of his offered him a position, so it was kind of the final push for him to come back. . . ."

His voice trailed off at the frozen look on my face.

"You're upset," he said. "I was afraid you would be."

"I'm not," I lied.

"Please, Val. Don't pretend to me."

"It's just . . ." I swallowed hard, forcing the words out, feeling terrible for speaking them, and even more terrible for feeling them. "It's not the end of the school year yet. What are we going to do if he stops sending us beauty products? We'll have nothing to sell. Nothing! And we have that bet with Wes. We *have* to sell more. Can't he just stay for a little bit longer? Just until the school year ends?" I hated myself for saying it when I knew how much this meant to Charlie, but I couldn't stop myself. *How did I get so low?*

Charlie gave me a long, steady look, his face pained like there was a battle going on inside his mind.

"What?" I said. "What are you thinking?"

He sighed deeply, rubbing his forehead. "Nothing, Val. It's just that sometimes I think you see me more as a business partner than as your cousin."

"What do you mean? You're both."

"Yeah, I am. But I'm first and foremost family. And to me, family has always come first. Not business."

My throat felt tight. I blinked back the sudden tears that threatened to spill. "What do you mean by that? You think I don't care about family?"

"I think sometimes you take me for granted." His voice wavered, but he kept his gaze steady, determined to say what he wanted to say. It made me wonder how long he'd been keeping this in. "I think sometimes you forget that I'm your family and you see me just as a business partner. Not even an equal partner, but someone to help you when you need me, like a handy sidekick, ready to jump in at your call. I think sometimes that if V&C ended, it would also be the end of our relationship, because you wouldn't need me anymore."

"That's not true." It couldn't be true. I wasn't so heartless, was I? Maybe I saw the other kids at school either as customers or competition, but I always remembered that Charlie was more than a business partner. He was family, and not only that, he was my friend. I knew that. He had to know that I knew that.

But what had I done to show him that I knew it? Maybe it wasn't so clear after all.

"Listen," he said. "I know . . . God knows I know just how important this business is to you. But we're talking about my parents and me coming back together for the first time since I was like eight years old. I know this isn't how either of us wanted V&C to end, but we still have enough products to last us a week or two. Is it so bad that I'm happy about this?"

I shook my head, tears brimming my eyes now. I wiped them roughly away. "No, yeah, I get it. Of course it's not bad. It makes total sense. I'm sorry, Charlie. I really do know how much this means to you." I took a deep breath, reaching into the part of me that wasn't completely terrible, that wasn't falling apart at this news and desperately thinking, *But what about me?* I offered him the small piece of me that wasn't tainted by my own selfishness and whispered, "I'm happy for you."

His face softened. "I know this is shocking and you must be feeling—"

I held up a hand, stopping him. "Can we not talk about how I'm feeling? Not right now? Because I don't think I can talk about how I feel and tell you that I'm happy for you at the same time. It's not because I'm lying when I say I'm happy for you. It's just that I'm both. Okay? I'm so glad for you and so messed up in my head about this and what it means for me that I just can't handle talking about both those things right now. Is that fine?"

He looked stunned, but he nodded quietly. "Yes. It's fine."

"All right. Okay, then. I'm gonna go."

"Where are you going?" he asked, but I was already out the door.

Roseman Hotel is one of the ritziest places around. It's the kind of place where you can spot celebrities walking in and out the revolving doors if you sit in the lobby long enough. A place with a rooftop swimming pool and spa that all the Instagram influencers go to, wearing monogrammed hotel robes and holding VIP lounge drinks. The view from these rooms is rumored to be among the best in the city. Mountains as far as the eye can see.

I wasn't planning on coming here. At first I just started walking toward the mountains, fighting to make sense of the chaos in my brain. Everything was falling apart. Who would I be without V&C? What did I have left? I would lose the bet. Paris would be over. Umma and Appa and Samantha would go on laughing about my cute high school business club, and I'd have nothing real to show for it but a couple of Halloween ribbons.

No. I couldn't let it end this way. I'd do anything to keep V&C alive. Even if it meant doing something I'd never thought I'd do before.

Determined, I headed straight for the hotel.

"I'm looking for Taemin Park," I said to the front-desk manager.

She nodded over my shoulder. "Good timing. He's right behind you."

I turned around to see Taemin in his maroon bellboy uniform emerge from the elevator. We locked eyes at the same time, his widening in surprise.

"Nuna," he said, approaching me. "What are you doing here?"

"Can we talk?" I glanced around. "In private?"

He nodded. "Sure. I'm just getting off my shift." He led me to a cluster of couches in the lobby, taking a seat in the corner tucked away behind a giant plant. "What's up?"

"The counterfeit items you mentioned," I said, lowering my voice. "Way back when, that time at church. You told me there's a guy who sells counterfeit beauty products. Can you still get those for me?" Guilt gnawed at my stomach, but I tried to ignore it. This was the only option left. I couldn't afford to feel guilty.

"Whoa," he said. "I thought Valerie Kwon didn't do knock-offs?"

"She doesn't," I said sharply. "And that's what you're going to keep on telling anyone who asks. Now, can you get them for me or not?"

His eyes widened in surprise, and I sighed, pressing the heels of my hands into my forehead. "Sorry. I didn't mean to snap. It's just that you would be doing me a huge favor. Can you help? Please?"

He surveyed me carefully. "Yeah. I can. But are you sure you want to do this? I know I'm not one to go around trumpeting about morals, but this doesn't sound like you."

I paused just for a beat. It was either my morals or everything I'd been working for gone out the window. *I'm sorry,* I thought. To who? My customers? My business? Myself? Everyone. *I'm sorry it's come to this.*

"Yeah." I nodded once decisively, like I was certain. Calm, cool, and collected, even though I was anything but. "I'm sure."

CHAPTER SIXTEEN

WES

Monday / April 13

The past two months had been a fog.

I felt more machine than man, going through the motions of school, dancing through conversations with Mom and Dad where I never said what I meant and they only heard what they wanted to hear, filling every spare moment playing the saxophone, practicing for my Senior Showcase solo until my fingers ached because it was the only thing keeping me afloat.

I tried not to think about Valerie.

But of course I failed.

She was constantly on my mind.

Before, I'd tried to avoid her at school, but now I felt like I was always on the lookout for her. Whenever we passed each other in the halls, I would try to catch her eye, but she'd look straight ahead like she didn't see me. Maybe she really didn't. Maybe all she saw was a rival. Maybe that was all she'd ever seen.

Mostly, I felt like I was running out of time.

Time to make enough money for the May deadline. Time to win the bet with Valerie. Time to tell Mom and Dad the truth about how I'd applied to Toblie School of Music. Acceptance letters would be going out any day now for the first-year jazz program. What if I got in? I would have to tell them sooner or later.

But what if I didn't get in?

The thought made my stomach churn. Maybe I should have applied to some of Dad's schools as a backup plan. He would be furious when he found out that I didn't. But even with a backup plan, I wanted to figure something out for myself, not just follow the path my parents chose for me. The lies kept growing. I wasn't sure how much longer I could keep all the secrets in, but I couldn't find the words to say what I wanted to. It was like Pauline had said. It wasn't just the one conversation. It was everything that came with it.

This whole year has been about building confidence, so why am I right back where I started?

"Earth to Wes," Pauline said. "The bell rang. We should start cleaning up."

"Right." I snapped out of my thoughts and started to clean up the leftovers from that morning's sale.

At least business was going well. Mom was extra busy with work meetings these days, preparing for Crown Tiger's new spring release, but her office was stocked with enough products that I didn't have to bother her for new merch all the time. I just grabbed what I needed from the pile of K-pop stuff gathering dust on her desk. The most recent Crown Tiger sunscreen sample tubes were doing really well. We barely had any left from today's sale.

"Listen, Wes," Pauline said. "I know we've both been busy lately . . ." True. We hadn't seen each other very much outside our Monday sales. On top of my music rehearsals and studying for final exams, Pauline's haenyeo info sessions at the aquarium had been a big hit, and now she ran them twice a week. "But I wanted to ask if you're doing okay. I know you always say you are, but you can be honest."

I sighed, leaning against a music stand. I'd avoided talking about it, even with Pauline, because it stung too much to recount. But it was getting too much to keep to myself. "I just can't figure it out, you know?" I said. "How Valerie knew about that deal I made with Lisa, Natalie, and Mimi. I asked them about it, and they all swore they didn't tell anyone. Other than you, there's no one else who knew."

I couldn't stop thinking about it. It was the one question I kept circling back to, again and again. How had this happened to us?

"Well, that's not exactly true," Pauline said.

"What do you mean?"

"One other person knew." When I stared at her blankly, she said, "Taemin. Remember? That day at the aquarium? I mentioned it when he was sitting there."

I blinked and then it hit me. *That's right. Taemin did know.* But Taemin wouldn't have told Valerie, would he? What reason would he have to do that? I had no clue, but I had an idea of someone who might know.

"Are you free to have lunch together today?" I asked, pulling out my phone.

"Yeah," Pauline said. "Who are you texting?"

"Charlie." I hit send and put my phone in my pocket. I couldn't believe I'd forgotten that Taemin knew. I wasn't sure what that meant yet, but it was time I found out. "We're going to meet him at the courtyard at lunch."

The weather was finally getting warmer, and it seemed like everyone was eating in the courtyard today. Pauline, Charlie, and I wove our way through kids playing Ultimate Frisbee, managing to grab a bench by the basketball courts.

"So why the emergency meeting?" Charlie asked, pulling a Tupperware of fried rice from his backpack. It had been a while since I'd had a conversation with Charlie about what was going on with the bet. I saw him in calculus class, but we never talked about business. Sometimes I'd casually try to ask him how Valerie was doing.

"You should ask her yourself," he'd say, his voice encouraging.

"I don't think she wants to talk to me," I'd say, and he would have nothing to respond with. But today I had a different kind of question for him.

He beamed at Pauline with a full-wattage smile. "By the way, can I just say how beautiful you look today? New turtle earrings, right?"

"Okay there, sweet talker," Pauline said, rolling her eyes and laughing. Ever since Pauline and Charlie had agreed to be honest in their friendship, he had truly done just that. He didn't want anything to go miscommunicated this time. While he was obviously still smitten with her, he was content to be friends, and it was nice to see them getting to know each other again. "Wes has something he wants to ask you."

"Fire away," Charlie said.

"Do you know Taemin Park?" I asked, jumping right into it.

"Taemin Park from church?" Charlie looked taken aback. "How do you know Taemin?"

"It's kind of a long story," I said. "We met Taemin at the aquarium one day, and when we found out that he knew you and Valerie, I kind of . . . hired him. To spy on your business."

Charlie stared at me. Then at Pauline. Then back at me. "No way," he said finally.

"I know, I know," I said. "It was shady. But it was just a one-time thing, when your sales were always overlapping with ours and we needed a way to—"

Charlie burst into laughter, his fist against his mouth. Now it was Pauline and me staring at him.

"What?" I said.

"Sorry, it's just . . ." He burst out into laughter again, now laughing so hard no sound was actually coming out. He clutched his stomach, his laughter coming out in silent wheezes. "It's just so ridiculous."

"I guess it is pretty ridiculous," Pauline said with a hesitant smile, clearly worried that Charlie had lost it.

Charlie waved a hand in the air, his laughter calming down.

"No, no. You don't understand. It's not the fact that you hired him as a spy that's ridiculous." His face suddenly grew serious. "It's that, uh . . . Shit, I don't know if I'm supposed to tell you this. Valerie will kill me."

"What is it?" I asked. The back of my neck prickled with sweat as I braced myself for whatever Charlie was going to say.

"Charlie?" Pauline said, her eyes widening like she was already putting the pieces together.

He chewed his lip, nervous now. "Okay. Well . . . Wow, this is so hard to say. Okay I'm just going to say it. Valerie hired Taemin to spy on *you*. That's how we knew exactly what you were going to sell, and we strategized our sales so there was no way you could win. The day you saw Taemin at the aquarium? He was probably there because we told him Pauline narrates the sea-otter show on weekends and he needed an in to spy on you." Pauline raised her eyebrows at this, and he lifted his hands like he was innocent. "I just overheard you telling someone in class that you were volunteering at the aquarium and we passed the info on."

Uncomfortable realization slowly dawned on me. "Then that means . . ."

Pauline nodded grimly. "It sounds like Taemin Park has been a double agent this whole time."

"Dude," Charlie said, definitely not laughing anymore. "That's messed up."

"Wait," I said, rubbing my forehead, trying to make sense of this new information. "So do you guys still see Taemin?"

"Here and there. He gave us info on a couple of your sales, and that was it for the spying, but we started hanging out more after that. I played basketball with him a few times, and the last time Valerie saw him was sometime in February, I think. She said they had bingsu."

"Sometime in February?" Pauline said. "Do you remember what day?"

"Yeah. It was a Saturday, the day after Valentine's Day. I remember because I was at her house dropping off the Valentine's Day package that my dad sent my mom. A bunch of lavender-scented beauty products, which is annoying as hell because he should know by now that my mom doesn't like anything flower-scented—"

Pauline cleared her throat. "Charlie. The story?"

"Right. So I was over at Valerie's house when she came home from meeting Taemin. She didn't say much more about it, but she seemed upset. She just went into her room and closed the door. Come to think of it, she never told me anything about what happened that day."

Bingsu. With Taemin. The day after Valentine's Day, which was the day before Valerie asked me to meet her in the courtyard.

"Oh my God," I said, burying my face in my hands. "I can't believe this. I have to talk to Valerie." I sprang to my feet, but Pauline grabbed my arm.

"Hold up," she said. "You said Valerie doesn't even want to talk to you right now. If you want her to listen, you need the cold hard facts, and we need to make sure we're not misunderstanding anything else before we move forward." Ever since her conversation with Charlie, she'd become doubly intentional about getting the facts. "Charlie?"

He sat up straighter. "Yes?"

"Text Taemin and ask him to meet you," she said firmly. "We have a spy to catch."

Friday / April 17

Waiting till the end of the week was torture.

Friday after school was the soonest Taemin was free. Charlie asked him to meet up at Snow Bunny, a trendy bingsu café in the city.

As soon as we walked into the café, I saw him right away. He rose from the booth when he caught sight of Charlie, a big dimpled smile on his face. And then he saw me and Pauline behind Charlie and his smile faded.

"Well, shit," he said, laughing nervously as we approached him. "What are you guys doing together?"

Charlie pulled out a chair for Pauline, and she sat down, folding her hands on the table. "Hello, Taemin," she said. "We thought we could all get together and have a chat."

"Over bingsu, I hope?" he said.

"No way are we treating you to bingsu, man," Charlie said, irritated. "You've been double-crossing us this whole time!"

"Whoa, what are these accusations flying around?" Taemin said, holding up his hands. He lowered them guiltily. "I mean, they're true. But I'm just proposing we get some bingsu at this bingsu café. It is a business, after all. We can't just sit here for free."

That made us all pause. This was true.

"Okay, I'll buy one," I said, sighing. "What flavor does everyone want?"

"Just get anything," Pauline said at the same time Taemin said, "Berry, please."

"Anything *but* berry is good, Wes, thanks," Charlie said.

Ten minutes later we were sitting around the table with a bowl of shaved ice topped with injeolmi, Korean rice cakes coated in powdered soybean.

"All right, bro, time to come clean," Charlie said. "You've been spying for both of us, haven't you?"

"Yes and no." Taemin ate a spoonful of bingsu and sighed, sitting back in his seat and looking around at all of us. His face grew serious. "Yes, I did gather and leak info at both of your requests. But it wasn't at the same time. Valerie asked me for help, so I helped her. After that was over, I got to know Wes a little more, and I felt bad that I'd put him in a tight spot. So when he asked me to help him, I helped him. The way I see it, me helping Wes canceled out me helping Valerie, so we're right back to the beginning of things, right as rain."

"No," Charlie said. "Not right as rain. What the hell, man! That's weird logic!"

"But also, it kind of makes sense," he pointed out. "I was trying to be helpful, okay? Besides," he added defensively, "everything I ever told any of you was true. I wasn't trying to hurt anyone. And may I remind you, *you* were the ones who hired *me*. In my opinion, I haven't done anything wrong here." He hesitated. "And, to be honest, I liked hanging out with all of you. It was fun."

We fell silent. As much as I hated to admit it, there was some truth to what he was saying. He was right that we *were* the ones who'd hired him. We'd started this whole thing, so who did we really have to blame here?

"Valerie Nuna was understanding about it when I told her," he said. "Well, eventually."

"Wait," I said. "Valerie knew?"

We all stared at him. He nodded. "Yeah. I told her a while back."

"Ugh, she doesn't tell me anything," Charlie said.

"Wait, wait, when did you tell her that?" I asked. "Was it the day after Valentine's Day?"

Taemin nodded again.

"What else did you tell her that day?" I asked.

He looked uncomfortable now, swirling his spoon around in the shaved ice. "Well. I may have told her that you were getting closer to her so you could spy on her business yourself. And that you made a deal with some girls from school to stop them from shopping with V&C."

My heart dropped, suspicions confirmed. More than confirmed. He didn't just tell her about Lisa, Natalie, and Mimi. He told her I was spying on her. "Dude, how could you tell her that? That's not what I meant!"

"What do you mean that's not what you meant?" Taemin said, his mouth dropping open. "That's literally what you said to me. So what was I supposed to do, huh?" He pointed at a booth across the café. "We were sitting right over there and she was over-the-moon happy about having a new boyfriend who I happened to know was leading her on. I was doing the right thing, telling her the truth. I even told Pastor Richard about it, and he said I did the right thing!"

"But it wasn't the truth!" I cried. "I just said that in the moment so you wouldn't ask me about it! I really, really like her!"

My throat got tight hearing she had been over-the-moon happy, only to be heartbroken moments later, but another hurt part of me felt angry with her. If she had just let me explain, we could have avoided this whole thing. Why couldn't she have just given me the benefit of the doubt and been honest with me instead of pushing me away?

Silence fell around the table. Charlie and Pauline stared somberly at the melting bingsu as Taemin looked at me, his spoon frozen in his hand.

"Well, shit." He slumped back in his seat and dropped his spoon. "I messed up, didn't I? Oh God. If my dad finds out about this, I'm going to have to work for the church this summer, aren't I?"

"Go on, Wes," Pauline said gently. "You have all the facts now. You need to talk to Valerie."

She was right. I pushed my chair back and ran out of the bingsu café, the bell on the door jingling as it slammed shut behind me. Moments later, the bell jingled again and Taemin's voice called out, "Yo, Wes! Wait up!"

I turned around, halfway down the sidewalk already.

He ran up to me, trying to catch his breath. "There's one more thing you should know."

"Listen, man, I really don't want to hear it right now," I said. "If it's about Valerie, I need to hear it directly from her."

He shook his head. "She won't tell you this. But I think someone should know, and she made me promise I wouldn't tell Charlie.

Seriously. I helped her with something, and I think it may have been a mistake."

I gave him a steady look. "What is it?"

Monday / April 20

Valerie is going to sell counterfeit products. I helped her get in touch with a guy who gave me his business card, but I haven't felt right about it since. And man, if I don't feel right about it, there must be something wrong, you know?

I'd turned over Taemin's words in my mind all weekend. I needed to see Valerie. I called her, left her voicemails, sent her text after text.

Me: Valerie, can we meet? I think we need to talk.

Me: I've typed and retyped what I want to say so many times, but I think I really need to say this in person.

Me: Please? Call me back.

She never replied.

I even asked Charlie to get in touch with her, but he said she wouldn't even reply to him.

"I swung by her house but she's not home," he'd said on Saturday. "Sorry, Wes. I don't know where she is."

So on Monday morning, I showed up early to school, earlier than I'd ever been, and I waited by her locker.

It wasn't long until she arrived, lugging a big cardboard box in her arms. She froze when she saw me standing by her locker, but then continued on, her lips set in a grim line.

"Excuse me," she said when she was right in front of me.

I didn't budge. She moved to the right, trying to get to her locker. I moved too, blocking her. She sighed and moved to her left, but I mirrored her again, getting in her way.

"What do you want, Wes?" she said, annoyed.

I looked her in the eyes. There was such deep fatigue there and something else. Something like desperation.

"What's in the box, Valerie?" I asked.

She tensed, her fingers tightening around the box in her arms. "Beauty products," she said. "It's Monday. I always come early to get my locker ready on Mondays."

I winced at the way she sidestepped the question, hating that this box was between us when all I wanted to do was pull her into my arms. I asked again, "What's in the box, Valerie?"

"I told you." Her voice rose as she put the box down on the floor, stepping in front of it like she was trying to protect it from my gaze. "Now please move out of my way."

She tried to move past me, reaching for her lock.

"Please, Valerie," I said. "Don't sell those products. I know they're counterfeit."

She froze. "How do you know that?"

"Taemin told me."

"Taemin." Her voice fell flat.

"I know he was spying for both of us, Valerie. It's a long, messy story, but the main thing I need you to know is that I never wanted to get close to you so I could get insider info on your business. I wanted to get close to you because—" My voice broke off. This wasn't how I'd imagined saying this next part, but I had no choice. I couldn't let us lose years like Charlie and Pauline just because I wasn't honest. It was now or never.

"Because I like you. Because you're smart and beautiful and independent and I learn so much every time I'm around you. What I felt for you—what I *feel* for you—is real. It has nothing to do with money or business or anything like that. It's just you. I like *you*. And I'm so sorry about that deal I made with those girls in school. I know how much your business means to you, and I hate that I tried to steal your customers in such a petty way instead of actually earning their sales like you did. Please believe me. And please don't turn me away. You can't keep doing that. I'm a human being, not just an obstacle in your life, and this isn't some business transaction. It's a relationship. I need you to talk to me."

For a hopeful moment, I thought everything might be okay. Once she knew the truth, we would laugh about it and finally talk and move on. Instead she just stared at me, absorbing everything I was saying, and then she looked away.

"Maybe what I heard from Taemin isn't true," she said. "But it doesn't change the fact that I've been losing focus on what's really important. Now, please get out of my way so I can set up my locker. I have a bet to win."

I stared at her in disbelief, so shocked that I stepped out of her way as she reached for her lock again. "You can't be serious."

"I am serious."

She dialed her combination, swung the door open. The battery-powered lights came to life inside her locker.

I shook my head. "No. No! I want to call off the bet. I don't want to take part in this anymore. Who are you going to bet against now, Valerie? Yourself?"

She whirled on me, anger blazing in her eyes. "You have to. We shook on it."

"You're the one who told me to stand up for myself more, so that's what I'm doing. I'm not going to carry on with this. Not if you're going to start selling fake beauty products. Are they even safe? What happened to sourcing ethical products for your business, huh? What happened to all the things that are important to you?"

"Don't," she said, her voice dropping dangerously low. "*Don't* pretend like you know what's important to me."

"Please," I said, begging her. "Don't do this."

Valerie gave me a long look. I willed her to see me, to see herself, to see that it wasn't too late to turn things around.

"Try and stop me," she said. And then she turned to her locker and started to fill it with products from the box. She picked them up one at a time—moisturizers, serums, toners, bottles with brand names that were all a little off if you knew what you were looking for—and slid each one onto its designated shelf. When she was done, she slammed her locker door shut, crushed the cardboard box with her foot, picked it up, and walked down the hall without looking back.

I stared after her. My heartbeat felt like a metronome in my ears, speeding up faster and faster. *Try and stop me.* I didn't want to try to stop her. I really didn't. But there was something in my gut that told me I would regret it if I didn't, and that, worse, maybe she'd regret it too.

My fingers tightened over my backpack straps as I walked down to the second-floor social studies wing, where I stopped at room 217.

"Wes?" Ms. Jackson looked up from her desk as I opened the door. "How can I help you?"

"Ms. Jackson. There's something I need to tell you."

CHAPTER SEVENTEEN

VALERIE

Monday / April 20

None of the beauty products smelled right.

I'd gotten the box from Taemin's contact over the weekend, just in time to refill my locker. Last week, I had officialy run out of the supplies that Charlie's dad had sent us in his final package. It was perfect timing, really.

Except it felt all wrong.

The colors were garish. The textures were off. And I didn't even recognize some of the ingredients on the labels. What was in these things?

But it was too late to go back. I had already invested in these products. And without them, I had nothing left.

I sat through all my classes that day, my knees jittering under my desk. My conversation with Wes this morning had left me shaken. So Taemin was wrong. Wes had never tried to get close to me so he could sabotage my business. He actually really liked me. He said his feelings for me were real. But that didn't change anything, did it? It didn't change the fact that I had money to make, a point to prove, and a business to salvage. Nothing was different.

Was it?

Wes likes you, a voice whispered inside my head. *And he said sorry. Remember what Halmeoni said? "See how much more fun life is when you let people in?" Besides, he has a point. He's a human being, not an obstacle. All he needs is for you to talk to him. So why don't you let him in?*

I couldn't. There was too much on the line.

The bell rang, signaling the end of class. I grabbed my backpack and shoved my books inside. It was my free period now, my last chance to tidy up my locker before customers started coming after the final bell. I had already Instagrammed my new products for the day. People were excited. *I* had to be excited.

But when I got to my locker and opened the door, the wrongness of it all washed over me again, making me feel physically nauseous. This wasn't V&C K-BEAUTY. This wasn't the business I had built up from the ground and worked so hard to manage over the past three years. This wasn't me.

Wes was right. I couldn't go through with this.

The sound of clicking heels came down the hall and I quickly closed my locker, locking it tight. I would figure out what to do with these products later.

I looked up to see that the person approaching was Ms. Jackson. She was heading straight for me, a grim expression on her face.

"Hi, Ms. J," I said, trying to keep my voice steady.

"Valerie," she said. "I thought I'd find you here. Can I see you in my classroom for a moment please?"

My stomach sank. I had a bad feeling about this. "Um, sure."

I followed her down to room 217, taking the same seat that I had sat in dozens of times before. Usually I felt right at home here next to her familiar WORLD'S BEST TEACHER mug, but today I felt like I was in the hot seat. My palms grew clammy. I wiped them against my jeans.

"What's going on, Ms. J?" I asked.

She folded her hands on her desk and gave me a long, searching look. "Valerie, you are an extremely smart and talented young lady," she said at last. "You've impressed me time and time again with your quick thinking and creativity. Not only that, but you are a student full of integrity. I know you are. It's one of the reasons I respect you so much. So please be honest with me when I ask you this next question." She took a deep breath. "I've received word from a source that you plan on selling counterfeit goods through your business. Is this true?"

My mouth went dry. "I— Who did you hear that from? Was it Wes?"

Her face betrayed nothing, but I knew immediately that it was him. "Why would he do that?" I said, my voice shaking, but even as I asked, I already knew why he would. He did it to stop me. Just like I had dared him to.

"Please answer the question, Valerie," Ms. Jackson said. "Is it true that if I were to open your locker right now, I would find it full of counterfeit products?"

I swallowed hard. I couldn't lie to Ms. Jackson. I nodded slowly. She shook her head, not understanding. "Why would you do that, Valerie?"

Why? Because Charlie's dad is coming back. Because my business is falling apart and I have no control over it anymore. Because I need to take Halmeoni to Paris so she can see the world like she's always dreamed. Because I need to prove to Umma that I can do something worthy of her attention, that Samantha's not the only one in the family who can make something of herself. Because I got rejected by a college and I'm scared I'll get rejected by more. Because without V&C K-BEAUTY, I don't know what I have or who I am, and I can't lose everything all at once.

But I didn't know how to say all of that to Ms. Jackson. I didn't have the words or the strength to speak them out loud. "Because," I said instead, my voice hoarse, "it was a fast way to make more money."

Ms. Jackson closed her eyes, pressing her folded hands against her face like she was getting ready to pray. In that moment, I felt so sorry for disappointing her. But the truth was too painful. I couldn't face it.

When she opened her eyes again, they were full of sadness. My heart ached. I had done that. I had put that sadness there.

"Valerie, I have always held you to a high standard because I believed so strongly in your entrepreneurial skills," she said. "This is extremely disappointing to hear. It also strictly violates the code of conduct for student-run businesses at Crescent Brook High to sell staff-approved products only. I'm afraid I have no choice but to suspend your business for the rest of the school year."

"Suspend?" I said.

"Yes. No more sales. No more promotion. V&C K-BEAUTY is officially closed for business."

I sat there, fists clenched against my knees, completely lost for words. I opened my mouth, closed it again. I had nothing.

No words. No business. No V&C.

"I'd like to see you in my classroom again tomorrow during lunch," Ms. Jackson said. "I've known you for several years now, Valerie, and I have a feeling there's more to this story than just your desire to make more money. You might not be ready to talk about it right now, but I hope tomorrow you will be."

"I understand," I managed to whisper.

Her face softened. "I want to make this clear. I'm not giving up on you. I still believe in you and your future. But I can't let your actions go unpunished. I will be recording the suspension of your business at the school office."

I nodded, swallowing the lump in my throat. "I understand," I said again.

Except I didn't really. How could she still believe in me after all this, even when she didn't know the whole story? *I'm not even sure if I believe in myself anymore.*

The final bell rang and she rose from her seat, walking me to the door. "See you tomorrow, Valerie," she said.

I stepped out of the classroom just as the halls filled with students shouting and laughing and bounding for their lockers. I wondered how many people would be lining up at my locker right now, expecting to see me there like I was every Monday after school.

I didn't realize my hands were shaking until I reached for my phone, my fingers quivering as I typed a message to Charlie.

Me: V&C is over. Officially.

It wasn't until I hit send that I remembered Charlie was at a basketball tournament all day today. He wasn't even in the building.

Still, when my phone rang a second later, I thought it would be him. But it was Umma's name on my caller ID. I let it go to voicemail. She only called me when I'd done something wrong. I couldn't deal with that right now.

Ten seconds later my phone rang again. This time it was Samantha.

Weird. She hardly ever called me.

I picked up.

"Samantha?" My voice sounded strange and hollow to my ears.

"Valerie, come quick." It sounded like she was crying. She never cried. "Halmeoni's in the hospital."

"What?" Time slowed. Someone bumped into me with their backpack as they jogged past, but I didn't feel a thing. I'd gone completely numb.

"Halmeoni. She fell down the stairs."

"Halmeoni is in the hospital?"

"Yes. Come on, Valerie, are you even listening to me? She's asking for you, so come quick."

She's asking for me. Halmeoni is asking for me.

"I'm coming," I said, and then I hung up. I had to get to the hospital. I called Charlie, praying that he might have his phone on him at the tournament, but it went straight to voicemail. *Shit. Shit, shit, shit. How am I supposed to get there? What bus do I take?* I fumbled with Google Maps, trying to map out the fastest route. It was an hour by bus. *Fuck.* I wanted to scream. *Fuck you, Google Maps. I don't have a fucking hour!*

"Valerie?" I looked up to see Wes staring at me in concern. He was holding his saxophone case, probably getting ready to leave school for the day. "Are you okay?"

I took a deep breath, shook my head.

He took a step toward me. "Can I do anything to help?"

My voice came out small. "Yeah, actually. Could you give me a ride to the hospital?"

We sat in silence as he drove.

I rested my head against the passenger window. I felt bruised all over on the inside. Was that even possible? I wasn't sure. All I knew was that everything hurt.

"Do you want to listen to some music?" Wes asked, breaking the silence.

"Okay." Somewhere deep inside, I was still angry with him, but I didn't have the energy to be angry at him right now. Besides, music sounded nice.

He turned on something instrumental, mellow and jazzy and full of light piano chords.

"Jazz always helps me clear my head," he said softly, not taking his eyes off the road.

"I guess it's like your version of Hi-Chews," I heard myself say.

He smiled. "Yeah. Something like that."

"Ms. J suspended V&C."

He looked sharply at me and then back at the road, the smile dropping from his face. "What? Valerie, I'm sorry. I just thought she might talk you out of it. I had no idea she would suspend your business."

"It's not your fault. It's mine." I meant it, even though it hurt to say. I stared out the window, speaking more to myself than to him. "When I was looking at all the counterfeit items in my locker today, I realized you were right. This isn't what I built my business to be. It's not V&C K-BEAUTY and it's not me. I just got so . . ." My voice trailed off. "Desperate. But I couldn't go through with it after all. I have nothing now. My mom was right. I never had it in me."

"Never had what in you?"

"The skills. The smarts. Anything worthwhile."

He shook his head. "You know you're more than just your business, right?"

I said nothing. He didn't press it. There was more I wanted to say about the things he'd said to me, how I treated people and relationships and saw them all through a business lens, but I couldn't find the words. We drove without speaking the rest of the way, the music filling the space between us.

It wasn't until we pulled up to the hospital that I realized I was crying. Silent tears rolling down my cheeks and dripping down my chin. I quickly wiped them from my face with the sleeve of my jacket.

"Thank you for the ride," I said, unbuckling my seat belt.

"Hey, wait." He opened the glove compartment, revealing a bag of Hi-Chews. He fished out a handful of strawberry ones and held them out to me. "Just in case you need the extra support."

I stared at the Hi-Chews in his palm. I had so many mixed feelings. Hurt. Pain. Gratitude. For a moment I thought about rejecting them. But right now I knew I needed the support more than I needed to prove a point.

"Thank you," I said. I took the Hi-Chews and got out of the car. And then I walked straight through the hospital doors.

The first person I saw was Samantha. She was sitting in the waiting room, rolling an empty paper cup of what might have once held coffee between her hands. As soon as she saw me, she ran forward and hugged me.

"You made it," she said, pulling back. Her face was pale and tired, totally drained of all energy. "Appa, Eemo, and Charlie are all on their way. Umma just went home to get some of Halmeoni's stuff. It looks she'll have to stay overnight."

"How is she?" I asked, anxious.

She hesitated and my stomach dropped. Seeing the terror on my face, she quickly replied, "Halmeoni's okay. No broken bones or anything, just some bruises. They just want her to stay overnight to run some tests while she's here." She didn't look directly at me when she spoke the next part. "The doctors think she has Parkinson's disease."

"Parkinson's disease?" The words fell out of my mouth, clunky and foreign. It couldn't be true. Halmeoni was healthy. She had to be healthy. "Why would they say that?"

She pressed her lips together and shook her head. "I don't know. They're doctors. I guess they see the symptoms." She looked away. "Halmeoni was asking for you. You should go see her. She's in room 402."

My mind was racing. I thought back to all the times we'd gone out, me pulling her around the grocery store, us walking together to the arcade, arms linked. A terrible thought hit me. Had I pushed her too hard? Was it my fault this was happening? My throat tightened. *I can't believe I let this happen.*

I immediately headed for the room, stopping only when I realized Samantha wasn't following. "Aren't you coming?"

"I saw her earlier," she said, already sitting back down. There was a different look on her face now, one that I couldn't quite place. She crumpled the empty paper cup in her hand. "Besides, she only asked for you."

When I walked into room 402, the first thing I noticed was how strange it was to see Halmeoni in a bed, and not her floor bed. She looked so small and frail, lying there with her eyes closed. My heart ached as I crawled into bed next to her, curling up against her side. My halmeoni.

Her eyelids fluttered open. "Valerie. You're here."

"Uh-huh," I said, resting my cheek against her shoulder. "Sorry it took me so long."

"It doesn't matter," she said. "As long as you are here now."

"Are you in pain?"

"A little," she admitted. "My knees hurt, and I feel very stiff. But they gave me some painkillers that make me very sleepy.

Your halmeoni is not so young anymore, it seems."

She laughed lightly. I couldn't help it. I started to cry again.

"Halmeoni, I'm so sorry," I choked between tears.

"Wae, my girl? Why? What's the matter?"

"I wanted to take you to Paris. We were supposed to eat maca-rons together and see the Eiffel Tower and eat real French cheese on real French baguettes with your travel-sized gochujang." I was full-on crying all over her hospital gown now as she stroked my hair with her wrinkled hand. "But now . . . but now . . ."

"The doctors say I have Parkinson's," she said, filling in the gap.

I nodded against her shoulder. "I thought that going on some kind of big adventure would give you new life, that you would feel better if we could make your travel dreams come true. But Umma was right. You're not as healthy as you used to be, and if I took you to Paris, I probably would have made it all worse. I was so focused on what I thought would be best for you, I didn't even see what was right in front of me."

"Oh, Valerie. Don't cry over that," she said, tears filling her own eyes. "I *like* the way you see me. It is so nice to have someone dream dreams for you. What a gift. Besides, don't you know? I am already the happiest I can be whenever I am with you. It doesn't have to be Paris. It can be our own backyard. If you are there, your halmeoni is happy. If you are there, it is enough for me."

"But what about wanting to go out and see the world?" I said. "It's too late now. I was too late. If I had just worked harder or raised money faster . . ."

She sighed. "Oh, Valerie. The world is so big. Of course I want to see more of it. When I lived in Korea, I dreamed so badly of going to America. Of giving my children and grandchildren every opportunity they could ever hope for. When that dream came true, it was very hard. Immigrating to a new country is very lonely. I made many mistakes. Your mother and Sunhee Eemo know. They had to put up with a lot from me. And it was so hard for them too. They had just lost their father, and they were nearly adults by the time we moved. Not young enough to absorb a new culture very quickly.

"But I look at you and Samantha and Charlie now and I think, yes, it was worth it. To see you live your lives to the fullest, to take every opportunity, to meet all different kinds of people, and to see a whole new world grow inside each of you. The world out there is big, Valerie, and of course I would love to see more of it. But your halmeoni is so, so content to be by your side and watch the world grow inside of you."

I wrapped my arms around her tight, letting her words sink deep into me. "What if the world inside me is not so good, Halmeoni?" I whispered, speaking my fear. "I've made so many mistakes."

"We all have, my girl. It's part of growing." Her voice grew faint, drifting in and out like ocean tides. She squeezed my hand, nodding off to sleep.

I curled closer into her side and closed my eyes too, feeling raw but more at peace than I had in a long time.

CHAPTER EIGHTEEN

WES

Monday / April 20

I sat in the car for a long time after Valerie disappeared through the hospital's sliding doors, not moving until the car behind me started honking. I drove out of the hospital drop-off zone, my mind bursting with endless questions.

Did I make a mistake telling Ms. Jackson about Valerie's plan? Is Valerie's halmeoni going to be okay? What happens now with V&C K-BEAUTY? What happens now with me and Valerie?

Somehow, without even realizing how I got there, I ended up back in my driveway. I turned off the ignition and pressed my forehead against the steering wheel. I had too many thoughts, too many emotions, and nowhere to put them.

I needed to play this out. I needed music.

I'll tell Dad I'm sick, I decided as I got out of the car. *And then I'll lock myself in my room and play until dinner.*

But as I walked through the front door, I could already sense that something wasn't right. For one, there were too many shoes by the door. I could hear voices coming from the kitchen. Mom's and Dad's voices. What was Mom doing home? She was never home at this time.

"Hello?" I called to let them know I was there.

Their conversation stopped immediately.

"Wes?" Dad's voice called out, stiff and unnatural. "Can you come in here for a moment?"

My immediate thought was: *We're moving again.* Why else would Mom be home at this time unless she was getting ready to pack our life away? A flare of panic shot up in my chest. *No. Not this time.* I couldn't leave yet.

I walked into the kitchen, practically expecting to see everything already packed away. But it was just as I'd left it in the morning. Mom's Vitamix on the kitchen counter, Dad's collection of magnets shaped like computers on the fridge. Mom was sitting at the table, clutching her phone, while Dad sat across from her, an open white envelope in his hands.

My eyes zeroed in on the envelope. An envelope marked with Toblie School of Music's seal.

"We were wondering why Toblie School of Music was sending you a letter," Dad said, holding up the envelope. "And why they'd like to congratulate you on your acceptance for the fall."

I sucked in a breath. *Holy shit. I've been accepted. Holy shit holy shit holy shit.* And yet, any happiness I was feeling was immediately tamped down by the look on Mom's and Dad's faces as Dad threw the envelope on the table, folding his arms across his chest.

"So?" he said. "Should we call them and tell them they've made a mistake? That my son never applied for this music school? Or do you have something you want to tell us?"

I opened my mouth, but no sound came out. *Come on, Wes. Don't wimp out now. Come on, come on.*

"It wasn't a mistake," I finally managed. "I applied. I auditioned. I got in."

Dad's face grew stormy. "And?"

And? "And . . ." My voice trailed off. "That's all."

"Oh really?" Now Mom spoke, holding up her phone and sliding it across the kitchen counter toward me. "What about this? Care to explain?"

Confused, I slowly picked up the phone. It was an Instagram picture of a girl holding up a bottle of sunscreen and smiling. My stomach sank. Not just any girl. It was Kristy Lo, her hair as blond as butter. She was holding the sunscreen with Shiyoon's tiger mascot, the orange one wearing sunglasses.

Can't wait to try my new sunscreen featuring my one true love, Shiyoon! the caption read. *Thanks, Wes, for the hookup!* 🐯 🖤 *#RoyalStripes.*

"One of my colleagues sent me this photo, asking me why this girl had a sample of Crown Tiger's new sunscreen that hasn't even been released yet," Mom said, her eyes boring into mine. "Imagine my surprise when we traced it back and found an account selling K-pop beauty products run by Wes Jung at Crescent Brook High."

Oh my God. I wiped the sweat beading on my forehead, trying to remind myself to breathe. This couldn't be happening. This was happening. *What the hell do I do?*

"Well, Wes?" Dad said.

The silence stretched between us like an elastic band ready to snap. There was no way out. The moment to speak up had finally come.

"I needed money to fix my saxophone and apply for music school, so I started selling the beauty products that Mom's been giving me. I knew you would oppose it, so I kept it a secret." I took a deep breath, plowing forward. "I'm so sorry I've been keeping this from you. I really didn't mean for you to find out like this. But I'm not sorry that I applied for music school. It's something I have to do. I can't live a future that you choose for me."

My heart pounded in my ears. Finally I was saying what I'd always wanted to say. It was a hundred times more satisfying than I'd thought it would be, but also a hundred times more terrible. The look on Dad's face was worse than anything I had ever imagined. It was disappointment, anger, and betrayal all at once.

"Why not?" Dad said, his jaw tensed. "You're too young to even know what you really want. And obviously you're not capable of making your own decisions yet. Look at the mess you've created for your mom! Do you know how much chaos you've caused for her team, selling products that haven't been released yet? You've thrown off their entire marketing timeline!"

I winced. *Shit. I really messed up.* "I'm so sorry. I had no idea. I just took them from Mom's office thinking that everything in there was old and fair game. I didn't know . . ."

"How could you think you could get away with something like this?" Dad said, practically yelling now. He slammed his fist on the table, making both me and Mom jump. "You think we're going to give you our blessing for this music school just because you got in? There is no way any son of mine is going down a path like this. I'm not going to support this."

"Yeobo, calm down," Mom said, resting a hand on his arm. She looked at me, disappointment etched on her face. "Wes, I don't understand what you mean by all of this. Where is this coming from?"

"Wait, Dad, what do you mean, 'a path like this'?" I asked. "A path like what? A path I actually want? A path I think I could be really good at?"

"A path that's for dreamers," he spat out.

"What is wrong with being a dreamer?"

"You want to live with no money, Wes? Huh? You want to be unstable your whole life? It's difficult. You have no idea how difficult. When I was your age, I had to support both myself and your uncle. You think I could have done that if I went into something like music? Why do you think your uncle struggles so much still? I didn't raise my son to live with his head in the sky. I raised you to be grounded and to make a difference in the world."

"You raised me to believe that I had to do everything your way," I cried. Now that I had started talking, I couldn't seem to stop. Everything rushed out of me at once, begging to finally be free. "You made me think that I could never say no to you. But I can make decisions for myself. I know the road will be hard. I know it won't be as stable as being a doctor or a computer scientist like you. But I have to try. Pursuing music isn't just some fantasy to me. It's what keeps me grounded. And believe it or not, I think music can make a difference in the world. It has in mine."

"Wes, please," Mom said, standing between me and Dad with her hands held out. "Both of you. Let's stay calm."

"I get that you're worried for me," I said, pleading now. "I really do understand. But I'm ready for it to be difficult. And even if I'm not, even if I have no idea how hard it will actually be, don't you think these are lessons I need to learn for myself?"

"No!" Dad yelled. "You don't need to learn lessons that I'm teaching you right now. How am I supposed to sit back and watch you struggle for the rest of your life? You have had every opportunity given to you and you're about to waste it all now. When will you come to your senses, Jung Hojin?"

We fell silent, Uncle Hojin's name hanging in the air between us. There it was again. For Dad, it always seemed to come back to his brother. He slumped in his seat, shaking his head. Mom covered her mouth with her hand.

"Dad," I said quietly. "Uncle Hojin, he's happy. I know you worry about him a lot, but for him, music was a calling he couldn't ignore. Just like it is for me. And I'm not your younger brother. I'm your son. Things can be different between us."

"How do you know what he does or doesn't regret?" Dad said.

"Uh . . . I may have been emailing with him since the school year started," I confessed. I guess today was literally the day all my secrets came out.

Mom and Dad both stared at me, saying nothing. Finally, Dad shook his head, rose from the table, and walked out of the kitchen. I watched him go in disbelief. That was it? He was walking away from this?

"Where are you going?" I said.

"Just let him go," Mom said. "He needs to cool off." She sighed, staring at me with a mixture of shock and disappointment and confusion. "Wes, I don't understand. I never knew you were this passionate about going to music school. Why didn't you tell me?"

"You're never really around," I said. "And I guess I thought because Dad is so against it, you would be too." Was I wrong? Could I have had Mom on my side this whole time if I hadn't been so scared to talk to her about it?

Her shoulders sagged. "You're right that I've been busy. I'm sorry I haven't been around to more, and it's definitely something I want us to talk more about later. But there are other matters to discuss right now. Wes, you've been lying to us for a very long time."

I hung my head. "I know. And for that I'm really sorry, Mom."

"Sorry is one thing. But to undo the mistakes you've made with my team . . . Wes, how could you just go into my office and sell whatever you found in there? The sunscreen? The makeup pouches? I know I've been using it as a storage room all this time, but when I finally decided to start using it properly and move new things in there, I never dreamed you would go in and sell them."

"I really am so sorry," I said. "What can I do to make it better?"

She shook her head. "There is nothing. The team will handle it now. But you will give me all the profit you've made from the products I've given you."

My mouth dropped open. "All the profit? From everything?"

"Good Lord, Wes, how much did you sell? Yes, everything. You need to understand that your actions have consequences. Do I make myself clear?"

I bit my lip and nodded. This was my mistake. I had to own up to it. "I understand."

"Okay, then." She sighed. "I'm going to go talk to your father."

She walked out of the kitchen, leaving me alone with my acceptance letter on the table. I waited until Mom's footsteps faded away and I heard the sound of a closing door before picking up the letter and opening it myself.

I read it once. Then twice. Then three times.

Dear Mr. Wes Jung,
Our faculty was incredibly impressed by your moving
and skillful saxophone audition. As such, we are pleased
to offer you a spot in Toblie School of Music's jazz pro-
gram . . .

I clutched the letter to my chest and breathed deep. Wow. I did it. I got into my top music school and I finally stood up to my parents.

I can't believe I did it.

I! Did! It!

I broke out into a smile. Even though Dad wasn't speaking to me and Mom was taking all the money I'd raised and I had no idea what I was going to do next, this moment was enough for now. This victory was enough for now. It was like an extraordinary weight had been lifted from my shoulders and I was, at last, untethered.

CHAPTER NINETEEN

VALERIE

Tuesday / April 21

Hospitals are a weird place. I stared at the vending machine, rows of chip bags and chocolate bars staring back at me. *Why don't they have Hi-Chews in vending machines?* I'd stayed the night with Halmeoni and run out of all my Hi-Chews, plus the Hi-Chews Wes had given me in the car. I begrudgingly chose a Kit Kat instead, the second-best option.

As I headed back down the hall to Halmeoni's hospital room, I spotted Samantha sitting cross-legged in a waiting-room chair, scrolling absentmindedly through her phone.

"Hey," I said, approaching her as I unwrapped my Kit Kat. "When did you get here?"

She didn't look up from her phone. "Just now."

"Are Umma and Appa here too?"

"They're in the room. Helping Halmeoni get ready to leave."

"Okay. Cool," I said.

The vibe between us was weird, but I wasn't sure why. She had that look on her face again, the one I couldn't quite place from yesterday.

"What about Sunhee Eemo and Charlie?" I asked.

"They're going to meet us at the house later. No need for all of us to escort Halmeoni home. We wouldn't even fit in one car."

"Yeah, that's true. You didn't have to come, then. Don't you have finals to study for?"

She tensed, finally looking up from her phone. I was surprised to see that her eyes were rimmed with red like she had been crying all night.

"You're missing school to be here," she said. "I can too."

Silence fell between us, awkward and heavy. I didn't know what to say, so I just took a bite of chocolate, the wafers sticking to my teeth.

"Okay," I said finally, just to say something. "Why are you sitting out here, then? Let's go into the room."

"Umma and Appa told me to wait. So I'm waiting."

I scoffed. "Whatever. I'm going in."

"It really must be so nice," she said, stopping me in my tracks as I turned to leave, "to be the youngest and do whatever you want. Is that why you're Halmeoni's favorite?"

I whirled around, narrowing my eyes. "What the hell, Samantha? What are you talking about?"

She glared at me, her lower lip quivering. I could tell she was trying to control it, to keep her face even and neutral, but her voice came out shaky. "You're Halmeoni's favorite. You always have been. She barely even notices me. I'm worried about her too, you know."

Seriously? Now I was angry. "Why do you need Halmeoni to notice you? You already get all of Umma's attention."

"It's not the same."

"What's not the same?"

"Forget it," she said, looking away.

"No, tell me. Umma is constantly comparing me to you. 'Why can't you be more like Samantha?' 'Samantha did this, so why don't you do it too?' 'You're not as skilled as Samantha, as smart as Samantha, as capable as Samantha.' She basically worships you. So what the hell do you have to complain about?"

I was getting so heated that the strangers in the waiting room were throwing dirty glances my way, putting fingers to their lips with shushing noises. Samantha looked up at me, her eyes filled with angry tears.

"Do you know how exhausting it is?" she said. "To try to please her all the time? To meet her expectations? We have the same mom, Valerie. You feel like nothing ever satisfies her? I feel like that too. Like if I slip up once, she won't see me the same anymore. At least you have Halmeoni to support you. You go to her every time you have a problem with Umma, but who do I have to go to? Appa's never around, and all the responsibility falls on me as the oldest. You can get away with disobeying Umma because you're younger, but I have no room to make mistakes. I've always been jealous of you for that."

Her voice broke at the end and she wiped the tears roughly from her eyes. I realized then that they weren't just angry tears. They were also tears of sadness.

"I had no idea you felt that way," I said quietly. I slumped into the seat next to her, the Kit Kat dangling from my hand.

"Yeah, well." She drew her knees into her chest. "I do."

We sat in silence. I held up the chocolate bar.

"Do you want a piece?"

She paused and then took it from my hand. "Thanks."

"We really don't talk about problems in our family, do we?"

"Never."

"What do you think would happen if we did?"

Samantha took a bite of chocolate as Halmeoni, Umma, and Appa appeared from down the hall, searching the waiting room for us. Halmeoni waved, smiling.

"Honestly?" Samantha said, waving back with a smile that didn't reach her eyes. "I think things would stay exactly the same."

Samantha's words stuck with me the whole day. Even after Sunhee Eemo and Charlie came and went with lunch, after Samantha left to go back to her college dorm, after Halmeoni went to bed, and after Umma and Appa tucked themselves away into their room to talk in low voices, I thought about everything that was said and unsaid in our family. I was sitting in the kitchen with my chin propped in my hand, staring out the window, when Umma came downstairs. She looked tired.

"Valerie, what are you doing in here?" she asked. "Do you want something to eat?"

I shook my head. "Just sitting."

"I'll cut you some fruit," she said, reaching for a bowl of giant

Korean pears on the counter. Korean pears are different from American pears. They're bigger and rounder with yellow skin and a sweet, almost floral taste. She sat across from me with a plate and a paring knife and started peeling a pear.

I watched her, taking in the dark bags under her eyes and the pinch between her forehead. "Umma," I said.

"Hmm?"

"Did you suspect? That Halmeoni had Parkinson's disease? Is that why you never wanted her to go out?"

"Yes and no," she said, not taking her eyes off the pear. "I didn't know it was Parkinson's. But I noticed she was getting clumsier. Slower and stiffer than she used to be. Here, eat this."

She held out a slice of pear to feed me. I let her.

"Halmeoni said when you first immigrated here, she made a lot of mistakes," I said. "She said it was hard."

"It was."

"Did Halmeoni ever treat you and Sunhee Eemo differently?"

She laughed. "Where's this question coming from?"

"I'm just curious."

"Sure, she treated us differently when we were kids. Sunhee Eemo is older, so she had a lot more responsibility. I was more carefree." She smiled wistfully. Maybe it was the hospital visit or the scare with Halmeoni that was bringing out the softness in her, but she was more open to talking than I'd ever heard her. "But after we immigrated here, it changed. There wasn't room to be carefree anymore. We had to survive in a new country with new rules, and the three of us had to depend on each other to live well. It was a difficult time. But anyway. It's all in the past. All I know now is that I don't want my girls to grow up in hardship like Sunhee Eemo and I did. You will have good, successful lives."

Her words struck a chord in me, forming a lump in my throat. She held out another piece of pear for me, but I didn't take it.

"Umma," I said, my voice coming out shaky. I folded my hands on the table and took a deep breath. "I know you're hard on us because you want us to grow up to be hardworking people. But sometimes when you do that, you know, you make me feel like nothing."

She slowly lowered the pear, her brow creasing. "What are you talking about?"

"I'm talking about the way you speak to me. You always talk down to me, always compare me to Samantha, always make me feel like I'm never enough."

"That's ridiculous," she said, shaking her head. "You're my daughter. Why would I make you feel that way?"

"But you *do*," I said, my voice rising. "You put these expectations on me that are impossible for me to meet. Do you know what that does to me?"

She looked at me in shock, like she truly didn't know where I was coming from. "What are you talking about? I've only ever wanted you to feel safe."

"Safe from what? Myself?"

"From the world! It's not easy out there. I worry less about Samantha because she is responsible and listens to my advice, but with you, I worry more," she said, her voice rising now as well.

"You're my youngest child, my maknae. I want you to live a good life, but you don't do what I say. Even as a little kid, you never wore the clothes I picked out for you. Sometimes at the playground, I could hear the other kids and moms laughing at your outfits, saying you looked ridiculous. My daughter! Ridiculous! If you'd just listen to me like Samantha does, things like that wouldn't happen and I would worry less."

"Why do you care so much about what other people think of me? What about what I think of me? Just because I'm not exactly like Samantha doesn't mean I'm not good enough."

"Good enough? What are you saying? How should I have treated you, then?"

"Like someone who's worth something!" I cried. "Like someone who has good, smart, interesting thoughts and can do good, smart, interesting things. I'm not just your youngest daughter. I'm a person with feelings and talent, and I feel like I've waited my entire life for you to tell me that so I can really start believing it." My voice was thick with tears now, but I pressed on. I needed to say these next words. "But I'm so tired of waiting, Umma. So tired. From now on, I'm going to believe it because it's true, not because you say so."

She sighed, rubbing her forehead. "This is so sudden, Valerie. I don't know where all of this is coming from. Let's talk about it another day when we're both less tired. Here." She nudged the plate of pears closer to me before rising from the table. "Eat this whole thing. I'm going to bed for now."

I watched as she walked out of the kitchen. As predictable as it was for her to leave at such a tense moment, it didn't hurt me when she left. Instead I felt something break free inside me. Maybe one day we really would talk about it again and she would come around. Or maybe Samantha was right and things would never change. I realized now that even if I did something big that Samantha had never done before, like traveling to Paris with the money I made from a business I started from scratch, Umma would continue to see what she wanted to see about me. Nothing I did would change her mind. But whether she stayed or walked away, I would stand by what I said. I would believe in myself because it was the truth, and I wouldn't wait for anyone's permission to do it.

I finally let the tears slide down my cheeks. They were bittersweet tears, but mostly they were tears of relief at finally having said what I had always wanted to say. I picked up a pear and took a big bite.

It tasted like freedom.

Friday / May 1

Somehow the day that Charlie had been waiting for all year had snuck up on us without us even realizing. Senior prom. I considered skipping out on the event altogether, but I couldn't resist an opportunity to dress up. Even more important, there was someone there who I needed to see.

Throughout everything with Halmeoni and Umma, Wes had constantly been in the back of my mind. I had to talk to him, and today was the day.

"Are you sure you don't want a ride?" Charlie asked over speakerphone. I stood in front of the bathroom mirror, curling my hair, the phone balanced precariously on the edge of the sink.

"No way," I said. "My dad is driving me. This is the moment you've been dreaming of since sophomore year. Don't let me third-wheel on you and Pauline."

"We're just going as friends," he said with a laugh. He cleared his throat. "But, uh, you saw the selfie I sent you, right? How's my hair?"

"Looks great. Perfect balance between putting in effort and not trying too hard."

"Okay. That's what I was going for." He breathed a sigh of relief. "I'll see you soon, then?"

"Yeah." I paused. "Thanks for calling and offering a ride. I appreciate it."

The words came out awkward and strange, but I was trying to practice saying them. To remind him, and myself, that I was grateful for him.

"No problem," he said. I could almost feel him smiling through the phone. "See you at school."

After curling my hair, I slipped into my prom outfit: a shimmery silver dress with a halter neck and a crisscross back. Simple but delicate. A perfect last-minute vintage find.

I checked the time and took a deep breath.

I had a prom to go to.

The school gym had been utterly transformed. Gold and silver balloons filled the room. Long tables decorated with antique candlesticks were laden with food, from finger sandwiches to ten different kinds of fancy chicken. Somehow the decoration team had even managed to hang an impressive chandelier from the ceiling. The DJ was set up in a corner of the gym, playing hit pop songs while students made their way onto the dance floor, screaming and grabbing one another's hands as they spun, on the high of senior year.

I scanned the gym. Kristy Lo waved at me from the dance floor, her bright red dress matching her newly dyed auburn hair. Beside her, Joanne Patel and Rebecca Sanders were wearing a dozen matching glitter bracelets that they'd crafted themselves, dancing up a storm. Natalie Castillo and Amelia Perry were cheesing it up at the photo booth, while Tina Pierce and Matt Whitman were making out in a corner of the gym. Just as Kristy had predicted at the beginning of the school year.

Charlie and Pauline were standing directly under the chandelier, surrounded by friends, the glimmering lights illuminating their faces. They talked and laughed like they had been friends forever without a two-year break. Pauline looked amazing in a sparkly aquamarine mermaid dress. Seeing them together gave me an odd sense of hope. Maybe if Charlie could find a way to start new friendships with unexpected people, I could too.

It was strange being at a school event where I wasn't V&C K-BEAUTY. I was just Valerie. The first few days after I had announced on Instagram that V&C was out of business, I'd thought my world would fall apart. But mostly I'd just gotten a bunch of DMs from people saying they were sorry to see me go, that shopping with me had been their favorite part of Mondays. Ugh! Heartbreak!! Best OG student business ever 😖, Kristy had texted me.

And then things had settled into a new normal. The world still turned. V&C was over, but I was still here.

My eyes landed on a boy in glasses standing by the punch bowl, hair gelled back. He looked handsome in his tux.

I took a deep breath as I got closer and tapped him on the shoulder.

"Hi," I said.

He turned and his eyes lit up. "Hi."

"I wanted to thank you again, for the ride to the hospital."

"Of course. I wanted to text you to see how things were going, but I wasn't sure if our no-talking, no-texting, no-calling rule was still in place."

"Right." I took a deep breath, looking down at my shoes and then up at him. "Listen, I wanted to say I'm sorry."

He looked surprised. "For what?"

"For never giving you a chance to explain. For shutting you out when I should have listened. For telling you that Valentine's Day was a mistake. It wasn't. I'm sorry."

He shook his head. "I should be the one apologizing—" he started.

"You already have," I said. "Many times."

"Still. I'll say it again. I'm sorry for what I said to Lisa and the others. And I'm sorry for saying all that stuff to Taemin. I really, truly didn't mean any of it."

"Apology accepted."

He smiled a smile that made me melt, like my words had released a huge weight off his shoulders. "Thank you. I accept your apology too." He cleared his throat. "I suppose there's nothing left to do then but to tally up the bet? All or nothing, right? Loser owes the winner all their earnings?"

I bit my lip. I hadn't been sure if Wes would want to go through with the bet, but I had come prepared with the number just in case. There was almost no way he hadn't won, what with V&C closing early and our sales being down from previous years. It wouldn't be fair for me to pull out of the bet now, especially when I had been the one to insist on it. I had to pay up what I owed. Even though I didn't need it for Paris anymore, it still stung a bit to part with my money. But fair is fair.

"Okay," I said. "On the count of three? We both say how much we earned from the beginning of the bet to now?"

"You don't want to see my spreadsheet?" he asked with a grin.

I laughed. "No. I trust you."

"Okay, then." He nodded. "Three, two, one."

"Nine hundred eighty-seven dollars," I said at the same time he said, "Zero."

I blinked at him, confused. "Zero?"

"Ah, yeah. See, I kind of made this mistake where I sold some products I wasn't supposed to. So I owe my mom everything I earned, leaving me with nothing." He laughed, running his hand through the back of his hair. "And that's not even all of it. I have to give her everything from the fall, too. And the money I already spent on my application, so I'm actually at negative dollars."

I whistled low. "Damn. That's harsh."

"Yeah. But fair."

"So that means . . ."

He grinned. "You win. But since I technically made zero dollars, I guess I owe you zero."

I burst out laughing. "Wow. Why does it feel like we both lost here?"

The hype dance song in the background faded to a slow pop melody. He smiled shyly, holding out his hand. "Dance with me?"

My heart fluttered as I took his hand. We walked onto the dance floor, his arms sliding down to my waist, mine wrapping around his shoulders. We were so close, I could almost hear his heartbeat pounding through his chest. Or maybe that was mine.

"Valerie," he said, his voice nervous. "I wanted to tell you something."

"Hmm?"

"I got into Toblie School of Music. And I told my parents that I'm set on going even if they don't support me."

A smile broke out across my face. "Wes! That's amazing."

"But that's not what I wanted to tell you," he said.

I cocked my head to the side, confused. "Oh?"

"I wanted to tell you thanks. Meeting you this year was . . ." He looked up at the ceiling as if searching for the right words. "It was life-changing. I know that sounds cliché or whatever, but it really was. I would never have had the guts to start my own business and pursue my dreams and take my life into my own hands if I didn't see you doing it first. I really respect you. I wanted you to know that."

At that moment, I truly understood what Halmeoni meant

when she said there was a world inside all of us. A world that grew as we let people in, allowing them to shape us in ways we could never do alone. Maybe I had changed Wes's life without even realizing it, but the same could be said the other way around.

"There's something I want to tell you, too," I said. I swallowed nervously. Thinking it and saying it were such different things. But I had to try. "Thanks for stopping me from selling those counterfeit items. And for saying a lot of things that I really needed to hear. Like how I'm more than my business and how people are people, not just helpers or hindrances. You asked me when I was going to wake up and get it, and I feel like I'm starting to."

He looked embarrassed. "Did I really ask you when you were going to wake up and get it? God. I'm sorry. What a choice of words."

"It had to be said." I laughed. "And also, that thing you said at my locker? How your feelings for me are real?" I took a deep breath. *Here goes nothing.* "I feel the same way about you."

He stopped dancing so we were just standing in the middle of the gym, dancing classmates swirling all around us. His face was full of surprise and raw, untampered hope.

"Really?"

I smiled. "Really."

The smile that spread across his face made my heart swoop. He leaned in and I wrapped my arms around him tighter as his lips pressed against mine. It was just as sweet as the first time we'd kissed, only this time there was nothing to hide.

CHAPTER TWENTY

WES

Monday / May 11

Now that Mondays were no longer for business, I used the extra time in the morning to practice saxophone in the band room. Auditions might have been behind me, but I still had my solo at the Senior Showcase coming up. I needed all the practice time I could get, and Mr. Reyes was more than happy to help me out.

Sometimes Pauline would join me, showing up at the band room every Monday out of habit. On this particular Monday, she was grinning from ear to ear with good news.

"Wes, guess what?" she said. "My dad and I are going to visit Jeju Island this summer!"

"What? That's amazing!"

"Yeah. I'm really excited." She beamed. "Anyway, I wanted to say thank you. For letting me be part of your business and encouraging me to not let go of my Korean heritage if I still have an interest in it. I didn't think that would impact me so much, but it did. And obviously my dad is thrilled."

"Hey, you did all the work," I said, laughing. "I just made a suggestion. You're the one who ran with it."

"Still. Thanks." She smiled and then glanced at the clock behind my head. "Don't you have somewhere to be right now?"

I did. I packed up my saxophone and jogged up to the second floor, where Valerie and Charlie were already standing outside room 217. Even from afar, I could tell Valerie was nervous by the way her jaw was moving. She was definitely eating a strawberry Hi-Chew.

"Yo," Charlie said, fist-bumping me as I approached. "Talk her down, will you? She's been nervous about this the whole morning."

Valerie scowled, pinching Charlie in the elbow. He yelped.

"I am not nervous," she said. "I'm just . . . a little on edge."

After much persuasion from both me and Charlie, Valerie had finally decided to tell Ms. Jackson the entire truth about what had happened with the counterfeit items. Why she had decided to sell them, and why she'd chosen not to go through with it. Business might be closed for good, but she could still lift the suspension and restore legitimacy to V&C for the sake of its legacy. Plus, she respected Ms. Jackson too much to let the school year end without telling her the truth.

She'd been avoiding meeting with her mentor for weeks while she tried to work up the courage to say everything she wanted to, but now she was finally ready. Or at least as ready as she would ever be.

"Hey," I said, putting my hands on her shoulders and looking her in the eye. "You can do this. You're Valerie Kwon. And you already know Ms. Jackson's on your side. She'll hear you out. Besides," I grinned, "you have to tell her that you got into RLU Wallace School of Business."

After being initially wait-listed, her acceptance letter had come a few days after prom. She'd called me screaming, and I'd gone over to her house, where her halmeoni was beaming and her dad kept saying, "I knew she'd get in all along! My daughter the business-woman." The school was close enough that she could visit her halmeoni every weekend, which was important to her. And it was only five hours and seventeen minutes away from Toblie, with traffic. Not that I had done extensive calculations or anything.

"You've been wanting to share the news with her since you got it," I said.

"You're right, you're right." She took a deep breath, shaking out her arms and muttering to herself, "Okay. Let's do this."

"Good luck," Charlie said. He opened the door for Valerie. She stepped inside, turning around and sneaking me one last look.

"You got this," I said.

She grinned and took a deep breath as the door swung shut behind her.

Friday / May 29

The night of the Senior Showcase came faster than I was ready for it to. Now that it was the end of the school year, it felt like time was just vanishing before my eyes.

I peeked out from behind the curtain. The auditorium was filled with people. Were Mom and Dad out there? I'd invited them last minute, sliding the poster advertising SENIOR SHOWCASE across the jade marble counter over breakfast. "We'll take a look at it, Wes," Mom had promised, while Dad received it with stony silence. We hadn't spoken much at all since my acceptance letter came in the mail. I was beginning to think we might never speak again.

"Wes," a familiar voice behind me said.

I turned, letting the curtain drop. My body filled with warmth, easing my nerves. "Hey, Val."

She grinned, tortoiseshell sunglasses perched on top of her head. "I just came to wish you luck."

Standing on her tiptoes, she kissed me lightly on the cheek. This would never stop being the best feeling ever.

"Wes!" another voice yelled from across the room.

Valerie and I both looked up to see Charlie and Pauline walking toward us. Not just Charlie and Pauline. Charlie, Pauline, and Taemin.

"Whoa," I said, my eyes widening. I hadn't seen him since that day at Snow Bunny. "What are you doing here?"

"Charlie invited me," Taemin said. He grinned sheepishly, looking back and forth between me and Valerie. "Listen, I wanted to say sorry to both of you. I mean, I still stand by the fact that you're the ones who hired me and I don't think I really did anything wrong in that department—"

"Taemin," Charlie coughed into his hand.

"—but I will admit, I almost screwed up your whole relationship by miscommunicating some info, and for that I really am sorry," he finished. "Believe me when I say I was trying to do the right thing. But honestly, I'm pretty sure I did more harm trying to do the right thing than if I had just done the wrong thing."

Valerie and I exchanged glances.

She sighed, glowering at Taemin. "You're a real pain in the ass, you know that? Hiring you was a huge mistake. But I guess I have to thank you for telling Wes about my counterfeit plan," she added. "I would've done something I really regretted if you didn't. So thanks."

Taemin raised his eyebrows and grinned. "So, I did do one right thing, then. Maybe I'm not a lost cause after all."

Mr. Reyes rushed up to us, waving his conductor's baton in the air. "Students! The show's about to start!"

Valerie, Charlie, Pauline, and Taemin all gave me one last thumbs-up before going to find their seats. I took a deep breath and joined the rest of the band on stage with my saxophone. Mr. Reyes took his spot in front of us. Today his socks had music notes. I was surprised I'd never seen them before.

"Welcome to Crescent Brook High's Senior Showcase, everyone!" Amelia Perry, the MC of the event, declared. "Tonight we'll be seeing performances from several of our seniors, showcasing what we've been working on all year. We've got music, dance, a theatrical performance by yours truly and the senior drama club, and much more. To kick us off for the night, please join me in welcoming Mr. Reyes and our senior band class!"

The audience burst into applause as the curtain went up and the spotlight shone.

Mr. Reyes lifted his baton and the music began.

No matter how nervous I feel before playing, once I start, I know I'm home. I let the music carry me, harmonizing with all the other instruments in the band. When it was time for my solo, I didn't even have to think about it. The music simply came, hours of practice taking over my muscle memory so all I had to do was focus on the emotion.

The audience didn't make a sound for the whole performance. Were they as captivated as we were up onstage? As we neared the final note, I thought I saw tears shining in Mr. Reyes's eyes. It was a moment to be proud of, for all of us.

He raised his baton, arms wide, holding the final note. And then he let it go and the audience erupted into cheers. People jumped up to their feet, whistling and stamping their feet. Adrenaline rushed through my body as we all stood up to bow.

"Wes, you were amazing," Valerie said, squeezing my hand as I joined her in the audience after my set.

"Yeah?" I knew I was smiling like a fool. I couldn't help it. "My live performance was as good as the video?"

She grinned. "Even better."

"Seriously, dude, you're a saxophone master," Charlie said, thumping me on the back. "I mean, I figured you'd be good, but I didn't know you would be *that* good."

"Agreed," Taemin said. "I think we should all go out to celebrate Wes's sexy saxophone playing after this. Bingsu, anyone?"

"Only if you're paying," Pauline said.

Valerie's hand wrapped around mine as we watched the rest of the Senior Showcase performances. I was happy. So unbelievably happy. But still, I couldn't help but glance around the auditorium every so often as the drama club and dance teams performed onstage, searching for two familiar faces. Were they here? Had they come? Had they seen me play?

As the a cappella group finished up their set, Ms. Jackson took the stage, Mr. McAvoy wheeling up a table of trophies next to her. I felt Valerie's hand tense in mine.

"What is it?" I whispered.

"Every year they acknowledge the student businesses with awards during the Senior Showcase," Valerie said. "Businesses that don't get suspended, that is."

"You had a great talk with Ms. Jackson though, didn't you? And she lifted your suspension after hearing your story."

"Yeah. But still. It was a big mistake." She bit her lip, nervous at what would happen, or what wouldn't happen. I squeezed her hand.

"This year, we have so many young entrepreneurs to celebrate," Ms. Jackson said into the mic, holding a stack of gold envelopes. "It's been my greatest delight as a teacher to see students taking chances and growing in ingenuity. Through trial and error, these students have grown to be wonderful entrepreneurs and even more wonderful human beings. Please join me as I call them up to the stage." She opened the first gold envelope. "For Best Teamwork, Joanne Patel and Rebecca Sanders and their bracelet business!"

The audience whooped as Joanne and Rebecca made their way

up to the stage, hands clasped together and held over their heads in victory.

"For Best New Business, Wes Jung and Pauline Lim for their K-pop beauty business!"

I froze, immediately looking at Valerie. Was this okay?

She smiled and nodded, knowing what I meant without words. "You deserve it. Go!"

Pauline and I made our way up to the stage to receive our trophies. The list went on as more and more students joined the stage. The trophies dwindled until there were only two left.

"Finally, for Best Overall Business," Ms. Jackson said, and I could have sworn she got a little choked up, "please join me in welcoming Valerie Kwon and Charlie Song of V&C K-BEAUTY to the stage."

The audience thundered with applause. I cheered loudly with the rest of them as Valerie, stunned, made her way up to the stage, Charlie steering her from behind with his hands on her shoulders.

They received their trophies, and Ms. Jackson leaned forward to whisper something in Valerie's ear. She nodded, still stunned, and took the mic from her mentor.

"Hi, everybody," she said.

"Hi, Valerie!" people in the audience shouted.

She laughed, her shoulders relaxing. "Ms. J asked if I could share a bit about my business and what I've learned over the past three years. I'll keep it short, but first, people love a good deal. Second, know what the values of your business are and do your best to stick to them. Even if it's tempting not to." She swallowed hard, glancing over her shoulder at me and then at Ms. Jackson and Charlie standing on either side of her. "Third, and this was a hard one for me . . . the best part of a business isn't the profit. That's part of it, for sure, and the part I focused most on for a long time. But profit doesn't forgive you when you make mistakes. It doesn't believe in you when you don't believe in yourself. It doesn't give you second chances when you don't deserve them. But people do. They're what make this whole thing worth it. So thank you to everyone who has ever supported V&C, whether you shopped with us or not. We truly could not have done it without you."

She cleared her throat and passed the mic to Charlie. "Did you want to add anything?"

"V&C forever, baby!" he shouted into the mic.

The audience burst into laughter and then thunderous applause. I felt a swell of pride, clapping until my palms tingled. She and Charlie deserved this so much. I could tell by the look on all the other business owners' faces that they thought so too.

As we made our way off the stage, a crowd of people immediately rushed around Valerie and Charlie. Their family. Her face was flushed with joy as she showed her trophy to her parents, her halmeoni beaming with pride. I hung back, giving her space with her family. This was her moment.

Then, from across the auditorium, I spotted them. Mom and Dad standing shoulder to shoulder by the back door like they had just come in. At first I wasn't sure if it was really them. I wiped my glasses on my shirt and put them back on, my trophy tucked awkwardly under my arm.

It was.

"You came," I said, walking toward them. "Did you, um, just get here?"

"No," Dad said. "We've been here since the beginning, but there were no more seats." He shoved his hands in his pockets, not quite looking at me. "It's a full house."

"It is," I said. Silence stretched between us. "Did you catch my performance?"

Mom nodded. "Wes." She squeezed my shoulder. "Your solo was . . . It was beautiful."

Hope rose in my chest like a music note set free. "Really?"

"Really. I can't believe I've never heard you play like that before." She looked down at the floor and then back up at me, her face a mix of emotions. "I suppose we've never been able to make it out to any of your shows in the past."

"Well. Thanks for making it out today," I said, my voice threatening to break. I cleared my throat and glanced at Dad, who still wasn't looking directly at me.

He was still disappointed. I could tell. My shoulders drooped, deflated.

"Wes," he said finally, looking at me steadily. I held my breath. "I'm glad I got to see you play. Thank you for inviting me." He cleared his throat. "I took a video and sent it to your uncle. I thought he'd like to see it."

My heart swelled. "You're welcome," I said. "And thank you."

It wasn't full acceptance yet, but today they'd shown up. They'd seen what I could do.

And maybe that was enough to give me hope for tomorrow.

CHAPTER TWENTY-ONE

VALERIE

Wednesday / July 15

"Halmeoni, hurry up! Paris isn't going to wait forever."

"Aigoo, arasseo, arasseo. Okay, okay. Always in a hurry, Valerie!"

I grinned as Halmeoni walked down the stairs, Umma supporting her on one side, her new walking cane supporting her on the other.

"Wait, Halmeoni, one last thing." I pulled out a purple beret from my tote bag and arranged it carefully on top of her perm. It matched the blue one on my own head. "Jjajan!"

"Ooh." Halmeoni examined her reflection in the TV screen, patting her beret. "Now I really feel like I'm in Paris."

Because of Halmeoni's condition, traveling to Paris didn't make much sense anymore. I suppose it never had, but now I really knew it. It would be too hard on her body, not to mention unpredictable. But that didn't mean I couldn't bring Paris to her.

As soon as summer break had started, we'd begun our local

Parisian travels. Samantha and I took her to a café on the other side of town that served the best macarons and the most buttery croissants. I printed out high-quality photos of famous paintings in the Louvre and hung them all around our house, creating our very own museum, complete with the *Mona Lisa*—with none of the crowds. And today we had some very special dinner reservations.

"Have fun, you two," Umma said, dropping us off in front of L'Éléphant, a restaurant in the heart of downtown. "And don't exert yourself too much," she added, waving at Halmeoni. "And make sure to get a comfortable seat!"

After Halmeoni's diagnosis, Umma got more flexible about letting her go outside, though her permission often came with a list of cautionary things to keep in mind. We didn't know how much time Halmeoni had left before it became difficult for her to walk at all. It could be months or years. We hoped it would be the latter, but we wanted to make the most of every day we had.

As for me and Umma, we still hadn't talked about everything I'd said that one night in the kitchen. I suspected that was how it would be for a long time. But she had made my favorite foods more than ever since that talk. I didn't know if things would ever really change with how she saw me, but for now the extra doenjang jjigae was nice, as were the plates of cut-up fruit that appeared on my desk. I think it was a sign that, at the very least, she had heard what I had to say.

The hostess seated us at an outdoor table in the courtyard, where wisteria vines hung from the red brick walls and the glass ceiling was strung with crisscrossing white lights.

"Would you like some drinks, ladies?"

Our waiter appeared at the table. He was tall and handsome with his hipster, not-fake glasses crooked on his nose. I reached up to adjust them and he blushed, smiling.

"Thanks," Wes said. He turned to Halmeoni and bowed. "Annyeonghaseyo, Halmeoni."

She grinned, reaching up to pat his cheek. "Hello, handsome Wes."

His blush grew deeper and I laughed. Wes had joined us for a couple of our Paris adventures, and Halmeoni was totally smitten with him. He'd snagged a job at L'Éléphant right after graduation. After much thought, he'd decided to delay his music school acceptance and take a year off to save up for tuition. "They said I'm welcome to join them next fall," he'd said. "This way I can save some money, and who knows? Maybe my parents will even warm up to the idea by next year."

"When does your shift end?" I asked now.

"In ten minutes," Wes said. "But then I play for an hour. You'll stick around for a bit, right?"

I nodded. "Of course. That's why we came tonight."

Halmeoni and I surveyed the menus. We ordered a duck confit and French onion soup to share. When no one was looking, Halmeoni pulled her travel-sized gochujang out of her purse. "For the duck," she said.

We ate until our bellies were full, talking about everything under the sun. We talked about my shopping list before starting college in the fall; how Charlie was going to take a year off to travel now that his dad was back home to keep his mom company; how

Pauline had sent us postcards from her trip to Jeju Island with her dad. We even talked about Taemin and how he'd somehow managed to avoid working at his dad's church this summer by finally snagging a volunteer role at the aquarium instead. He was officially the magician for special events, and, much to Pauline's delight, he had to dress up as a dolphin for every shift.

Just as we were perusing the dessert menu, the live band began their set. This was my favorite thing about L'Éléphant: how they had live music in the courtyard for dinner. Well, more like my second favorite thing. My first favorite thing was definitely the saxophonist in the band.

It was one of the best parts about Wes getting a job here. He split his time between working as a waiter and playing live music along with a pianist, bass player, and drummer. Halmeoni and I leaned back in our seats, soaking in the moment. Chocolate soufflé and jazz were a great combo.

"No hurry at all, but here's your check, ladies," our new waiter said, arriving with our bill. "And also, your previous waiter asked me to give you this."

I glanced down at the check. On top of the bill were two pineapple Hi-Chews.

"What does the pineapple one mean, Valerie?" Halmeoni asked.

I caught Wes's eye and winked. His mouth curled into a grin around his saxophone, and he winked back, cheeks pink.

I popped the pineapple Hi-Chew into my mouth. "It means that everything is just as it should be," I said.

And everything was.

ACKNOWLEDGMENTS

A few years ago, I thought to myself, *I want to write a book about teens who sell K-beauty products at school*. I didn't know at the time what else they would get up to—that they would fall in love, fight for their dreams, and struggle to feel seen by their families. It's been a journey discovering Valerie and Wes's story and there are so many people who walked alongside me through the process. My heart is full of gratitude for these people, so much so that I'm not sure I have the words to properly express my feelings, but here we go! Let me give it my best shot.

Thank you to my editor, Jennifer Ung. I feel like I won the lottery having you as my editor. Working on this book with you has been one of the best experiences of my life and that is by no means an exaggeration. From the beginning, you just *got* it—the story, the characters, what I wanted to say. Not only did you get it, but you also made the book stronger and deeper with each edit letter. YOU ARE AMAZING! All caps because I want you to imagine me shouting it from a rooftop.

To my agent, Linda Epstein. Where to even begin? You are my champion, my advocate, my literary fairy godmother. The real-life human version of a strawberry Hi-Chew, always there to calm me down when I need it. Thank you for pulling me out of the slush pile and for believing in my words. I will never not be grateful for you and the magical library where I always seem to be for your life-changing calls.

When I first saw the cover for this book, I immediately fell in love with the colors and the character details (the treble clef! Valerie's necklace!). Thank you to Sarah Creech for the cover design and to Anne Pomel for the art. I love what you created.

All my gratitude to the team at Simon & Schuster BFYR for championing *Made in Korea*, including Justin Chanda, Kendra Levin, Dainese Santos, Morgan York, Karen Sherman, Tom Daly, Sara Berko, Lauren Hoffman, Chrissy Noh, Lisa Moraleda, Christina Pecorale, Victor Iannone, Emily Hutton, Michelle Leo, and Anna Jarzab.

Sending my deepest appreciation to all the librarians, book-sellers, and bloggers who have supported this book. Thank you for all that you do!

Thi Tran, thank you for the coffee dates and brainstorm sessions, and for being the first person to read the earliest drafts of chapter one. Getting started can often feel like half the battle and I wouldn't have been able to do it without you.

Many thanks to Jane Cho for meeting with me to talk about the experience of being a third-culture kid. I appreciate you so much!

At times, publishing can feel like Wonderland, especially as a debut author. That is to say, a strange new world that's at once exciting, magical, confusing, and full of uncertainty as to what's coming next. Thank you to Kat Cho, Nafiza Azad, and Rachel

Lynn Solomon for your guidance through it all. Your advice, humor, and friendship have been grounding.

In the summer of 2019, I went to Ireland for a writing retreat/ tour where I met Julie Dao and Thao Le. Thank you to you both for your valuable insights and for all your encouragement. You have no idea how much you impacted my writing journey and the trajectory of this book!

To my friend Julie Abe. Or should I say fellow pizza lover, French-fry fiend, and professional croissant-eater? Your endless support has been such a balm for my soul. Let's meet in Japan one day and visit all the melon pan stalls.

Kaya Tomash, you are a light in the world and in my life! I always feel so inspired and refreshed after our talks. Thank you for cheering me on and for celebrating every step of this journey with me.

To the Kimchingoos—Jessica Kim, Susan Lee, Grace Shim, and Graci Kim—where would I be without you? Thank you for the bellyaching laughs and for being there through all the daily ups and downs. P.S.: it's ddeok.

To Sarah Harrington, Carly Whetter, and Grace Li. You are my safe haven. My critique partners before I even knew what critique partners were. Because of you, I have never felt lonely on this pursuit of publication, and I am so excited for my debut novel to meet its godmothers.

Farisia Thang, thank you for taking my headshots, reading the first draft of this book, and obsessing over K-dramas with me. Sometimes Sue O will catch a glimpse of the literal essays we send each other through iMessage and wonder how we have so much to talk about. I'm nearing the end of these acknowledgments, so . . . *gets ready to play song from *Goblin**. You know which one.

Shout-out to Frances Lu, Enoch Choi, and Paul Choe, a.k.a. Sony Samsung, Vance Blundstone, and DM. (That's right, I just immortalized your D&D characters in print. Oh, and can't forget to include Sue O's character, BBG.) Thanks for all your support in my writing projects and for the impromptu brainstorm sessions. I hope by the time you read this, we have plans to go to Hawaii. XOXO, Gnocchi Gnomington.

To my family—아빠, 엄마, 언니, John, 오빠, and 세연언니. I am who I am because of you. Thank you for everything, and by that, I really do mean everything. Your support means the world to me. I love you more than we love the strawberry-mango mousse cake from Anna's. And to Emory. My joy and my style icon. When you're old enough to read this book, I hope you still think I'm fun and cool, and that you will always want to paint unicorn rocks with me.

Sue O Lee. You have listened to me talk about fictional people for way longer than anyone should, but I hope you know this is just the beginning. You have a lifetime ahead of listening to me talk about imaginary things. I hope you're excited! You are my person and my tether to the present. *Insert Kakao sticker here of Ryan pouring out hearts from a basket* I love you.

Lastly, to you, reader. It is wild to me that somewhere in the world, you're out there reading these words that I wrote. Thank you for picking up this book. Thank you, thank you, and thank you again.

SARAH SUK (pronounced like "soup" with a *K*) lives in Vancouver, Canada, where she writes stories and admires mountains. When she's not writing, you can find her hanging out by the water, taking film photos, or eating a bowl of bingsu. *Made in Korea* is her first novel. You can visit Sarah online at sarahsuk.com and on Twitter and Instagram @sarahaelisuk.